SHADOW AVENGERS

Peter Parker rubbed his bleary eyes as he ascended the subway steps into the bright daylight of early fall. As he crossed the street, a loud, repetitive clanging noise caught his attention.

Clang! Cling-clang! SHING!

"Typical Parker luck," he muttered, pulling his mask on, the chrome-plated lenses cutting the harsh rays of the midday sun. He crept toward the ongoing sounds. When he finally got a good look at the action he paused in shock, barely able to believe what he was seeing.

Loki and Venom were engaged in an epic swordfight, if you could call it that. Loki carried a sword, but Venom wielded a broken off streetlamp. As he exchanged brutal blows with the Asgardian, black symbiotic tendrils extended from his back, holding aloft a hose that dribbled a disgusting green glop onto the ground. Its other end terminated at the Oscorp tanker truck.

Peter knew he needed to put a stop to this, but he wasn't sure which side to take...

T0018587

ALSO AVAILABLE

MARVEL CRISIS PROTOCOL
  Target: Kree by Stuart Moore

MARVEL HEROINES
  Domino: Strays by Tristan Palmgren
  Rogue: Untouched by Alisa Kwitney
  Elsa Bloodstone: Bequest by Cath Lauria
  Outlaw: Relentless by Tristan Palmgren
  Black Cat: Discord by Cath Lauria

LEGENDS OF ASGARD
  The Head of Mimir by Richard Lee Byers
  The Sword of Surtur by C L Werner
  The Serpent and the Dead by Anna Stephens
  The Rebels of Vanaheim by Richard Lee Byers
  Three Swords by C L Werner

MARVEL UNTOLD
  The Harrowing of Doom by David Annandale
  Dark Avengers: The Patriot List by David Guymer
  Witches Unleashed by Carrie Harris
  Reign of the Devourer by David Annandale

XAVIER'S INSTITUTE
  Liberty & Justice for All by Carrie Harris
  First Team by Robbie MacNiven
  Triptych by Jaleigh Johnson
  School of X edited by Gwendolyn Nix

MARVEL
CRISIS PROTOCOL

SHADOW
AVENGERS

CARRIE HARRIS

ACONYTE

FOR MARVEL PUBLISHING

VP Production & Special Projects: Jeff Youngquist
Associate Editors, Special Projects: Caitlin O'Connell & Sarah Singer
Manager, Licensed Publishing: Jeremy West
VP, Licensed Publishing: Sven Larsen
SVP Print, Sales & Marketing: David Gabriel
Editor in Chief: C B Cebulski

Special Thanks to Tom Brevoort

© 2022 MARVEL

First published by Aconyte Books in 2022
ISBN 978 1 83908 102 6
Ebook ISBN 978 1 83908 103 3

All rights reserved. The Aconyte name and logo and the Asmodee Entertainment name and logo are registered or unregistered trademarks of Asmodee Entertainment Limited.

This novel is entirely a work of fiction. Names, characters, places, and incidents are the products of the author's imagination or are used fictitiously. Any resemblance to actual events, locales, organizations or persons, living or dead, is entirely coincidental.

Sales of this book without a front cover may be unauthorized. If this book is coverless, it may have been reported to the publisher as "unsold and destroyed" and neither the author nor the publisher may have received payment for it.

Cover art by Xteve Abanto

Distributed in North America by Simon & Schuster Inc, New York, USA
Printed in the United States of America
9 8 7 6 5 4 3 2 1

ACONYTE BOOKS

An imprint of Asmodee Entertainment Ltd

Mercury House, Shipstones Business Centre

North Gate, Nottingham NG7 7FN, UK

aconytebooks.com // twitter.com/aconytebooks

To Emily and Jen, with gratitude for the
sanity-saving pandemic talks.

PART ONE
A GROWING STORM

ONE

Eddie Brock's stomach rumbled. He stopped in the middle of the busy New York City sidewalk and tried to remember the last time he'd eaten, eliciting annoyed glares and swear words from the pedestrians who had to go around him. He didn't even notice. He'd been working long nights in the seedy local paper's bullpen on a column about the club scene, and the days had melted together. He squinted up at the sun as if that might clue him in on the date. Was it really Thursday afternoon? He'd had steak and eggs at a greasy spoon on… Tuesday?

It didn't take super-senses to pick up on the delicious smells that wafted down the street. Ever since Sal's Pizza had opened up beneath his apartment the entire block had been coated in a miasma of scrumptiousness, an irresistible pepperoni haze of monstrous proportions. It seeped through his open windows and haunted his dreams.

His stomach growled again.

Let's get pizza, Eddie, said his Other, its voice echoing in his mind. *We're hungry.*

He almost replied aloud but cut himself off before he squeaked out more than a syllable. People got edgy when you held conversations with yourself, even in Brooklyn. If he explained that he was talking to the alien symbiote that lived inside his head, they'd shove him into a hospital bed before he could blink. He needed to hold it together, but that had gotten more difficult lately.

You also need pizza, persisted the symbiote. *If you don't take care of us, I will.*

"Yeah, yeah," Eddie muttered, but he couldn't muster up much heat. No matter how bad things got, or how far he fell down, at least he wasn't alone.

He went into the restaurant and bought himself a medium pepperoni from Sal, who gave him a wide smile under his slick white mustache.

"Medium pep for Brock!" he shouted towards the kitchen. "Add some extra meat to that one, because this guy looks like he might waste away from hunger!"

"Thanks," said Eddie.

The old man squinted at him, his happy expression fading into concern.

"You OK?" he asked.

"Peachy. Why do you ask?"

"You got blood on your shirt."

Startled, Eddie glanced down to see a gory spray across the front of his plain T-shirt. After he'd interviewed the owner of Broadway10, a hot new nightclub in a historic old theater, he'd run across a couple of guys who fancied themselves carjackers. He must have gotten a little carried away. But they'd been breathing when he left. He was almost sure of it.

They deserved it, said his Other. *Hunting in our city.*

But we hunted them back. It's no different, he thought in return.

Hunting kids is bad. Hunting predators is right. And fun. You know it was fun, Eddie.

The Venom symbiote was right. He didn't regret stepping in. But sometimes he couldn't remember what happened when he transformed. After the carjackers, things became hazy. He'd passed out in the alleyway behind the club at some point, but he wasn't exactly sure when or what he'd done afterwards. He didn't like those holes in his memory. Venom didn't understand human morality, and sometimes things went too far for Eddie's comfort. Maybe that was why he couldn't remember. He didn't want to.

Sal's rheumy eyes searched his face in worry. Eddie pasted a smile on his face. He'd never liked liars, but he'd always been a good one.

"Oh, *that*?" he said, laying it on thick. "You know how people are always talking about the alligators in the sewers? One of them crawled up through my toilet this morning."

Sal relaxed, shaking his head. "That so?" he asked.

"Yep. I wrestled it down, stuck my feet inside, and made it into a pair of boots right on the spot. It must have nicked me, though."

Sal leaned forward over the edge of the counter to cast a significant look at his feet, which were encased in battered boots of the non-alligator type. He arched one eloquent eyebrow. Eddie shrugged.

"They didn't go with this outfit," he said.

Chuckling, the old man fetched his pizza and handed it

over. "Guess you need your calories, if you're gonna be fighting 'gators. Here you go. You take care."

"Thanks."

The bell jingled as Eddie pushed through the door, glancing at the time. If he ate quickly, he could catch a nap before he had to work on that column. He pulled out one perfect slice, drooping under the weight of the cheese, and stuffed the end into his mouth.

Heaven, Eddie, said Venom.

"You got that right," he muttered.

He chewed, closing his eyes in blissful appreciation. His gustatory delight carried him across the street, where he was narrowly missed by a crosstown bus. He skirted the honking vehicle and continued down the sidewalk, chowing down steadily as he went. He was halfway through a second slice when his blissful food-coma-in-the-making was interrupted by the sight of Loki Laufeyson behind the wheel of an Oscorp chemical truck.

He stopped in his tracks, frowning. Dread filled him. The Asgardian did not belong on the streets of New York City, and he definitely didn't belong behind the wheel of one of Norman Osborn's vehicles. Eddie didn't like the implied idea of a partnership between the two of them one bit. As he stared, the cheese slid off his half-eaten slice of pizza and splatted onto the ground, unnoticed.

Eddie made it a habit to keep on top of the local action. Reporting and lethal protecting were both easier when he knew the current players. He'd heard through the grapevine that Loki was in town. The Asgardian's profile – the pale, angular face framed by long, dark hair and topped with a golden headdress – was unmistakable. Eddie debated punching his face in as a precautionary measure. The trickster god brought chaos with him wherever he went.

The Oscorp truck only put him more on edge. Norman Osborn was bad news, and Eddie loathed him almost as much as he did Peter Parker. Maybe Loki had just swiped the first truck he'd seen, but Eddie had been around the block too many times to believe in coincidence. He crammed the rest of the crust into his mouth without noticing the absence of toppings, tucked the pizza box under his arm, and followed the truck. He dodged through masses of pedestrians, losing himself in their numbers, keeping a careful eye on the vehicle lest he lose it in the dense city traffic.

Loki maneuvered down the street, past rows of cars parked bumper to bumper, before backing into a narrow alleyway between an auto body shop and a shuttered electronics repair place. The space was so tight that the side mirrors nearly scraped the brick on either side, but he guided the vehicle with supernatural precision. Eddie craned his neck as he strolled on by, but he couldn't stand at the mouth of the alley and rubberneck without Loki spotting him. He'd have to take another approach.

To do that, he would need to transform. To merge with his Other. To become Venom.

The mere thought of it sent adrenaline coursing through his veins. If he could, he would bond with his symbiote all of the time, riding high on the sense of common purpose and the strength their merger lent him. But turning into Venom sometimes left him with holes in his memory and blood on his hands. He tried to tell himself that the blood belonged to someone who had deserved it. Sometimes he even believed it.

But he needed the symbiote, whether he liked it or not, and he reveled in the power that flowed through him when they merged.

He relaxed the iron-clad hold he kept on himself, allowing the symbiote to ascend. Alien biomass seeped from his pores, chilly tendrils creeping over his skin like he was drowning in a pool of cold slime. At first, the transformation had overwhelmed him. But now he welcomed the sensation. The symbiote merged its body with his, building slabs of muscle on top of his already substantial frame. Slick pseudopods closed over his face, stretching his mouth into a giant maw. His teeth lengthened, growing to razor points.

The transformation didn't hurt a bit. In fact, it felt great.

He looked around for a proper vantage point. The auto repair building stood about five stories tall, with dark, shuttered windows flanked by rusted air conditioners. The other building on the opposite side of the alley was short enough that he might be spotted looking over the edge. That made the decision easy. A quick flick of his wrist sent a stream of symbiote-generated webbing to the top of the taller building. He swung up to the top of the building before he could attract attention. Underneath his arm, the pizza shifted in its box, but that couldn't be helped. A scrambled pizza was better than none at all.

When he reached the roof, he set the box down carefully atop a vent pipe. Hopefully the curious pigeons would hold off long enough for him to figure out what mischief Loki was up to.

Far below him, the truck door slammed. He leaned over the

edge of the building to take stock of the situation just in time to see a giant metallic dumpster flying straight toward his head. He threw himself to the side, dodging instinctively. The trash receptacle scraped along his bicep, but the symbiote easily absorbed the damage. The dumpster landed with a deafening clang just a few short feet behind him, scattering flecks of dirty green paint and bits of rusted metal. As it rolled to a noisy stop, it knocked the pizza box down, narrowly missing the pipe, and squashed the pizza beneath its bulk. The box crunched flat, emitting one last gasp of delectable pepperoni steam.

Venom threw his head back, screeching in fury.

"That was mine!" he yelled.

In lieu of an answer, a lamppost came hurtling towards him, borne aloft by an eerie greenish glow, wires trailing from the bottom where it had been ripped from the street. A swing of one mighty arm sent it careening off to one side. The magic user couldn't keep this up forever. Either he'd have to move out into the street in search of more things to throw, or confront Venom hand-to-hand. The sound of rapid footsteps suggested the latter. But the Asgardian didn't appear. It sounded like he was retreating down the alleyway. Hoping to hide behind the truck, perhaps? It wouldn't help.

With a shriek of challenge, Venom stepped off the edge of the building, using a web to slow his descent. Still, when he landed at the end of the alleyway, it sounded like a bomb had gone off. His feet crunched into the pavement, his alien musculature easily absorbing the shock. In the distance, a car alarm went off, bleating like a frightened animal. Somewhere nearby, a window slammed as the people inside washed their hands of whatever was happening in the alleyway. The residents of this rough neighborhood tended to keep to themselves when stuff went down. They wouldn't interfere.

From a spot near the back of the truck, Loki stopped to stare. The Asgardian had frozen in place, a long, flexible hose held in one hand. The other end of the hose had been hooked up to the tanker truck in preparation to pour out its contents. Loki's green eyes glittered as he took in Venom's black, glistening form.

"Well, aren't you a sight?" he said.

"Drop the hose," Venom ordered.

Loki arched an aristocratic brow, the corner of his mouth quirking up into a smile.

"Let me guess," he said. "Or you'll make me?" He paused for a moment before shaking his head. "I don't suppose it matters either way. I'm quite delighted to acquiesce."

He released the hose. The end bounced twice, and then landed in the open sewer grate at his feet. Loki held his hands out, making a show of how harmless he was without the oh-so-dangerous hose.

"There," he said. "I can be a reasonable man. Can you not be a reasonable… creature as well?"

Eddie wasn't sure what to make of him, but the symbiote had no problems deciding. It didn't like being called a creature. As a result, it didn't care for Loki one bit, and it had a default reaction to things it disliked.

Kill, Eddie? the symbiote asked, speaking mind-to-mind.

At least this time it was asking. Sometimes it ordered.

We need more information, Eddie thought back. Not yet.

A glowing green glob of something that could only be described as toxic waste spat from the end of the hose. Loki glanced down at it with an expression of surprise too extreme to be real.

"Oh dear," he said. "That might be a problem."

Another spurt of goop came out. Then it began to flood into the sewer like a polluted river flowing into the sea. Eddie didn't like that one bit. Loki plus Oscorp plus a surreptitious dump site didn't add up to anything good. Maybe the water treatment plants would filter this stuff out, but he couldn't chance it. No one poisoned the water in his town without paying the price. He'd beat Loki's face in and then sell the story of the plot he'd foiled to the highest bidder. This time, he'd have proof, so the big papers wouldn't be able to write him off as a nutjob again.

"I think *you* have a problem. That problem is me," he said, the symbiote twisting his voice until it sounded like iron nails on a chalkboard.

But Loki's smile merely widened. He pressed his hands together and bowed as if saluting an opponent. As he did so, a glass pendant about the size of a quarter swung to and fro, dangling from a golden chain slung around his neck. Inside the pendant, the same glowing liquid sloshed around.

If he'd been able to think, Eddie wouldn't have been reassured by this strange behavior, but he was beyond rationality. His mind merged more deeply with the symbiote, and they both had one singular goal: they would pummel Loki Laufeyson into a bloody pulp.

He shrieked a challenge as Loki straightened, pulling a sword from thin air. Mystical runes covered the hilt, and the bronze blade glistened in the midday sun. The Asgardian fell into an easy swordsman's crouch, the blade held at the ready.

Either he wasn't afraid of the monstrosity looming over him, or he did a great job of hiding it.

"Come, my friend," he said. "I'd like to introduce you to the weapon of my ancestors. This is Laevateinn."

"Bring your sword!" Venom snarled. "We will break it for you."

"With such an invitation, how can I refuse?" responded Loki with elaborate politeness.

As if on cue, they charged at each other.

TWO

Peter Parker rubbed his bleary eyes as he ascended the subway steps into the bright daylight of early fall. After a long week of working overtime on a freelance project, he'd overslept. His mind still swam with barely remembered dreams. He needed a pick-me-up, so he decided to go a few blocks out of his way and try out that new pizza place everyone had been raving about. He could pick up some lunch and still make it to the Shadow Avengers meeting on time.

But as he crossed the street, a loud, repetitive clanging noise caught his attention.

Clang! Cling-clang! SHING!

It kept on going, a steady metallic rattle that begged to be investigated. He took in a deep and exasperated breath and let it out slowly. Sal's was just around the corner, and he could smell the pizza from here. His stomach growled. But it would have to wait while he checked this out.

"Typical Parker luck," he muttered. "Just typical."

He stuffed his hands into his pockets and casually strolled down the street, following the noise to a narrow alleyway. A short distance inside, a large tanker truck idled, blocking his view. On its front was the Oscorp logo, painted in a bright and glaring green.

If Oscorp was involved, he needed a better look. The cab of the truck sat empty, its door wide open. It would be tight, but he'd changed into his suit in worse places, and he didn't want to waste any more time than necessary. The more he listened to it, the more that noise sounded like swordplay.

With a quick backwards glance to ensure that no one could see him, he slid into the driver's seat and removed his outer layer of clothing to reveal the Spider Suit beneath. The skintight fabric fit him like a glove, so comfortable that sometimes he forgot he was wearing it. He pulled his mask on, the chrome-plated lenses cutting the harsh rays of the midday sun. Now he could investigate without risking his loved ones. They tended to pay for his screw-ups, which was why he kept his mask on and his identity locked down tight.

He slid silently from the cab and contemplated his options. The long metal tank blocked his view of most of the action behind the truck. He needed a better vantage point. A quick blast with his web spinners, and he could be atop that auto body building in seconds, but the movement would almost certainly draw the attention of the swordfighters in the alleyway. He needed a stealthier approach.

His fingers grazed the side of the tanker truck, tingling as electrostatic force built nearly to shock-point between his skin and the slick metal. Then he climbed easily up the curving surface, his atoms sticking to the metal like a magnet and releasing at his whim. He crouched low to the truck's surface as he crept to the top, his limbs jutting out at arachnoid angles. He'd been doing this for years, and it still amazed him every time.

Atop the truck, he crept toward the ongoing swordplay. When he finally got a good look at the action he paused in shock, barely able to believe what he was seeing.

Loki and Venom were engaged in an epic swordfight, if you could call it that. Loki carried a sword, but Venom wielded a broken off streetlamp. As he exchanged brutal blows with the Asgardian, black symbiotic tendrils extended from his back, holding aloft a hose that dribbled a disgusting green glop onto the ground. Its other end terminated at the tanker truck.

The two seemed fairly evenly matched. Loki swept his weapon around in a wide arc, waiting for his opponent to commit to a block before changing trajectory at the last moment. The sword's razor edge slid down the lamp and grazed Venom's ribcage, eliciting a grunt of pain. But the Asgardian didn't notice the black and glistening tentacle that swung at him from behind, smacking him in the side of the head. It knocked him off balance, sending his return swing wide. The sword took a chunk out of the apartment building, spraying brick dust in all directions.

Peter knew he needed to put a stop to this, but he wasn't sure which side to take. He'd worked with Loki in the past, and although they'd been on the same side, he knew that the God of Mischief didn't do loyalty. And of course, he had a history with Eddie Brock. It wasn't a pleasant one. On the surface, he and Eddie had a lot in common, with one major exception: Eddie had embraced the Venom symbiote, while the mere thought of what he'd done under the sway of the bloodthirsty alien made Peter sick to his stomach. Eddie might have things under control for the moment, but Peter had been there once, too. The symbiote was patient. It would strike at the most inopportune moment, and Eddie might not be able to resist.

Peter could only hope that that moment wasn't today.

At the end of the day, he wouldn't trust either of them with a dribbling hose full of presumably toxic sludge. So, he'd just have to take control of the truck and sort out the logistics later.

Easy peasy.

He stood up and said, "That looks like fun. Can I play, too?"

They stopped trying to kill each other for just a moment, goggling up at him with an almost comical surprise. Before they could recover, he leaped off the tanker, all of his senses alert. He would defend himself, disarm them if possible, and wrest control of that hose before whatever was inside it hurt somebody.

But before he could do any of that, something unexpected happened. Loki took a step back, lowering his sword.

"Good day, old friend," he said, saluting Peter with the blade. "I'd love to chat, but I have places to go and things to do. I'm sure the two of you can carry on without me, as painful as that might be."

"No!" Venom shrieked.

"As for you, my skilled adversary, we will meet again." Loki pulled a small object from his pocket and flung it at the hulking black monstrosity. It glittered as the sun hit it – a green glass pendant on a long gold chain. "You've earned it."

"Now, wait just a minute…" said Peter.

But Loki did not in fact wait a minute. In fact, everything happened so fast. The chain landed around Venom's neck as if guided by sorcery, which it probably was. The symbiote grabbed it and yanked once before breaking off to screech in pain. Then Loki blinked out of existence with a flash of magic. His afterimage hung in the air for a second after he was gone, the air stinking of ozone.

Venom didn't even pause. His baleful alien eyes remained fixed on Peter's masked face. Behind him, the hose drooped toward the ground as the symbiote's grip loosened, all his attention fixed on his enemy. Sludge began to dribble on the ground again, pattering down into an open manhole with a wet plunk.

"The hose!" Peter exclaimed. "Don't drop it!"

"Traitor!" Venom growled, ignoring him completely. "You are on his side. Don't try to fool me."

"We barely know each other!" Peter protested, but it was no use.

Venom swung the lamppost, putting all his considerable strength behind the blow. Peter dodged out of the way, his augmented reflexes moving his body at superhuman speeds. But Venom wasn't exactly slow. The lamppost missed Peter by millimeters. He grabbed it, twisting it out of the symbiote's grip, and tossed it down the alley with a deafening clang and a shower of sparks.

"I'm not taking sides here," Peter said. "I just want to know what's in that truck."

He couldn't believe he was trying to rationalize with Venom, but here he was. It wouldn't work, of course. The symbiote fed on aggression and anger. Eddie might have been a smart guy and a decent reporter when he kept his head on straight, but his animosity ran too deep. It was futile, but Peter had to at least try so he could sleep better at night.

Not well, but better.

Venom looked down, and for a moment, Peter thought he'd actually gotten through to the big lug. He must be thinking about what Peter had said. But then the symbiote picked up a stray trash can and tossed it at him.

Once again, Peter dodged easily, and the can clattered to the ground behind him.

"If you're thinking of taking up baseball, I wouldn't quit your day job," he said in conversational tones. "You couldn't hit the side of a barn."

"Always a comedian," said Venom, the harsh alien tones running cold fingers down Peter's spine.

"It's one of my many talents," he said, pushing the fear away. "You working for Oscorp now? Or was Loki?"

"Stop trying to distract me and fight!"

"Come on, man. I know we don't see eye-to-eye, but can't we table it for the moment? At least we could stop trying to kill each other until we shut down the truck. After that, we can get back to our regularly scheduled violence if you want."

"Trickery!" shouted Venom. "Lies!"

He was beyond rational thought. This wasn't going to end well, and although Eddie Brock had caused Peter Parker a lot of pain and grief in the past, he couldn't stop the regret that swelled deep within him.

"For what it's worth, I'm sorry. I wish I'd been wrong about you," he said.

Peter meant it, too. For a long time, Eddie Brock had been a cautionary tale of what could have happened to him if Peter hadn't come to his senses, but he'd held out hope that maybe the other man would turn out to be stronger willed. He would have been thrilled to be proven wrong about the dire fate that awaited anyone who gave in to the symbiotes but, time and again, he'd seen it firsthand. All they brought was death.

Venom launched himself at his opponent, but Peter was ready. They'd fought a hundred times before. Eddie Brock would always be his enemy. But this fight was uniquely dangerous in one important way: as Venom rushed toward his opponent, he dropped the hose. It fell in what felt like slow motion. Peter shouted, but to no avail. Venom didn't care. He didn't even appear to have heard.

The end of the hose fell to the ground, rolled, and settled into the open manhole with a clunk. Peter could hear a slow-motion glug-glug, like a hundred two-liters were simultaneously being poured down some massive drain. He flung out a web, intending to pull the nozzle from the manhole, but Venom barreled into him, knocking the webbing wide and carrying the two web-slingers down to the concrete.

The truck would empty itself into the water supply, and even though he didn't know what was inside, it was a safe bet to assume that it wasn't fluoride.

"Look, just grab the hose, would ya?" he begged, as they rolled across the dirty ground. "You don't want to see people die any more than I do."

Venom's beefy hands closed around Peter's neck, cutting off his air. He scrambled to dislodge his attacker. His superhuman stamina would allow him to remain conscious for a while without oxygen, but not forever.

His fingers struggled for purchase on the symbiote's slick skin. That weirdly incongruous green pendant swung between them as they grappled for dominance, bonking him in the nose. Fetid breath washed over his face. The mask muted some of the stench, but still… Peter yanked at Venom's wrists, loosening his grip just enough to pull in a lungful of air.

"Ever heard of mouthwash?" he gasped.

The fanged maw opened in response, letting out a tortured screech. Apparently, Venom was a little sensitive about his dental hygiene. Peter would have felt bad about pushing his buttons if not for the fact that the symbiote had been trying to kill him.

Strangely, Venom didn't pursue his advantage. Instead, the symbiote stood up with his hands to his head, continuing to shriek loud enough to wake the dead. That was one good thing about living in NYC. People stayed out of the way when things got sticky. Sometimes. Anything was better than nothing.

"No!" said Venom, staggering backwards. "Stop!"

"I'm… not doing anything." Peter stood up, bracing one hand against the back of the truck, and hesitated. He would have suspected a trick, but the symbiote didn't have that kind of subtlety. Or any subtlety, for that matter. So, he asked a question that was a bit ridiculous given the circumstances. "You OK?"

For a moment, Venom didn't answer. Then, Peter's Spider-Sense leaped into overdrive, and he tucked and rolled just in time to avoid a sweeping blow from his symbiotic adversary. A massive fist smashed into the back of the truck right next to where his head had been moments before. Some mechanism inside the vehicle gave way with a clang and a hiss of steam that made his suit cling wetly to his face and shoulders.

"Ugh!" he exclaimed, pawing at the damp fabric. It smelled like oil and mold. Guess he'd be washing the suit early this week.

This would have been an ideal time for Venom to make his move, but the symbiote crouched on the ground instead, clawing at his own head in what looked like another wave of agony. Peter took a cautious step toward him, trying to figure out what was happening. But he saw nothing out of the ordinary except… were the symbiote's eyes green? They'd never had color before, and that was odd.

He took a deep breath, regretted it, and then steeled himself to make another offer of help that Venom would ignore. Again. But he had to continue to try to talk some sense into the guy. It didn't mean they had to be buddies and sing kumbaya.

"Look, Eddie," he said.

Before he could get any further, the symbiote crouched, gathering his considerable strength, and leaped into the air. A stream of webbing spurted from one outstretched arm. For a moment, Peter debated stopping him, but it wasn't worth it. His repeated entreaties weren't getting anywhere. Besides, he needed to deal with the hose. In all of the chaos, he'd nearly forgotten about the green substance being pumped into the ground.

He hurried toward the back of the truck and heaved the tubing free of the street. A thick liquid splashed sluggishly onto the ground, glowing a putrid green. His Spider-Sense flared as he picked up the tube, and he paused, ready for anything. But he sensed and heard nothing. No, this was a generalized sense of danger, like he got when he tried to take his mask off without noticing a security camera pointed right at him. Sometimes, if the danger was great enough, even inanimate objects could trigger his Spidey-Sense. Picking up the hose had triggered his warning system, and that meant one thing: this stuff was really dangerous.

Ugh, thought Peter. *I'd better be careful. Last thing I want to do is take a bath in that yuck, if it's bad enough to give me the heebie-jeebies.*

His stomach sank as he looked down into the open manhole. How much of this stuff had poured out while he'd been distracted by Venom? Had that been Eddie's plan all along, to distract him while the truck emptied?

The next time Peter Parker saw Eddie Brock, he wasn't going to allow himself to be diverted by his own Boy Scout tendencies. He wouldn't try to reason or redeem. He wouldn't be cruel, because he wasn't that guy, but he couldn't let the symbiote get away with this.

But first, he needed to get this situation under control. The hose continued to dribble, so he found a convenient garbage bag to wipe it on. Then he held it up high over his head, hoping that gravity would keep it from spilling all over him while he shut down the truck. He'd never worked one of these before, but how hard could it be?

It turned out that the mechanism was quite easy to figure out thanks to the big red sign labeled "Emergency Stop." Unfortunately, the space beneath the sign had been pulverized by Venom's fist. If there had been an emergency stop button, it was no more. In fact, none of the controls seemed to do anything, and although Peter could have figured out how to jury rig the system with time and tools, he had neither right now.

He was stuck here for the moment. He'd be late for the meeting, but it couldn't be helped. He couldn't just leave this truck unattended. Everything else would have to wait. As he began to spray webbing to cover the dribbling hole, his stomach growled.

He'd never gotten that pizza, either, darn it.

THREE

T'Challa checked the dashboard clock for the third time in as many minutes. He disliked tardiness on principle. When he was a boy, he'd constantly shown up late for everything, from mealtimes to matters of state, until his father, King T'Chaka, had sat him down and explained, in the gentlest tones possible, that timeliness was an expression of respect, and lateness a mortal insult. Ever since then, T'Challa had made it a point to be early whenever he could.

Some tardiness couldn't be helped, though. His attendance at the League of Nations scientific committee meeting had been essential, and his presentation on alternative fuel sources well received. Sometimes, he marveled at the backward thinking of some world leaders, but then he reminded himself that everyone started somewhere. After all, he'd once been a boy who routinely showed up half an hour late for dinnertime.

He sat back against the smooth tan leather of the hired car and tried to relax. Outside the tinted windows, the New York streets were jam-packed with commuters and cabs. At regular intervals, horns honked and angry voices shouted out of open car windows, but these gestures failed to have their desired effects. If this traffic didn't improve, he'd get to the Sanctum Sanctorum more quickly on foot. In fact, he might even make it faster if he crawled.

But kings didn't suggest such things. Instead, he checked the time again. When he lifted his eyes from the watch's gleaming face, he found Okoye's amused brown eyes staring at him via the rearview mirror. The captain of the Dora Milaje had insisted on driving him today, even though there were many younger warriors who would be more suited for such a menial task. Not that he minded. After their long acquaintance, she felt as much like family as his sister, Shuri.

"We will make it, my king," she said in the traditional Hausa dialect.

"Am I that transparent, Okoye?" he replied.

"I have served you a long time. I know you as well as I know the grip of my own spear."

"Nicely said."

T'Challa's teeth flashed in appreciation of the imagery, and the bodyguard's smooth brown head bowed momentarily in acceptance of the compliment. After a pause broken only by the hiss of the luxury car's air conditioning unit, she added, "Although, I am beginning to think that it would be quicker to walk."

He needed no further urging. After a morning spent sitting in board rooms, he needed to move. But just as his hand grazed the door handle, Okoye's Kimoyo card beeped. Although the car boasted an exceptional GPS system, it couldn't hold a candle to the processing speed and capability of the Wakandan tech. The Kimoyo card made a top-of-the-line cell phone look as basic as an abacus. She'd been using hers to navigate her way around town ever since they'd arrived.

"Hold, please," said Okoye. "I may have a way through."

With a quick twist of the wheel, she pulled off the road and into a narrow alleyway. Brick walls closed in on the car, blocking the glare of the midday sun. The car passed beneath a flapping banner stretched across the narrow passage and out onto another packed street. Okoye wove through the traffic and into another alleyway, guided by the gentle voice of the Kimoyo card.

Here, the ground was scattered with refuse, and Okoye drove with care, trying to avoid the broken glass strewn over the dirty concrete. Although they'd brought their Kimoyo cards, they hadn't had the time to change out the hired car's tires for something a little more durable. The last thing they needed was a flat.

As she drove, Okoye leaned forward, peering out the front window at something he couldn't see. Before he could inquire, she said, "Damisa-Sarki? My scanners tell me that the avatar of Anansi is engaged in battle up ahead. How shall I proceed?"

Okoye had always held tight to traditions. She called her king "Damisa-Sarki," or "the panther" in the Hausa dialect, and Spider-Man was "the avatar of Anansi," the West African spider god. T'Challa thought Spider-Man secretly liked that. After all, who would balk at being called the god's chosen? Men had died for lesser honorifics.

He didn't hesitate, activating his Panther suit with a thought, and as its vibranium-laced microweave fabric enclosed him, he reached for the door handle once again. Part of him still delighted in the same blissful sensation he'd experienced the first time he'd donned the Panther mask: the feeling that he was finally whole, the way the gods had intended him to be. But there was no time to dwell on such things. After all, he didn't want to be late for the fight any more than he wanted to be tardy for anything else.

"Maneuver the car as close as you can. We'll need it. I will go ahead," he said, opening the door while the car still moved.

Okoye's lips pursed in frustration. She hated seeing anyone go off to battle without her, and least of all her king. But she couldn't argue with his orders.

A dark colored blur streaked toward the car, moving so quickly that it was barely visible in the dim light. T'Challa threw open the door and leaped out into the alleyway, but it was too late to interfere. Venom's glossy black bulk landed on the roof of the car, denting the metal, and continued down the alleyway.

Okoye sprang from the driver's seat, her spear at the ready. Although she was dressed for the day in a neat black suit, T'Challa knew that her armor sat beneath the fancy clothes. Her keen eyes tracked the symbiote's movement away from them.

"Follow Venom," ordered T'Challa. "I will assist Spider-Man. Rendezvous back here when you have tracked him to his lair, and if we are already gone, meet us at the Sanctum Sanctorum."

"As you wish, my king."

Okoye took off, running with the easy stride of a woman who could keep up the blistering pace for hours without tiring. If anyone could track an airborne alien symbiote, it would be her. T'Challa turned his attention down the alleyway. An Oscorp truck blocked the space up ahead, its blinkers filling the space with yellow light. On and off. On and off.

Where was Spider-Man? Over the past month or so, T'Challa had gotten an opportunity to work with him more closely, and he knew that the intrepid web-slinger wouldn't allow an opponent to escape without a fight. It didn't bode well.

"Spider-Man?" T'Challa called, the suit amplifying his voice to carry down past the truck with ease.

"Panther? Is that you? Down here! I could use a hand."

T'Challa followed the voice, hurrying toward the back end of the truck where he found Spider-Man holding a long hose up over his head with one hand while he fumbled with the valves on the back of the truck with the other. The end of the hose had been sealed by a thick wad of webbing, but glowing green goop had begun to seep out the edges. It threatened to spill over at any moment.

"How may I assist?" asked T'Challa.

"The control panel is shot, and I can't jury rig it from here. Can you figure out some way to shut this thing down? I'm not sure what this stuff is, but I'm pretty sure taking a shower in it would be a bad idea," said Spider-Man.

A single glance at the control panel told him that Spider-Man's assessment was an accurate one. Not that he was surprised. The web-slinger had proven to be a potent ally, and their lively discussions about technological innovations had made T'Challa's participation in the Shadow Avengers initiative a pleasure.

"Perhaps I could close off the tanker from above," he suggested, indicating the juncture where the hose plugged into the truck.

"I had the same idea, but it's not easy to do while you're juggling toxic waste."

T'Challa smiled at his friend's attempt at humor, although his mask hid the expression. But the suit would protect him from a wide variety of hazardous materials, and it seemed prudent to continue to wear it until the truck was decommissioned.

Although he'd never used this type of truck before and the equipment was caked with grime and worn down by repeated use, he was easily able to intuit the operational mechanism after an initial inspection. Within moments, he had shut the valve manually and turned off the hose.

"That should do it," he said. "I believe I have something in the car that would help seal the hose off more effectively. Unless you'd like to stand there like the Statue of Liberty all day?"

Spider-Man chuckled. "I'd appreciate that. You think it would work down there, too?" he asked.

T'Challa followed the web-slinger's pointing finger to the open manhole. Globs of green goo clung to its edges. It didn't take a genius IQ to figure out what had happened here. Venom had been pouring this mysterious glowing substance into the water supply. The implications of such a thing were sobering indeed.

"I can stop up this section of the pipe," said T'Challa. "But I'm afraid that's the best I can do at the moment. Then we can liaise with the city and offer our assistance in evaluating further damage."

"I'll take anything at this point," said Spider-Man. "My hand's falling asleep."

"Hold tight, brother," said T'Challa, hurrying toward the car and tapping on his Kimoyo card as he went.

Almost instantaneously, the card opened up a voice channel to Shuri's lab. Her voice came through as clear as if she stood next to him, and it dripped with amusement.

"I told you that I should have come with you," she said in lieu of a greeting.

"You were right, sister," he said, because she wouldn't let it go until he admitted it. "As usual."

"Laying it on thick, aren't you, brother? Things must be very bad. Did you get arrested?"

"No."

"Too bad. That would have been very funny," she joked.

He outlined the situation in a few brief words. Shuri listened in silence, her playfulness drying up as the implications hit her. Although her youthful nature sometimes got the best of her, she was one of the most intelligent people he'd ever known. Over the years, he had found himself relying on her as a sounding board with increasing frequency.

When he'd finished, she responded briskly, all business.

"You'll have to bring me a sample," she ordered. "I'll conduct a full analysis since you're too busy rubbing elbows to work in the lab anymore."

"Of course," he said, ignoring the jibe. "I am fetching the sample containers at this very moment."

"Show off."

His lips curled in amusement as he opened the passenger door of the car and looked around for the emergency kit. Okoye always packed one, but he wasn't sure where she'd stashed it. In the trunk, maybe? He could contact her via the Kimoyo card to ask, but he hated to interrupt her while she was tracking. In an ideal world, she would catch Venom and pump him for information.

The emergency kit wasn't in the passenger compartment, so he popped the trunk, sagging in relief as he spotted it. The oversized briefcase was packed with Wakandan technology, each item seated snugly in a cutout of dense foam. He pulled a lined and sealed specimen cup from its spot in the corner, and then let his fingers trail over the rest of the supplies. "What do you think of using the impact foam?"

"To block the contaminant from reaching the water supply?" Shuri replied, picking up on his meaning without needing an explanation. "Not a bad idea. It's quite absorbent. It's probably your best option, although the locals won't be able to remove it. The city authorities will likely throw a fit over having to replace the pipes. It wouldn't be great for diplomacy."

"It'll be better than poisoning the populace with whatever this is. We'll pay for the replacements. Will it work?"

"Anything that reached the main pipe is long gone. But if the contaminant is as thick as you say, and Spider-Man interceded early on in the dumping process, the foam should soak up most of it. As soon as you can get the sample back to me, I'll begin the analysis. I can be in touch with the EPA and the city officials if further action is necessary."

"Once I reach the Sanctum Sanctorum, I'll ask Doctor Strange to teleport the sample to you immediately. I'm sure he'll be happy to help."

"Ask him to deliver it outside my lab, please. His portals always set off my sensors."

"Maybe your sensors need adjusting," he said mildly, and cut off the connection while she was still sputtering.

FOUR

Stephen Strange, the Sorcerer Supreme, did not fidget. Perhaps he paced in thought while he waited for the Shadow Avengers to arrive for their meeting. It was entirely possible that he drummed his fingers in deep concentration while he sat at his desk, surrounded by piles of arcane texts. But he most certainly did not fidget. Such a thing would be beneath him.

Still, he could not deny his concern. The city – the world – had been too quiet in the few short months since the Guardians, Iron Man, and Ms Marvel had foiled Dormammu's plan. The Dread Sorcerer wouldn't go down without a fight. Out of everyone in the universe, Doctor Strange probably knew that better than anyone.

As if summoned by that train of thought, a portal opened in the corner of the library, near the stack of Atlantean histories he'd been meaning to read but hadn't managed to get to yet. He tensed momentarily. Perhaps this was it, the source of his foreboding. Perhaps he'd instinctively anticipated the attack that would come through this portal, striking directly at the heart of the Sanctum Sanctorum. Or maybe the portal would disgorge a herald who would bring news of Dormammu's next strike. He stood, summoning his power like a cloak around him, ready for anything.

But the figure that emerged from the portal was neither attacker nor herald. Her disembodied spirit shone with crackling energy. Although this astral form held no color and was partially translucent, he would have known her heart-shaped face and luminous eyes anywhere. He often saw them in his dreams.

Clea. His former wife.

Although they had unfinished business between them, she didn't often darken his doorstep. Something had brought her here.

"Are you well?" he asked. "Do you need assistance?"

Her lips curled. "Stand down, Stephen," she said. "I have no dogs on my heels. Not yet, anyway."

He relaxed his hold on the arcane energies he'd held at the ready and gestured toward the sofa against the wall.

"Please, sit," he said. "I'd offer refreshment, but…"

"It's an empty platitude given that I'm not really here," she finished for him. "I know."

"Why send your astral form?" he asked as they settled down onto the smooth leather. "Of course, I appreciate the visit, but…"

"I'd prefer not to attract attention by traveling in my physical body," she replied. "And even if that weren't the case, I'm otherwise occupied. But I needed to talk to you."

"About?"

"I have put some thought into your offer to join the Shadow Avengers. I am afraid I must regretfully decline."

He frowned. "May I ask why? You of all people know what is at stake if Dormammu should succeed in his efforts to unite the entire Multiverse under his rule. We must unite to stand against him if we are to prohibit this reality from coming to pass." He hesitated. "If it is a matter of our personal issues…"

She patted him on the hand. All he could feel was a cold tingle as her astral form intersected with his physical one.

"Our feelings are irrelevant," she said. "This is what must be."

"Why?" he asked. "I have hand-selected this team, and we are uniquely suited to stand against Dormammu regardless of his next step. But I am in dire need of your magic, Clea, as well as your counsel. As his niece, you understand Dormammu better than anyone. Even me."

"I can offer my counsel at a distance if you like, but no more. My presence will only attract my uncle's attention. Furthermore, I am pursuing a promising lead in Avalon. Perhaps the new spells I have discovered here might help us defeat him. I cannot leave now."

"Even if it means losing the nexus to the Multiverse? You know what it will mean if your uncle takes over our world. It is the stepping stone to countless other realities ripe for conquest."

"I am playing the long game, Stephen, and that requires sacrifice. You know this as well as I do," she said gently.

He let his head fall. As the Sorcerer Supreme, he didn't often let down his guard. The world needed him at his best, and Stephen Strange had always performed well under pressure. But Clea had a way of breaking down his defenses.

"I do," he admitted. "But I refuse to accept such an avoidable loss. Clea, he destroyed Praeterus. The entire planet. All of those Kree lives wasted. He won't hesitate to do the same to Earth."

"He needs your planet. He won't destroy it."

"So he'll just enslave us." Strange gritted his teeth, mastering his growing frustration with effort. "You know what will happen. I will stand up to him, and the outcome of this encounter is unclear. I am not guaranteed to win."

She hung her head, sorrow written clearly on her face despite its watery appearance.

"I know," she said.

"I ask not as the Sorcerer Supreme, but as someone you once loved. You know I don't beg easily, Clea, but this time…" He shook his head, unable to shake the growing sense of foreboding that had haunted his every waking moment since the destruction of the planet Praeterus a few short weeks earlier. "I have done everything possible to prepare, but this time it is not enough. I need you here."

She shook her head again, and the refusal nearly broke him. But he let none of his emotions show on his face. He couldn't afford to fall apart. Not now. Especially if he would have to face Dormammu, the Dread Sorcerer, in a magical battle alone. He had done it many times before and won, but something told him this time would be different. The destruction of Praeterus hadn't been without its purpose. All of the planet's magical energy had to go somewhere. A great deal of it had been absorbed by the planet killer, but Earth's heroes had defeated her after a mighty battle. If his calculations were correct, she hadn't sucked up all of Praeterus's magic. Thirteen point three percent remained unaccounted for.

Stephen Strange had never been a superstitious man, but that number struck him as very unlucky indeed.

He took in a breath, intending to explain his calculations, to make Clea see that this time was different. That her magical research could wait until the world – his world – didn't hang in the balance. But he had already explained it all in his letter. He'd made his arguments. She had refused, and he had his pride.

He would find a way to defeat her uncle without her, but he would never forget this moment. He had begged, and she had refused him. Abandoning his arguments, he stood, drawing himself up to his full height and straightening his shoulders.

"I suppose this conversation is over, then," he said. "If you'll excuse me, I have work to do. Preparations to make."

She reached out to him as she stood, but he evaded her hand. Such a gesture meant nothing now. He knew where her priorities lay.

"I should go," she agreed. "But you're wrong about one thing."

"What?" he asked, despite himself.

"You said you were someone I used to love. I still do."

But he had no time for emotion. His need for her support had been nothing but a momentary weakness. After all, how many times had he faced Dormammu before? He would do so again and set this juvenile need for support aside. The Sorcerer Supreme had to be strong enough to stand alone.

He nodded coldly. "I am sure you think you do," he said. "Now, if you'll excuse me."

He went to his desk and turned his attention to the tomes gathered there, even though he had no real use for them at that moment. After he rifled through the pages of the Grimorium Verum for the third time, magic washed over him as she departed back through the portal without a word.

Stephen Strange remained at his desk, staring down at the book, until Wong came to fetch him for the meeting half an hour later. During all that time, he didn't comprehend a single word.

FIVE

As she approached the rear entrance of the Sanctum Sanctorum, Kamala Khan adjusted her mask for the third time. She still wasn't used to walking around in her super hero costume and couldn't shake the feeling that people were staring. Once he'd discovered her discomfort, Doctor Strange had kindly made arrangements for her to enter the building through the back, which required navigating a labyrinthine maze of narrow alleyways and up and down a pair of dubious fire escapes. But it was way better than marching straight up to the Victorian brownstone that housed the universe's mightiest sorcerer while people took pictures with their cell phones.

Maybe with time, she'd get less neurotic. Most of the other Shadow Avengers walked around without masks on all the time. Then again, their circumstances were different. Doctor Strange was the Sorcerer Supreme as a full-time job; he had no alternate life to hide. The Black Panther was a freaking king, so no one would dare give him any grief about putting on spandex and running off to fight crime. Mr Cage was literally unbreakable, so it didn't matter if people knew who he was or not. The only other member of the group who showed up masked was Spider-Man. It made Kamala feel like the two of them were part of a club. At the very least, she didn't feel like such a wuss for refusing to take hers off.

She adjusted it one final time before stopping in front of a plain brick wall. It took her a moment to find the right place to knock, and then a long wait until a black outline appeared in the wall, and the bricks disappeared, revealing an opening into the Sanctum Sanctorum kitchen. Silver appliances and neat counters gleamed under the bright fluorescents. Wong stood silhouetted in the doorway, a beatific smile on his aged features, the light shining off his bald head and robes.

"Good afternoon, Ms Marvel," he said, bowing. "Please come in."

"Thanks, Mr Wong."

He sighed. "How many times do I have to ask? Wong. Just Wong. Not Mr Wong. Not Sir Wong. Not Dr Wong. Just Wong."

"It's a habit!" she protested, her cheeks going red. "I'm sorry."

He clucked his tongue at her, his dancing eyes making it obvious that he was just teasing. Slowly, she relaxed as she followed him through the kitchen and into the foyer. The first few times she'd been here, she'd goggled at the ornate furnishings and interesting artifacts hung on the walls. Mysterious gas lamps flickered into flame as they passed and then extinguished themselves when no longer needed. She wondered what would happen if she ran up and down the halls, but she'd never had the chance to find out.

But she'd visited a few times a week for the past month now, and she'd gotten used to the place. Now, she had to admit that nothing on the walls was as interesting as Wong himself. Was he

Doctor Strange's employee? Friend? She'd come in once while he was working in the kitchen, and he'd been nonchalantly juggling knives. Not small ones, either. She'd been worried he'd take a finger off, but he'd escaped without a scratch.

"You can take your mask off, if you like," he offered as they crossed the foyer to the study. It seemed much further away than it had last time, but sometimes this place did that. It stretched like taffy, and no one even blinked, so Kamala pretended it didn't weird her out.

"I'll change out of my mask if you change out of your robes," she blurted. Immediately, she clapped her hands over her mouth. "Oh, jeez. I'm so sorry. That was insensitive. I shouldn't make fun of your religion or whatever."

But instead of getting angry, he threw his head back and laughed, stopping right in front of the drawing room door.

"That was a good one!" he exclaimed. "Can I tell you a secret?"

She was so relieved not to have shoved her foot into her mouth that she nodded without even thinking about the question.

"I only wear these robes because they're more comfortable than jeans. I can have a nice meal without loosening my belt, eh?" He elbowed her as if this was a joke.

"I hate jeans," she replied, because he seemed to be waiting for her to say something. "Leggings are where it's at, man."

"See? You are picking up what I'm putting down."

He winked at her, and after a moment, she smiled. She liked Wong. Maybe at some point, he'd teach her how to juggle. Unless he did it with magic? Before she could ask, the doorbell rang.

"Let yourself in," he urged. "I've got to get that."

But she didn't want to go in alone. Last week, she'd arrived before everyone else and spent an awkward five minutes alone with Doctor Strange while he inquired about her studies and feigned interest in the frog dissection they were doing in science class. After it was all over, she realized how dumb it was to brag about getting an A for dissecting an amphibian when you were talking to a man who had performed some of the most difficult brain surgeries in the world. She didn't want a repeat of that humiliation if she could avoid it, so she waited.

It was a good thing she did, too, because the rest of the Shadow Avengers arrived all at once. Her relief quickly gave way to concern when they hurried past her without any more than a brief greeting. Of course, Spider-Man's mask hid his expression from view, but the other two wore identical expressions of determination. Jaws locked. Eyes intent.

Something had happened, and Kamala was willing to bet that it wasn't good.

She followed them into the drawing room, shutting the door behind her. As her fingers closed on the knob, she realized they were shaking. Logically, she knew she belonged here. She'd stood against the planet killer with the rest of the heroes like Tony Stark and the Guardians of the Galaxy just a month earlier. She'd made an alliance with the Kree student in her school, Halla-ar, which gave them the information necessary to unravel the mystery. Without her, Earth might have gone nuclear, just like Praeterus.

Still, she couldn't help but feel like she was about to get in over her head. Again.

SIX

The drawing room had been set up for their meeting with a round wooden table and heavy, ornate chairs awaited each member of the Shadow Avengers. Luke Cage held out a chair for Ms Marvel, and pushed it in for her once she'd taken her seat. He had all the faith in the world in her abilities, but becoming a father had changed him. He couldn't help but pick the safest spot at the table and deposit the teenager into it. It wouldn't guarantee her safety if attackers burst in through the door or windows, but it put her in the position least likely to take immediate fire, and that was enough for him.

He sat to her right, in a spot that gave him a good vantage point of the door and the long row of windows swathed in heavy velvet curtains. A quick glance told him that everything was as secure as it could be, and if he knew Strange at all, the sturdy locks on the windows were the least of the Sanctum's security measures.

Of course, that failed to make Luke relax his guard because such a thing wasn't in his nature. He might be unbreakable, but the people around him were always a different story. It was his job to do something about that. The Shadow Avengers could hold their own better than most, but he still had a responsibility to them, and he didn't take it lightly.

He folded his hands and scanned the table. Ms Marvel squirmed in her seat, fiddling with her mask. The young woman hadn't yet gotten used to the weight of heroism. She alternated between eagerness and nerves with whiplash-inducing speed. It was adorable, if exhausting. Sometimes, he looked at her and wondered what his daughter would be like at that age. If she was anything like Ms Marvel, he'd consider it a success. Despite her nerves, the young super hero showed up, even under the direst of circumstances. That was all anyone could ask for.

On her other side sat Stephen Strange, as calm and inscrutable as ever. His keen eyes under the dark brows missed nothing. But those long, delicate fingers toyed with the clasp on his cloak. The Sorcerer Supreme never fidgeted. He'd always remained cool as a cucumber even when it seemed certain that the world would end and there was nothing any of them could do about it. Still, everyone had things they cared about. Buttons to push. Unless Luke was mistaken, someone had found one of Strange's and pushed it hard. He'd have to keep an eye on that.

Next to him sat Spider-Man. Luke knew his true identity from way back in the day, but he respected Peter's decision to keep his mask on, even in the relative safety of the Sanctum Sanctorum. The sociopaths they fought against didn't play fair, and they'd take their ire out on family and friends if given the chance. That was why Luke had eventually realized that he could only be with someone who was able to hold their own.

Jessica Jones could do that and more. She'd keep their daughter safe while he took care of business here. But Peter didn't have that luxury. Luke's heart went out to him.

Today, the web-slinger hunched eagerly at the table, his gloved fingers drumming an impatient tattoo on the glossy wood. On his right, T'Challa, King of Wakanda, glanced at the fidgeting Avenger and smiled slightly at Luke. The two Black men exchanged respectful nods. T'Challa's keen eyes softened for a moment, and although no words were spoken, Luke understood his meaning as well as if they'd talked for hours. They were brothers, if not of the blood, then of the spirit. They'd taken each other's measure long ago, and although T'Challa wasn't his king, Luke would die for the man if necessary.

Doctor Strange gestured, and the empty glasses before them filled with their beverage of choice, as if the liquid had been pumped up from some hidden bar beneath the table. Luke couldn't help but flash his teeth in a grin. The sorcerer could never resist the urge to show off, just a little, before they began. Otherwise, he would have filled the glasses before they arrived.

He picked up his iced tea and took a sip to be polite.

"Shall we begin?" asked Strange, his low voice carrying easily across the lengthy table. "I am sure you all have important things to do, and I don't want to waste your time. With your kind permission, I would like to give you an update on my research into Dormammu's whereabouts, and then I'll open the floor for updates."

He paused to take in their nods, but before he could continue, a loud snarl broke the silence. It sounded like an animal ready to break its leash, and Luke tensed, his eyes flickering from the door to the windows and back again. But he saw nothing.

Spider-Man shifted uncomfortably in his chair. He flipped the bottom edge of his mask up over his clean-shaven chin and chugged the entire glass of soda that sat on the table before him. Then he wiped his mouth with the back of his hand before settling the mask back into place. The empty glass slowly began to refill.

"Sorry," he said. "I'm starving. I meant to eat on the way here, but I was unavoidably detained."

Luke chuckled, Ms Marvel snickered, and even the corner of Strange's mouth quirked up into a smile. The sorcerer tilted his head, looking off into the distance.

"Wong?" he said, even though his housemate was nowhere to be seen. "Could you bring down some snacks? I'm worried that our friendly neighborhood arachnid might digest himself if we don't feed him." He paused as if listening to some unheard response. "Thank you." Then he focused on the table. "We'll have some food here in a minute. Shall we continue in the meantime? I've been searching for signs of Dormammu's next move, and to date, he continues to lie low. This worries me."

"But…" The word tore from Ms Marvel's lips. "I want to hear what happened to Spider-Man. It seems like the kind of thing the Shadow Avengers ought to know about." She paused. "Please."

Doctor Strange's lips tightened almost imperceptibly. "I assume if his news was important enough, he would have made such a thing known when he arrived," he said. "Is that the case?"

The red masked face froze in thought as Spider-Man considered. Then he hitched a single shoulder. "Not sure what to think of it, to be honest," he said.

Luke leaned forward, the chair creaking under his considerable weight. Spider-Man had been around the block quite a few times, and Luke had learned to trust his fellow hero's instincts. If something nagged at him, it would be unwise to ignore it. "I think I would like to hear more about this," he said.

There it was again, that flash of displeasure across Stephen's face. It was gone almost as soon as it had arrived, but Luke had been watching for it. He'd never seen the sorcerer lose his cool, and he didn't want to start now.

"We do not have the time for this," said the sorcerer. "I have no quarrel with your outside activities, and I would not presume to ask you to set aside your important work. But I hope I do not need to remind you of the importance of our task. Dormammu destroyed a planet. If we do not remain vigilant, you won't have streets to patrol any longer."

"If a short report is enough to tilt the scales, we deserve to lose," Luke said, folding his massive arms. "Spider-Man has brought us information, and I for one would like to hear it."

Strange sighed.

"After all this time, you still do not understand," he said.

"No, you don't understand. Micromanage your students all you like, but we each bring skills to the table. If you don't lay off, we'll take them elsewhere. Or maybe that's just me."

It had needed to be said for a long while. Strange was smart – Luke had no illusions about that – but he held on too tight. Luke didn't fancy being led around by the nose, and he didn't regret standing up to the man. Well, maybe a little. Panther and Spider-Man both seemed to be taking the quarrel in stride, but Ms Marvel's wide eyes darted back and forth in what looked like panic. He hadn't meant to worry her. If this came to blows, he'd move her out of the way first.

But Strange slipped his placid mask back on and nodded, stroking his short beard. "If you insist," he said. "I will table my report for the moment. But I must register my objections. We are here for one purpose, and I beg you to consider whether you can put it first when it counts."

"Understood," said Luke. "Spider-Man? What do you have?"

"Uh… yeah," said Spidey, clearing his throat awkwardly. "I gotta admit, this one has me confused. On my way here, I saw Venom and Loki sword fighting over an Oscorp truck that was pouring toxic waste into the water supply."

That statement got attention. Even Doctor Strange jerked upright, his eyes glued to Spidey's mask.

"That doesn't sound good," said Ms Marvel faintly.

"No kidding," Spider-Man replied. "I had no idea who I was supposed to be helping. I don't know much about Thor's brother, but I wouldn't have pegged him as the sort to throw in with the likes of Norman Osborn."

"He'll throw in with anyone if it suits his purposes," said Strange, frowning. "But what purpose that is, I cannot say."

"What happened?" asked Luke.

"I decided it would be better to stop the truck and figure out who was to blame later. Loki poofed off through a magic portal, and Venom tried to rip my head off before he started arguing with himself. Then he ran off screaming," said Spider-Man.

"Odd," said Luke.

Spidey sighed. "Wish I could say I didn't see it coming, but that symbiote plays with your head. It was only a matter of time before Eddie lost the few marbles he had left." His stomach snarled as if to underscore the point.

Luke took this in silently. Although he didn't argue, he wasn't sure he bought that explanation. There were too many players in the mix for his liking. As far as he knew, Venom and the Green Goblin weren't buddies, and the Asgardian had no reason to associate with either of them. Something must have brought this disparate group together. Something big.

He wouldn't make an issue about it for now, but if the group opted not to follow up, he would seek out Spider-Man himself and offer his assistance. Once again, he met T'Challa's gaze across the table. The concern he saw mirrored in the Panther's eyes reassured him that at least some of his companions shared his desire to look into this further. They would pursue this together, regardless of Strange's protests. After all, it was their job. Avengers could not pick and choose their fights, no matter how badly they wanted to.

"My car arrived at the end of the fight," said the Wakandan king, drawing their attention. "My warrior Okoye followed Venom as he fled, while I assisted the avatar of Anansi in shutting down the truck."

"Any luck capturing Venom?" asked Strange.

"I am afraid not. He led her on a merry chase through the streets, and only after they had gone a considerable way did he take to the skies where she could not follow. I suspect this was designed to draw her away from the site and insure that as much of the liquid as possible made it into the water supply, but I cannot prove this. She did report that he seemed unwilling to engage in battle."

This news gave even Spider-Man pause.

"That makes no sense. If the symbiote is taking over, he should be ripping everyone's heads off. Those symbiotes love that kind of thing." He tried to turn it into a joke, but his revulsion was clear. "They see a head, they rip it off."

The door to the drawing room opened, and Wong entered with a cart burgeoning with random foodstuffs. A bowl of steaming Chinese dumplings nestled next to a plate piled high with potato pancakes. A precarious tower of unidentifiable cookies dusted powdered sugar down onto an intricate arrangement of fresh sashimi. In the corner sat a few steaming burgers, still wrapped in paper from the fast-food joint down the street. Under different circumstances, they would have fallen on the food with relish, but none of them so much as blinked. Not even Spider-Man, whose stomach still hadn't stopped growling.

"What about the liquid?" asked Strange.

"Shuri is analyzing it now," replied T'Challa. "We have taken the liberty of notifying the appropriate city authorities, as well as the EPA, and we will work with them on identification and cleanup. We were able to block off that section of pipe, but we don't yet know how much of the material made it into the water supply. For the moment, they have concocted a story about contaminated water and are encouraging residents in that neighborhood not to drink or bathe."

Luke shook his head. That was all well and good, but these people needed to live. And in that neighborhood, they didn't have a lot of spare cash around to go buying bottled water. A lot of those folks struggled to pay the bills as it was.

Although T'Challa couldn't relate, he had never been the kind of royalty who lost touch with the realities of life outside his walls. Luke had always admired how T'Challa made decisions that betrayed his extensive study of people of all walks of life. He leaned forward to catch Luke's gaze and said, "I have ordered deliveries of water to every home in the affected area. You and Spider-Man live here. You know the area better than the rest of us. I hope you will advise me on what else we can do to make sure that these people are adequately supported."

The tension in Luke's shoulders relaxed as he nodded. "Of course," he said. "Thank you."

"It sounds like we have reached a conclusion, then?" asked Strange. "Very good. I hope you will update us during our next meeting. But in the meantime, let us return to the topic at hand. Our reason for existing as a group. Dormammu."

He fixed them with a stern look that lingered on Luke. Luke gazed back steadily, unwilling to engage in a fight for control of the group. They would stay or not, and he would support their right to choose for themselves. But after so many weeks of discussing an enemy who hadn't shown his face, they weren't as eager as they'd been at the beginning. Luke had begun to wonder if they were chasing shadows, but the sorcerer remained adamant that the danger was real. Whether it would turn out to be prescience or paranoia remained to be seen.

"Let's hear it, then," said Luke, folding his arms. "I'm listening."

SEVEN

The meeting had ended long ago, but Stephen Strange remained at the empty table, staring at nothing whatsoever. His mind whirled with questions and conundrums. Normally he took delight in unsolvable problems, but lately he couldn't find the same pleasure in them. Which only served to bring up more questions about what had changed.

So, he sat in the study, trying to reorder his thoughts. As he contemplated, clouds crept over the sky bathing the room in shadows. The heavy air promised rain. Perhaps he'd go for a walk in it. The water might reorient him in a way that his usual tricks had not achieved. Meditation, fasting, quiet contemplation: all had failed to bring him the understanding and focus he needed.

The door opened on silent hinges. Wong entered the room, making a beeline for the food cart. The Shadow Avengers had eaten quite a bit, but their consumption had barely dented the extensive spread. Wong didn't seem to mind. He surveyed the half-full plates with evident delight, rubbing his hands together. Then, with careful deliberation, he selected a cream puff and shoved the whole thing into his mouth.

As he tried to chew the sizeable confection, his eyes fell on Doctor Strange's shadowy figure. He betrayed no surprise. Instead, he swallowed hard, held out a plate, and said, "Cream puff?"

"How can you think of confectionery at a time like this?" snapped Strange.

"How can you not?" Wong replied, unruffled.

"I have bigger things on my mind."

Wong moved with a deceptive lightness that seemed in contrast with his stout figure and blunt, thick fingers. He set the plate down without disturbing the rest of the laden cart, and then took a seat at the table.

"Out with it," he said, gesturing. "What's bothering you?"

"It's nothing."

"Obviously not, or you wouldn't be sulking in the dark."

"I am the Sorcerer Supreme. I do not sulk."

"Ah," Wong said, and left it at that. He began to collect the empty glasses and dishware, making a small mountain of them. "How did the meeting go?"

"I'm losing them."

The truth put his poor temper into stark perspective. He had created this group for one purpose: to counter Dormammu's inevitable attempt to invade the planet. But then the attempt didn't come. The enemy didn't show, and his troops grew restless. Once they disbanded, the Dread Sorcerer would strike. He knew it deep in his bones, but he couldn't do a thing about it. He could bear many burdens, but he'd never been good at feeling powerless.

"Why do you say that?" asked Wong.

"In the middle of my report on Dormammu, Ms Marvel interrupted me to ask Spider-Man a question about Venom's lair. I don't think she heard a word I said."

"So? You had nothing new to report, did you? The situation is unusual enough that it bears following up, and it might do them some good to have something to do. Most people get restless when they sit around too long. They aren't conditioned for stillness. Heroes in particular."

"You don't need to tell me that," replied Strange. "My point remains valid."

"As does mine." Wong settled back into his seat behind the pile of crockery and folded his hands. "Stephen, you selected the Shadow Avengers because they have the strength of will to stand up to Dormammu. You can't turn around and complain that they're too independent."

Doctor Strange arched a dark eyebrow. "Lecturing me now, are we? What would you have me do, then, since you have this all figured out?"

"Allow them their own interests while you locate their ultimate target. You've said it yourself. Dormammu is planning something. Instead of waiting for him to come to you, why not take the fight to him?"

"I had intended to do so once Clea arrived, but she isn't coming."

Wong sighed. "Well, should you require another body for a ritual, you know you only need to ask. Otherwise, you will just have to… how do the kids say it? Put on your big boy pants."

He stood up and began to pile the soiled dishes onto the

cart. As he did, he snagged another cream puff and stuffed it into his mouth.

"You should try one," he said, after he'd swallowed. "It would sweeten your disposition."

"You sound like Luke Cage," said Doctor Strange. "I bid you both to remember this when Dormammu comes, and I stand between you and eternal servitude."

"Ah, but that's the point, isn't it? You can't stand alone. Like it or not, you need people. Friends." Wong patted him on the shoulder as he reached across the table for the dishes. "And I am your friend. The Shadow Avengers are, too, so perhaps you should stop treating them like servants."

"I'm trying to help them! To help everyone!" exclaimed Strange.

"Yet, here you sit, with the accumulated wisdom of countless sorcerers at your disposal, brooding when you could be looking for something that would help. There must be some spell or artifact that would do it."

"That wouldn't keep these Avengers out of trouble. They are determined to rush around chasing shadows while the enemy works in the background."

Wong clucked his tongue.

"What I hear you saying is that you are afraid, and you do not know how to handle it. I forgive your quick temper under these conditions. But if you do not face that fear, you will fall. That would be a pity," said Wong, not unkindly.

The Sorcerer Supreme opened his mouth to protest that he felt no such thing, but the words refused to come. Perhaps his longtime companion had a point. His iron-clad self-control, honed over years of contemplative study, had begun to slip.

His growing concern over Dormammu was only a part of it; Clea's rejection had pushed him over the edge. He had best get his head on straight before he lost his edge.

He stared off into the distance, lost in thought. When Wong let himself out of the room, Stephen Strange didn't even notice.

EIGHT

Eddie Brock waltzed right in through the loading dock of the Oscorp headquarters. He wore a dirt-streaked jumpsuit with a pair of worn work gloves sticking out of one pocket and a grimy baseball cap pulled down low over his face. No one would give him a second look in these duds. He was just another maintenance guy showing up for his shift. Nothing to see here.

No one bothered him as he crossed the open bays toward the entrance. No one expected a delivery this late in the day, and they definitely hadn't expected a symbiote to foil their fancy security cameras and vault over their expensive electric fence. That was the problem with employees these days. They couldn't think outside the box.

The problem was that Eddie couldn't either. Not now. His head still pounded from the beating it had taken earlier. One minute, he'd been choking the life out of that cursed web-slinger, and the next, it felt like an atomic bomb had gone off inside his noggin. Squealing noise filled his ears, and pain lanced through every cell in his body. Even more frightening was that the racket had hurt the symbiote, too. It had begged him to make it stop in a broken voice that nearly broke Eddie as well. For a moment, it felt like this would be the end. They'd both be taken down by some unseen attacker, linked to them through that blasted pendant.

The pain radiated out from the spot near his clavicle, just below the glass globe full of glowing green liquid, but he couldn't remove it no matter how hard he tried. That cheap-looking chain should have given way at the slightest tug, but it refused to budge, and tugging on it too much made the pain worse.

So he'd retreated. It hadn't been a conscious choice. Both he and his symbiote had been driven to near madness with agony, and when it finally eased, he found himself at the end of an alleyway with no idea how he'd got there. He didn't even know what part of the city he was in. But the running footsteps behind him suggested he wasn't alone, and although Eddie could be accused of a lot of things, he was no dummy. He knew he wasn't in any shape to defend himself. So, he shot a long stream of webbing off a nearby fire escape and swung up to the top of the apartment building it was attached to. There, he didn't even chance looking back. He just fled and hated himself for it.

Although he felt like he'd been stuffed into a bag with a pile of bricks and rolled down a hill, there had been no time to go to ground and lick his wounds. The pendant could start its agonizing assault on him at any moment. He didn't know why it had started or what made it stop. He had no idea how to find Loki, or if the Asgardian was even still on the planet. That left one possible lead.

Oscorp.

He had come to the headquarters to get answers. Norman

Osborn would give them to him, or Venom would snap his neck. It would be a public service.

All he had to do was find the megalomaniacal businessman with the answers, and that meant going up. He'd considered climbing up the exterior of the building, but that attracted more attention than he was prepared to entertain. On a good day, he might have relished the opportunity to disarm a bunch of goons and break their assault weapons into pieces in front of their shocked little faces, but not today. He had to save every remaining ounce of strength to face Osborn and come out with all his limbs intact.

He pushed through the door at the back of the loading bay and nearly ran face first into a wall. He was so tired, and his head wouldn't stop pounding. The pendant sloshed on his chest, a constant reminder of the mess he'd gotten himself into. If he saw Loki again, he was going to shove that stupid headdress down his throat.

"You OK there, buddy?" asked a concerned voice.

He looked up to see an elderly security guard watching him from a chair near the employee elevators. The chair creaked as the guard half stood, ready to catch him if he fell over.

Eddie feigned a cough to keep the man at arm's length. Nobody wanted to approach a sick person, and worry over catching a nasty bug might keep the guard from noticing little details like his lack of an employee badge.

"Sorry," he croaked. "I should probably be in bed, but I'll get fired if I don't show."

The guard backed away with an almost comical speed, holding his hands up like that might ward off any wayward germs.

"Hope you're feeling better soon, but stay away from me, will ya?" he asked. "I can't afford to get sick neither. I'm saving up my off days for a trip to Atlantic City."

"Good luck with that," Eddie rasped, punching the elevator button.

The door opened immediately, saving him from having to make more painful small talk punctuated by fake coughs. He pushed the button for the highest floor he could and then stabbed the one that closed the doors, hoping to escape before his ruse fell apart.

"A hot toddy will clear that cough right up," said the guard as the doors began to close. Then his eyes sharpened. "Hey! You forgot your–"

The doors cut off the rest of the sentence and the questions that would have inevitably followed it.

"Good deal," Eddie said. "I think we're in."

His Other didn't respond. That worried him, but he could feel the symbiote lurking at the back of his mind. Maybe it, too, was conserving strength, just in case. He sure hoped so, because getting the crap pounded out of him by the Green Goblin would not be a great way to cap off an already tough day.

Besides, he still had to get to the man. This elevator only went up to the nineteenth floor without a key card. An egomaniac like Osborn would be in the penthouse, and that meant Eddie had to get up to twenty.

Before the doors could open on nineteen, he pushed the emergency stop. A flashing red light on the control panel warned him that this approach would not hold for long before it attracted too much attention. He had to move, and fast.

He drew upon the symbiote, opening his mind and body to

allow it free rein. Normally, it seized at the opportunity to take control, straining at its mental leash like a killer dog with prey in its sights. But today, it came out sluggish. Reluctant. The transformation took place in slow stages, the way it had in the beginning, when he could feel every alien tendril as it sucked him in and remade him into something new and powerful.

If it had been someone else, he would have asked, "Are you OK, man?" But he didn't need words to know that the symbiote was hurting, too. Transforming into his symbiote form didn't alleviate the headache that stabbed at his eye sockets. If anything, it got worse.

He grew as he changed, tall enough to reach the access panel at the top of the elevator and tear it free with the sweep of one powerful arm. Alien tendrils reached up to pull him through the tight opening and onto the top of the elevator car. The dimly lit shaft smelled strongly of burned rubber and damp concrete. A few feet above him, he could see the outline of the doors to the twentieth floor. With his shoulders hunching against the lingering pain in his head, he climbed.

A normal man might have struggled to open the shaft doors, but they posed no challenge to Venom. A polymorphic pseudopod slipped through the miniscule crack between the doors, prying them open with ease. One heave of his substantial muscles, one leap, and he stood on the polished tile of the twentieth floor. His landing shook the ground beneath him, and a delicate painted vase standing on a plinth opposite the elevators teetered over in slow motion and fell with a crash.

He paid it no mind. Opposite him was a single door. The golden placard mounted to its center read, "Norman Osborn, CEO." Light seeped around the edges of the door.

Venom threw it open, leaped through, and landed in the middle of the opulent office. A quick sweep of his alien gaze told him everything he needed to know. The layout, dominated by an immense steel and glass desk strewn with papers. The security system, controlled by a panel covered in blinking lights on the far wall. The windows, shuttered against the midday glare. Osborn himself sat at the desk, his piercing eyes punching holes through the intruder as he reached for the security panel. But Venom got there first, a single alien tentacle emerging from his shoulder and shooting toward the delicate machinery. It hit hard, the panel exploding into a spray of sparks.

Osborn didn't even flinch. Instead, he turned his attention back to Venom, leaning back in his desk chair and looking him over with obvious calculation. Eddie had run into him plenty of times, and he'd always found Norman's face to be more intimidating than the Goblin mask he sometimes wore. Something about those angular features topped off with those cold eyes gave Eddie the willies, and he'd never been easily rattled.

Of course, he would never show it. Not even when he was still staggering from whatever that pendant had done to him. He opened his monstrous jaws and said in a voice like iron nails on a rotten chalkboard, "Nice office."

Norman's mouth quirked. "It was. To what do I owe this social call?"

The man gave an appearance of relaxation, tilting further back in his chair and lacing his hands behind his head, but Venom knew better. Osborn was like a coiled snake waiting for the right opportunity to strike. Besides, Venom wasn't in the mood for conversation. He had been hurt, and he itched to set the scales straight again.

In the dim recesses of their merged awareness, Eddie wondered if this was the right course of action. If Norman wanted to talk, it would be stupid not to take advantage of that. He might be able to glean something useful from the conversation.

For one passing moment, it seemed like violence might be averted. A flicker of surprise crossed Osborn's face, quickly hidden beneath his mask of urbanity. Eddie began the difficult process of putting the symbiote back into the bag without satiating its unending bloodlust. But his Other had changed its mind. First it didn't want to come out, and now it didn't want to retreat. It was nothing if not stubborn. Maybe that's why they got along so well.

As they struggled, his eyes remained on his enemy. If Osborn picked up on their conflict, he might take advantage of it, and Venom knew it. The mad scientist leaned forward, dropping his elbows to his knees and studying the symbiote with evident interest. As he did, a chain worked its way free of the unbuttoned collar of his shirt. The pendant at the end dropped down, swinging to and fro beneath his chin. A familiar green liquid sloshed around inside.

All questions and restraint vanished. Eddie had been running on a theory, but now he knew for certain that Osborn was to blame for his pain. Maybe Osborn's pendant controlled Eddie's, or something similar. The details didn't matter. He would release Eddie, or Venom would rip him into pieces.

He shrieked, all restraint forgotten, and charged toward the desk. Osborn didn't wait. He rolled out of the way with inhuman speed, pulling one of his hands out to point at the hulking symbiote. A metallofabric purple glove enclosed his fingers, the fluorescents glittering off the circuitry woven into the palms. He tensed his fingers, sending a surge of electrical current toward his attacker.

The crackling ball of electricity blasted Venom in the chest like a freight train. It locked all his muscles in place, seizing them in pain. The impact flung him into the opposite wall, shattering the framed diplomas that hung there. He fell to the ground in a shower of broken glass.

Venom shook his head, pushing through the pain. If he could just get to that pendant, he'd be free. Any amount of agony would be worth it to achieve that goal. The symbiote had been a slave before, and he refused to return to that wretched existence. He'd die first.

The symbiote scrambled to his feet and leaped. This time, he was ready for the concussive blast that the Goblin flung at him. He shot out a sticky web, reorienting in midair to dodge around the crackling ball of power. He landed with a thump in front of the heavy desk, picked it up overhead, muscles straining, and threw it at Osborn.

The businessman dodged out of the way as best he could, but there wasn't anywhere to go. The desk hit the ground and shattered, flinging broken glass and torn metal in all directions. A chunk of steel hit him on the side of the head, dazing him. Minute cuts opened on the arms he flung up to protect his face. When he lowered them, blood trickled down from the corner of his eye socket. He'd been quick, but not quite fast enough.

The symbiote pressed his advantage, grabbing onto Osborn's hands and pushing them out of the way. He would destroy Osborn's pendant and see if that released him. Then he would have his vengeance. Venom would not be leashed. Anyone who tried to do so would pay.

But the moment that the symbiote's hands closed on the pendant, the pain began again. It crackled through his head like fire, twisting his insides. It felt like someone had stuffed his head with a million ghosts, howling in torment. His back arched, and he shrieked in pain, falling to his knees.

The agony subsided in slow stages. When Venom could think again, he realized that Osborn stood over him, staring down with a satisfied smile twisting his lips.

"You wear the Master's pendant, too," he said. "Now I understand what brought you here."

"Let me go!" demanded the symbiote, struggling to his feet.

He launched himself at the tycoon once again, only to be struck down by another bolt of intense agony. Norman waited it out patiently, tucking the pendant back into his dress shirt. Once the symbiote lay quiet again, he cleared his throat.

"We can do this all night," he said. "Or we can talk."

Venom groaned.

"Yes, I know. Take your human form, if you please. Then I will explain."

The symbiote knew he had no other choice. Following orders rankled, but he would do it for the moment. He would discover the eldritch power behind the pendants, and then he would use it to bash Norman Osborn's smug face in. Both Eddie and the alien liked that idea. They liked it a lot.

NINE

The flight was abnormally bumpy. T'Challa had spent a lot of time in planes, between his duty to represent Wakanda on the world stage and his continued commitment to stand against evil as the Black Panther. For some reason, evil rarely came to his door. It always required a commute.

As a result, he'd gotten used to living on planes and in the backs of cars. He'd become quite adept at catching a wink of sleep in uncomfortable seats whenever the moment arose. Wakandan transports had luxurious facilities that made travel more than bearable, but Shuri was in the midst of upgrading his hyperjet, and he'd chosen to rent rather than inconvenience some of his people by commandeering another aircraft.

So, he curled up in the uncomfortable confines of his leather chair and napped. He'd just managed to doze off when his Kimoyo card beeped. Wiping the sleep from his eyes, he tapped the device to reveal the excited visage of his sister. Shuri leaned close to the communicator, her large brown eyes filling the screen.

"Brother!" she exclaimed. "I have something important to tell you." She paused. "Are you drooling?"

T'Challa wiped his mouth but found no moisture there. He shot her a look of exasperation. Someday, she would learn to be serious, just as he'd learned to be punctual. He loved her, but sometimes he thought that day couldn't come soon enough.

"What is it?" he asked. "Is there some problem?"

Behind him, Okoye woke from her own doze, shooting to instant attention. She approached on soft feet, easily maintaining her balance despite the lurching plane. Perhaps there was some weather approaching. That would be good. Wakanda needed the rain.

"My king?" she murmured, a question in her eyes.

He held a finger up, urging patience. "Shuri?" he prodded.

"I'm not entirely sure," she said. "I'm still working on the molecular analysis of that sludge you sent. It's a complex liquid that contains a few trace elements not found on Earth, so it will take some time."

"Really?" he asked, leaning forward. "It may not be of terrestrial origin?"

"Either that, or someone went to a great deal of trouble to make it here," Shuri replied. "But that's not the least of it. It's magic."

"Explain," said T'Challa, stroking his chin in thought.

"It emits energy. At first, I thought it was radioactive and took the necessary protective steps, but the energy isn't physical. It's mystical. I scanned it for magical energy and the readouts went off the charts."

T'Challa frowned. Next to him, Okoye wore an identical expression of concern.

"And a great deal of it was poured into the water supply. Is the system still shut down?" he asked.

"For the moment, but the authorities are getting restless. Their systems aren't calibrated to identify this type of contaminant. By all their tests, the water is clean. If I can't come up with something substantial soon, I'm worried they'll turn it back on."

"I'll notify Doctor Strange about the magical traces. He should still have some of the sample left. Perhaps he can help us identify the magical processes at work here."

Shuri nodded. "That would be wise. I'll continue to work on it from my end as well. Hurry home. I could use your insight."

He nodded back. "I'll be there as soon as I can. Take care, sister. It would pain me to lose you."

In response, she stuck her tongue out at him.

"I'm always careful." She paused. "Love you."

Then she cut off the communication. That last comment more than anything else she'd said made him realize how concerned she truly was. Shuri had never been the demonstrative type. It took a lot to make her declare her feelings.

The plane lurched abruptly to the left, throwing T'Challa about. Okoye stumbled but caught herself quickly on the back of a nearby seat. Their eyes met, and they shared a moment of wordless concern.

"There were no weather disturbances on the radar when we left New York, were there?" asked T'Challa.

"None." Okoye pulled herself into the chair and strapped in, pulling out her Kimoyo card. "Let me see what I can find out."

He left her to it, producing his own communication device and opening up a channel to Doctor Strange. Although the Sorcerer

Supreme refused to carry his card around, he'd performed some spell that linked it to him so he could still be contacted. Shuri and Okoye had tried to explain that the card was much more than a simple cell phone, but Strange preferred his magic and his artifacts. He'd said he had a rep to protect, and to this day, T'Challa couldn't decide whether he'd been joking or not.

Their conversation was brief and to the point. The surgeon-turned-master of the mystic arts came to attention when T'Challa explained the magical signature imprinted on the mysterious glowing fluid, and he promised to examine it as soon as possible.

"Thank you, my friend," said T'Challa. "Might I ask one more favor?"

"Anything in my power," replied Strange.

"We have encountered a strange weather pattern over Wakanda. I was wondering if it—"

The connection cut off in a burst of static which was quickly replaced by a rapid and repetitive beep. The Wakandan king stared down at the small metallic card for a long moment, overcome with surprise. Cell phones might cut out. Towers and phone lines might go down. But Kimoyo cards required neither. He could not recall an occasion when one failed.

He pushed the button that connected him to the cockpit. Although they flew a rented plane, he'd brought his own flight team with him, and he had every confidence in their abilities. Still, it would be prudent to check in with them. Something wasn't right.

"Yes, my king?" asked Yona, the Dora Milaje pilot.

"Just checking in. How is the plane handling the unexpected weather?" he asked.

"Very well, sire," she responded, in a tone of voice that made it clear that she meant the exact opposite but was too polite to say so.

"Perhaps we should have taken one of our own aircraft," he muttered, his concern growing. He hated the idea of putting his people at risk. There was nothing to be done about it now, and he hated that, too.

"Sire?" asked Yona. "I didn't catch that."

"Nothing," he said. "It's nothing. I'll let you get back to–"

Once again, his words were cut off, not by the crackle of static or the buzz of a broken connection, but by the loud crackle and boom of a bolt of lightning that enveloped the plane in a ball of electrical current.

They'd been hit!

TEN

Eddie Brock adjusted his collar and brushed the plaster dust out of his hair before taking a seat as Norman Osborn had ordered. He would set aside their fight for now. But if his change in heart pleased the business tycoon, Norman didn't show it. He surveyed the wreckage of his fancy desk with something that might have been regret.

"Eddie, Eddie, Eddie." Osborn clucked his tongue and shook his head. "You are a wrecking ball in disguise. Whatever will I do with you?"

"Got anything that needs wrecking?" Eddie replied.

If he'd been asked just that morning, he would have said that he'd ride a unicorn through Central Park before he chummed it up with the likes of Norman. Eddie hated everything the businessman stood for. While they might share a common hatred of Spider-Man and his perfect Boy Scout superiority, the similarities ended there. Osborn was a man of cold calculation and self-serving manipulation. He never gave. He only took.

Maybe Eddie wasn't perfect, but he did his best with what he had. That was part of what rankled him about Spider-Man.

Out of everyone in the world, he knew how hard it was to lasso the symbiotes. They were alien through and through, with a completely different sense of right and wrong. But he'd maintained his humanity – mostly – and achieved a kind of balance with his Other. Spidey looked at him and only saw a monster instead of the lethal protector he truly was. If Spider-Man hadn't been so judgy, they might have been able to be in the same room without trying to kill each other, but that would never happen. Even when Eddie tried to do the right thing, as he had earlier with the Oscorp truck, Spider-Man the do-gooder would assume the worst of him.

But that wasn't worth dwelling on. Not here, and not in this company. He had to be on top of his game, or he'd pay the price.

Norman crossed the room to the bar, broken glass crunching under the soles of his fancy leather shoes. They probably cost more than Eddie's rent.

"I think we got off on the wrong foot. Drink?" asked Osborn.

"I'm good, thanks."

Rich brown liquid glugged into a crystal highball glass. Osborn took a single sip before leaning against the wall, watching Eddie. Blood still oozed down the side of the mogul's face, winding a slow trail toward the corner of his mouth, but he didn't even seem to notice. Either he didn't feel pain, or he held it at arm's length through sheer force of will.

"How did you get that necklace?" asked Osborn.

"I saw Loki pouring toxic waste into the water supply. We had words about it."

"Ah. How did that go?"

Eddie swallowed the smart comment that came to mind and threatened to escape out his mouth. Osborn clearly knew what was up with the pendants. While Eddie had no desire to buddy up with the guy, he was willing to play nice until he got what he needed. And he needed to get this necklace off before it went crazy on him again. His noggin still throbbed, and if the necklace attacked him again, it just might explode.

"Not entirely sure. He ran, but he tossed this thing over my neck first," he said, pointing toward the green orb that rested against his chest.

"Ah," Norman repeated. He took a slug of his drink.

"What is it?"

"You might call it a monitoring device. That's a good word for it."

A wave of anger engulfed Eddie, making his breath quicken. He steeled himself to resist his Other's violent urges. They always got worse when Eddie was angry. It was like having an overprotective older brother, only the brother came from a different planet where the strong ate the weak.

But the symbiote remained quiet. If not for the persistent presence in the back of his mind, Eddie would have worried that it had gone for good.

Heck, he still worried. Had it been hurt beyond repair?

Not hurt, Eddie, it responded to his mental poking. *Resting. Tired.*

It was probably for the best. The symbiote's silence allowed Eddie to concentrate fully on his conversation with Osborn. He needed every ounce of wits he could scrape up.

"Who's monitoring me? You?" he asked, trying to sound like that would be just fine and dandy with him.

Maybe he laid it on too thick, because Osborn's perfect teeth shone in a brief smile before he responded.

"Not me. The Master," he said.

Eddie cocked a brow. "You don't seem like the type of guy to pay homage to a master."

Osborn drained the rest of his drink. Was it Eddie's imagination, or had the man's fingers tightened on the glass? The businessman had a good poker face, but Eddie's years of journalism had taught him to read what others tried so desperately to hide. Osborn wasn't as happy with the situation as he wanted Eddie to believe. Good. Maybe Eddie could find some way to use that.

"I pay homage to no one," said Osborn. "It is a mutually profitable business arrangement, and nothing more."

"OK. So now I'm in on that, since I have a necklace, too?"

Osborn's smile thinned. "No, Eddie," he said. "You're more like a dog on a leash. How does that make you feel?"

Once again, Eddie's fury flared, but he held it at bay. This felt like a test. Osborn watched him with hooded eyes, eager to take in his reaction. Trying to tear his head off would accomplish nothing, and that blasted necklace would start hurting him again.

So he swallowed his ire and said, "Well, Norm, I'm thinking about taking a leak on your carpet. Since I'm a dog and all."

Norman set the empty glass back onto the bar.

"Call me that again, and I'll rip out your fingernails and feed them to you," he said.

"Promises, promises."

They grinned at each other, a shark-like baring of teeth that betrayed no amusement whatsoever.

"Is Loki a business partner or a dog like me?" asked Eddie. "And who is this Master?"

"You're both dogs, and dogs don't deserve answers. They follow instructions. If I tell you to sit, I want your tailbone on the carpet. And if I tell you to kill..."

"Yeah, yeah, I get it." Eddie didn't want to, but he got the meaning quite clearly. If he didn't follow Norman's orders, the necklace would hurt him. If he tried to kill one of the other pendant carriers, it would hurt him. Norman wasn't willing to revolt against the mysterious Master – not yet – but maybe Loki would deal. Or let some important bit of information spill, just to enjoy the chaos that ensued. Maybe they were dogs, but Norman Osborn had forgotten one thing. Sometimes dogs bite their masters, and Eddie intended to do just that.

Osborn wouldn't know what bit him.

ELEVEN

Electrical current surged down the length of the plane, frying the delicate wiring that controlled the lights and air compressors. They died in an explosion of sparks, plunging the interior of the aircraft into dimness punctuated only by the slivers of light that crept in beneath the window shades. Up in the cockpit, multiple alarms beeped and whooped, and his stomach sank as the jet abruptly began to lose altitude. Did the engines still run? His ears rang from the lightning, and he couldn't be sure.

Yona turned to her youthful copilot, Anani, giving a quick series of instructions that T'Challa couldn't quite catch. The young woman nodded in response, tossing her headphones down onto the control panel.

"Can we recover?" he shouted, unwilling to wait any longer.

"We've lost half of our right wing," she said. "The best we can do is buy some time."

The plane was going down. His team burst into action without needing instructions. Yona remained at her post, fighting the yoke in an effort to keep them aloft just a few seconds longer. Sinewy muscles bulged in her arms as she struggled against the forces of gravity. Okoye opened the emergency cabinet, moving with swift efficiency. Although his people didn't jump out of airplanes very often, they remained calm and cool under pressure. They had faced down certain death too many times to be flustered by the fact that they were falling from the sky.

The sharp scent of smoke reached his nostrils. He leaned over to release the window shade, searching for the source. A single glance outside more than adequately illustrated the problem. Red flames flickered from the burned slag that was once the engine on the left-hand wing. The lightning had fried it.

Some part of T'Challa's mind filed the details away for future contemplation. He had been on planes that were struck by lightning before; it happened more than people realized, and the aircraft flew on. But something made this storm special, more deadly. He would think on that once he'd seen his people safely to the ground.

He stood, shrugging off his suit jacket and summoning his Panther suit with a mere thought. Cool metalloweave fabric closed over his body, encasing him in lightweight body armor laced with vibranium. It fit him like a second skin.

Okoye threw him a parachute. He promptly handed it off to Anani, whose face remained placid despite the fear lingering in her eyes. He turned back just in time to see Okoye's exasperated expression. She threw a second chute, and he handed that one off, too.

"One for you, and one for Yona," he instructed the copilot.

"Yes, my king."

Okoye clucked her tongue but said nothing. They'd had this conversation so many times that words had become unnecessary. That click of her tongue meant: "You are our king, and it is my job to protect you. You get the first parachute." His answering smile meant: "What kind of king would I be if I saved myself and let my people die?" They would never resolve the argument, and so the words remained unspoken.

Okoye tossed him a third parachute. Then, instead of pulling out a fourth, she shut the closet door, her face expressionless. Meanwhile, the plane rocked back and forth, the wings creaking with strain as the heavy winds buffeted the small aircraft.

"Where is yours?" he asked.

"There are only three. I asked for the chutes. I specified four." Okoye paused, her jaw clenching with strain. "But the rental company cannot count. We do not have an extra harness to jump tandem. I will remain behind, and I will take no arguments." She paused. "You are my king and my friend. You will let me do this."

They had no time to waste, but still, he couldn't help but pause to take in those words. He couldn't allow her to do it, of course, but her quiet sincerity touched him to the core.

"I am honored, Okoye. But none of us will die today. I will not accept it," he answered, clenching her hand in his. "Ready the emergency door while I think this through."

Her lips firmed, but she followed his orders, making her way down the rocking aisle to the emergency exit and grasping the red handle to unlock it. T'Challa took a quick inventory of the closet and closed the door with a frown. He'd been hoping to find an extra harness, or some spare equipment that would allow him to create one and jump tandem. Given enough time, he could have figured something out, but they didn't have a second to spare. Besides, none of them were light. Even if they stripped off their body armor, every occupant of the plane was corded with muscle. The combined weight of any pair of them would get dangerously close to the limits that the chutes could handle. It wasn't worth the risk.

He would have to come up with something else. An idea occurred to him, and he did some swift mental calculations. He could use the laws of physics in his favor. Everything would have to line up precisely to make it work, but with the help of his Panther suit, he could make it down safely without a chute.

"The door is unlocked," called Okoye. "Pull this lever, and it will open."

"Go now!" responded Yona. "I will keep the plane steady, and then I'll follow." •

"Actually," T'Challa corrected them gently, "here is what we will do."

He gave them their instructions. For once, Okoye didn't argue, but only due to lack of time and not to lack of disagreement. Either way, he enjoyed the respite. Once he was finished, he handed her the final parachute.

"Put it on," he said, in a tone that brooked no argument.

She did, grumbling the entire time. He summoned his mask, activating its sensitive neural receptors with a single thought. The protective gear surrounded him, augmenting his senses in such a subtle way that he barely noticed. Everything stood out in stark relief: the shaking plane, the eddies of smoke swirling in the cabin, the concerned yet resolved expression on Okoye's face.

He tore the emergency door free of its moorings with one

convulsive yank. Metal screeched as the hinge gave way. He tossed it into the back of the plane where it crashed against the mini fridge.

"See you on the ground," he said, his voice steady. He was not afraid. He trusted the Dora Milaje with his life.

"You'd better," Okoye responded, jumping out.

TWELVE

After a long meditation, Doctor Strange finally stirred, stretching his neck and allowing his eyes to adjust to the light once more. His friend and companion had been right about one thing: he could no longer afford to sit around and wait for Dormammu to make his appearance. He had hoped that Clea's arrival would draw her uncle out into the open where they could face him together as they'd done before. But now he would have to improvise.

On the surface, the task seemed impossible. Magically locating a single person on Earth was difficult but doable, especially with the availability of biological samples. Hair and nails retained their owner's unique magical signature long after they'd been severed. All one had to do was sift through a few billion people until the two of them matched. Easy.

But he couldn't use this strategy to track Dormammu. Strange and the Sorcerer Supremes before him had locked Dormammu out of this universe time and time again, imprisoning him away in punishment for his magical crimes. He could be anywhere. Tracking someone across the

Multiverse was a much more difficult task, and the amount of power necessary to do it would only attract attention he didn't want to risk.

His alternative was to watch for Dormammu's magic, which he would use to cross over into this world. But spells had a much smaller footprint that made them tougher to locate, and they faded quickly. It would be like tracking someone across a sandy beach while the water washed their footprints away at regular intervals. It would strain even Doctor Strange's considerable magical talent.

But Stephen had always been good at thinking outside the box. Time and time again he'd taken on surgeries that everyone had called impossible. He'd rarely turned down an opportunity to challenge his skills and more often than not he'd succeeded in the most unlikely endeavors. This time would be the same, if only he could figure out how.

He needed an amplifier, some artifact that would help him weed out the people and focus only on the magical traces left behind by deliberate spells. They'd fought enough times that Doctor Strange could have recognized his adversary's magical signature in his sleep.

After an hour's worth of study, Doctor Strange had to conclude that the creation of such an artifact would be possible, but in order to work it would have to be narrow in scope. He couldn't create a tool that would find any spell cast by anyone; that was simply too many variables to manipulate by a single construct. But he could build something that would alert him once Dormammu's magic reached the Earth and give him an approximate location. He should be able to narrow the search from that starting point.

With a huff of relief, he leaned back in his chair, stretching his aching neck once again. How long had he been sitting here, lost in these dusty magical tomes? As usual, he'd lost track of time. Ironic that a master of time would do such a thing, but libraries did that to him, and this library in particular sucked him in quite often.

As he stretched, his eyes fell on the small metallic vial that sat on the corner of his desk, almost completely obscured by the grimoire of Trismegistus, which had contained a few notes on the topic that had finally put Strange onto the path toward a solution. Inside the sealed chamber sat a small sample of the green liquid that the Shadow Avengers had been so concerned about. Strange wasn't so callous as to disregard a danger to innocent people, but he also had a perspective that they sometimes lacked. If Dormammu took over their world, millions would die. Once the door had been opened to allow him in, it would be nigh impossible to close it again.

So, while he understood the importance of reviewing the sample to determine if Shuri's theory was true, and the liquid was indeed magical in nature, Doctor Strange had to set priorities. He would finish his artifact first and then, once he could rest easy knowing that he would have an early warning when Dormammu made his move, he would turn his attention to the liquid.

Once again, he rifled through the scrolls containing the notes of the sorcerer Morphesti, every inch of which was crammed full of spidery handwriting faded with the passage of years. The enchantment would work, with the right vessel to house it. He stroked his beard, scanning the shelves for something that might suffice. On his travels, he often picked up bits and baubles, small and useful trinkets that could be enchanted when the need struck. A small porcelain doll sat next to a glittering crystal pendulum that swung to and fro in endless arcs. One row down, a plain wooden rack held a selection of prayer beads and semiprecious stones strung on gold chains. Next to it sat an ornate iron lantern, its shutters closed to keep out the dust.

The lantern called to him. It would be perfect. He took it down from the shelf and set it next to the scrolls. Then he skimmed them one last time, reviewing the incantation that would start the enchantment, and the series of steps he would follow afterwards. He must be fully prepared before he began, lest the entire thing explode in his face. He rubbed his chin in remembered pain. Although it had been some time, his early mistakes under the tutelage of the Ancient One still loomed large in his memory.

He took a deep breath, summoning the arcane power necessary to begin the spell. Swirling energies gathered around him, invisible to the untrained eye. He could feel the web of creation beyond them, the magical life force from which all living things derived. It washed over him, over the perfect symphony of his physical body and the balanced harmony of his spirit. He emptied his mind of all distraction. His concerns about Dormammu, his frustrations with the Shadow Avengers, his hurt at Clea's rejection all faded away to be replaced by a singular purpose, consumed by his magic.

It was time to work his magic, and Doctor Strange was ready.

THIRTEEN

The wind whipped at T'Challa's face despite the protection of his mask. The cold stung his cheeks. A heavy crosswind tossed him around, driving the breath from his lungs. With acrobatic litheness, he flipped himself over, reorienting himself in midair. He tucked his limbs in and pointed his head down, reducing the wind resistance in order to catch up with the others.

If his hurried calculations were correct, the Panther suit would allow him to survive the fall under the right conditions. In the past, it had successfully absorbed the impact from fifty feet up, although Shuri had warned him that it couldn't bear much more without injuring him. At greater distance, his body accelerated to an impact speed that the suit couldn't counteract. He had to slow his descent in order to walk away from the landing.

His plan would allow him to do just that while spreading his weight around so that it wouldn't overtax any of the individual chutes. His suit would offer some measure of protection from a fall, but the Dora Milaje had no such defense. This was their best hope to get them all onto the ground.

Above him, the smoking plane roared downwards on autopilot, its trajectory taking it well away from the landing zone and from any signs of civilization. Yona had aimed it towards a small lake that sat on the very edge of Wakanda. The pool was too shallow to fish, so no one would be harmed when the aircraft landed. That left T'Challa with one fewer concern to worry about.

A long stretch of sandy dunes grew beneath them. T'Challa oriented towards it, hoping that the soft ground would absorb some of the force generated by their hasty landing.

As he drew even with Anani, she turned to face him, her hand fumbling for the release toggle. He flipped downwards, allowing her to grab him around the waist from behind. They fell together.

"Now?" she shouted, her voice barely audible over the loud roar of the wind.

"Now," he confirmed, nodding.

She pulled the toggle, releasing the chute with a whump. The harness jerked her backwards as the air caught the heavy canvas, and her arms tightened around T'Challa with such force that it drove the remaining breath from his body. His airspeed slowed dramatically, and for a moment, he thought that the rest of the plan would be unnecessary. Then a sharp ripping sound caught his attention. One of the lines that attached the chute to the harness had torn free.

The ground swayed sickeningly beneath them for a moment as their angle of descent changed. The chute hung slightly crooked now, but it still held them aloft. He didn't dare risk remaining here. A second rip could prove fatal.

"Let go!" he ordered, turning his head.

She shouted something in response, but the wind whipped her words away.

He took her hands and loosened them from his waist. After a moment's hesitation, she let him go. Without his added weight on the chute, Anani could land safely despite the broken tether. She would be safe.

T'Challa accelerated downwards toward Yona, the sandy steppes beneath him growing larger and larger in his view. The mask protected his eyes enough to allow him to look down. There. There was the spot he would land, and hopefully walk away from.

Off to their right, the plane struck the lake with a loud and earthshaking smack, sending up a geyser of water. The burning engine exploded with a second clap of noise, but T'Challa could spare no time to monitor it. The water should keep the fire from spreading. He would follow up once he was safely on the ground.

He shot towards Yona, his body gaining speed as it continued to fall. As instructed, she was ready for him. They had three chances to get this right. Even if the chutes couldn't hold them, or one of the women lost their grip on him, the process should slow him just enough that he could survive the final drop. He was nearly sure of it.

As he drew closer, the wind intensified, stinging his face. It came in sharp, heavy bursts now that flipped him around like a coin, top over tail overhead, with no way to stop his tumble. He stretched out his body, trying to resist the blasts of air that seemed to be coming from all directions, but it didn't do much good. His stomach protested, a queasy feeling that he tamped down firmly. Vomiting in his Panther mask would not be pleasant, and he refused to allow it to happen.

Yona drew close, reaching out to grab him as instructed. But as she did so, another blast of wind caught her parachute, tugging her sharply off to the right. She struggled against it, swimming toward him in midair. He spun and flipped, trying to generate enough force to change his trajectory. He stretched his hands out to the point where his muscles groaned in protest and watched as she did the same. Their fingertips grazed but failed to gain purchase.

He slipped free. She shouted something after him. It was probably an apology, but the wind carried him too far away too fast to allow a response. Besides, now he was falling in the wrong direction, and he had to get to Okoye, or he would die.

Luckily, he had enough time to work his way towards her, and his acrobatic skills proved quite useful in a skydiving context. He couldn't change direction quickly, but he had no problem angling his body to move him inch by painstaking inch back towards the captain of his guard. She waited for him, her expression placid despite the sandy ground that loomed beneath them. If she didn't open her chute soon, it would be too late for them both. How high were they?

As she grabbed him, her strong hands moving with steady assurance, the sky opened up above them, and another bolt of lightning split the air with a crackle of electricity. The bolt arced harmlessly overhead, but a shiver of power ran over him, making his hair stand on end. Okoye turned wide eyes toward him as they held each other tight. She'd felt it, too.

Something pattered on the goggles of his mask, coating them with moisture. A low and heavy rumble of thunder split the air. White flakes swirled between their faces before floating off toward the ground.

He couldn't make out the words, but he could read Okoye's lips easily as she said, "Thundersnow?!"

He looked down through the snowy air toward the ground. It sat maybe two hundred and fifty feet beneath them, well below the usual limit for a chute, but still survivable. They had to pull it now. He groped at her harness while she was still distracted by the unseasonable weather, and yanked on the cord.

Her hands tightened on him, but they hadn't gotten into position. He slipped through the ring of her arms despite their best efforts, and barely managed to grab onto her ankles as the chute snapped out above her with a convulsive jerk. The abrupt impact nearly tore his grip free. He dangled from one hand, looking down towards the looming ground.

One hundred feet. Not close enough.

Crosswinds buffeted them, pelting them with stinging snow. The ground whirled crazily as the heavy air caught the parachute, swinging them around like they sat on a carnival ride. Okoye reached toward him, trying to catch his free hand, but the random twists and turns made every movement difficult. Their hands swung past each other over and over again.

T'Challa's hand began to work loose as the wind continued to buffet them. He looked down at the sandy ground, hoping for a miracle. Seventy-five feet. Another burst of air hit the chute, and one of the seams gave way with a loud tearing sound. The weather would tear it apart. T'Challa couldn't risk Okoye like that. He would take the chance.

He let go.

He plummeted toward the ground, orienting his body to land feet first. The energy regulators in his boots would absorb most of the shock and he knew how to land safely, but this would take him to his limits. He pointed his arms down toward the ground, pulling all the kinetic energy that had been stored in the suit to accumulate in his hands. With a grunt of effort, he discharged the energy in a long stream toward the ground as he fell toward it at bone-breaking speeds. The blast of energy pushed against the sand, and the counterforce that was generated slowed his descent just a little.

His boots hit the ground with a jolt that not even the Panther suit could absorb. He rolled into the fall, trying to divert as much of the kinetic energy as possible, but the impact still hurt him badly. He could feel his bones strain under the impact, hairline fractures traveling up from his ankles to his overtaxed legs with a crackle that he must have imagined. He swallowed the pain and sat up as Okoye landed next to him with a soft thump against the sand.

"My king! Are you hurt?" she demanded.

"I will survive," he said, bowing his head. "Thanks to your assistance."

"If you were not my king, I would smack you on the head," she declared.

"I am glad you're safe, too."

Her lips tightened, but she couldn't suppress the smile that rose on them. They waited as Yona and Anani landed safely a few yards away, looking up at the sky. T'Challa welcomed the opportunity to rest. They would need to walk soon enough, and he could use every available minute to allow his superhuman healing to repair the damage from the fall. He had survived, and that was the important thing.

"Thundersnow," said Okoye, looking up into the still-falling flakes. Another deep rumble shook the ground. "In all remembered time, I do not think such a thing has happened in Wakanda before."

"If it has, I have not heard of it," T'Challa responded.

"What do you think it means?"

"I don't know. But I intend to find out."

FOURTEEN

Doctor Strange frowned at the magical lantern that sat on his desk. He had been scowling at it for a good five minutes with no effect, but he kept at it. Perhaps some brilliant idea would occur to him if he frowned and stroked his beard just right.

The door to his study opened, and Wong stuck his head in, his dark eyes alert with interest. But he hovered at the door, unwilling to come in and disturb any ongoing spells.

"Any luck?" he asked, in a light voice that made it clear he considered their earlier argument to be over and done with. "Is it done?"

Strange beckoned him in, a brusque gesture that betrayed his frustration. Normally, he disliked being interrupted at work, but perhaps Wong could make sense of the strange output from the new artifact.

"The Lantern of Morphesti is complete," he said.

"Morphesti?" asked Wong. "Why not call it the Lantern of Wong, since I was the one who got you to quit brooding and do something about it?"

"You did not tell me anything I could not have determined for myself."

Wong clucked his tongue. "Fine, fine. Don't get all huffy with me. I cook your food."

"You do." Strange paused. "And thank you."

Although he didn't elaborate, Wong understood his meaning. The old man nodded, waving a hand as if to say it was nothing. Strange was more than happy to table the topic. He gestured toward the artifact. One of the shutters was open, and the magical light that churned eternally in the depths of the lantern projected a detailed map of the Earth onto the opposite wall. Wong could easily make out the wavy light that outlined familiar continents and bodies of water. But a series of flickering lights near New York and Wakanda caught his eye.

"How does it work?" asked Wong.

"If you feed it a magical signature, and if the target has sufficient magical power to stand out on a global scale, the map will light up. A yellow light signifies a weaker signal, such as a spell or an artifact. When the target is located, that is designated by a red light."

Wong leaned over, looking more closely at the map. "Then why are there two red lights?" he asked. "Clones?"

"I thought of that. Dormammu has enough power to duplicate himself, although I shudder to think of it. But I refuse to believe that he has opened multiple portals and sent duplicates through. Such a thing would reorder the magical energies of the Earth itself. Even you wouldn't have a problem feeling it."

Wong put a hand to his heart in mock hurt. "Ouch. I remind you again, I cook your food."

"Sorry," Strange muttered. "I dislike this situation, my friend. I do not mean to take it out on you."

"It's fine. I know how you are." Wong frowned, and the two men stood side-by-side, stroking their chins in simultaneous thought. "Any chance that the spell misfired?"

"Dormammu's signal is unmistakable. No mortal could duplicate it. I would assume that Clea is the only being in the universe that could come close, and it's not her. I double-checked. She's still in Atlantis."

"Perhaps it's time to call in your Shadow Avengers?"

"They're all otherwise occupied. I even tried Tony, but he's off on some remote island with Pepper and can't be reached. Doctor Voodoo seems to have gone missing. The Guardians are too far to get here in time. I've got no other resources."

"Well, then, I think the next best bet is to go to the source and see what you're picking up," Wong suggested.

"I've thought of that, too. But the artifact isn't particularly accurate. You can't zoom in on a street level view, and that gives us a lot of ground to cover. I assumed we would be able to zero in on his magic once he appeared, but I sense nothing," said Strange, his fist clenching in frustration.

"And even if he managed to cloak himself, his entry would reorient ley lines. You're right; there's no way a portal of that magnitude could go undetected." Wong squinted, leaning closer to the map. "You've got activity over New York and Wakanda. I urge you to reconsider calling your Shadow Avengers in if we're going to track this down. We'll cover ground faster that way."

"We?" asked Doctor Strange.

"You get too broody when I let you leave by yourself."

"Broody?" asked Strange, his brow rising.

"Like a hen."

The corner of Strange's mouth quirked despite his efforts to keep it under control. After his long meditation, he could accept the teasing without wanting to rip Wong's head off. In fact, it was rather funny. Few people dared to tease the Sorcerer Supreme.

"Very well, then," he said. "Far be it for me to stand in the way of your self-sacrifice."

"See? After all these years, you can be taught." Wong clapped him on the shoulder. "I'll go turn off the stove. Call up your friends."

Thunk!

A sharp impact against the window rattled the glass in the frame. The noise was followed by a rapid *rat-a-tat* of further impact. Gunfire? Shrapnel from some new energy weapon? Dormammu himself? Doctor Strange didn't know, but he was out of his seat and halfway across the room before his mind had run through the possibilities. He had pulled the heavy velvet curtains closed to better see the light of the lantern, and now he tugged them open, letting in faint mid-afternoon light.

Thunk!

A piece of hail the size of a baseball impacted against the window. A purple streak of energy distorted the window in its wake as the magical defenses of the Sanctum Sanctorum protected the glass. The spell was a bear to maintain, but better than having to replace all the glass. For some reason, villains always went for the windows. Maybe they hoped that worry over the repair bills would keep the Sorcerer Supreme busy while they robbed him.

Another giant chunk of hail impacted against the building, eliciting a second magical surge. Small pieces of ice pattered against the glass. On the street below, a huge ice ball punched through the roof of a car. The security alarm went off, blaring a too-late warning. The car's headlights flashed, illuminating the fleeing backs of pedestrians who rushed for shelter beneath the sudden onslaught.

"I didn't see hail in the forecast today," said Wong slowly. "I've never seen hail that big, either."

"Nope."

The stocky wizard lifted his arm, tapping on the fancy smartwatch on his wrist. He frowned in thought as he read the tiny screen.

"Nice watch," said Strange.

"Thanks. It was a birthday gift from me to myself." Wong frowned more deeply. "I don't like this."

Strange jerked upright, trying to read the smartwatch's screen, but even he had a problem making out such small print upside down.

"What?" he demanded.

"The news is saying that this hail came out of nowhere, and it's brought the five boroughs to a standstill. There's also an unexplained weather pattern over Wakanda. It's snowing there. During a lightning storm." His gaze flicked over to the map still projected on the wall, its lines fainter in the bright light streaming from the window. The twin lights still glowed on its surface: yellow and red over New York, and the same over Wakanda. "Quite a coincidence, don't you think?"

Strange's eyes lit on the vial sitting on the corner of his desk. A vague suspicion had begun to grow in his mind. All of these seemingly disparate clues might just tie together after all. If so, they pointed in a direction that he did not like one bit.

"Highly coincidental," he said aloud. "You're right. We need the Shadow Avengers, and we need them now."

Wong needed no further urging. For all his jokes and teasing, he was a master of the martial arts and one of the most formidable fighters Kamar-Taj had ever produced. Although he lacked a mastery of the mystic arts, he never backed down from a fight when the world was on the line. Strange had long been honored to fight by his side, and from the looks of things, today would be no exception.

"I'll get my staff," said Wong.

"I'll contact the Shadow Avengers. They need to know what's happening."

Strange reached for his Kimoyo card, his mind whirling as he tried to make sense of what exactly *was* happening. Although he hadn't put together the pieces yet, one thing was clear to him.

Dormammu was making his move.

Now he just had to convince his fellow heroes of that fact without any firm evidence save the workings of a possibly malfunctioning magical artifact.

Easy.

FIFTEEN

"The leg is broken, Darisa-Sarki," said Okoye.

T'Challa looked down at Anani, whose eyes remained downcast in shame. Her leg stretched out on the sand before her, its normally smooth contours misshapen from the injury. She had landed well enough, but before she could release her chute, a sudden gust had dragged her back up into the air, ripping the chute and dropping her unceremoniously to the ground. She'd landed poorly the second time.

Lightning struck the sand just a few yards from their shelter beneath a rock outcropping. It would keep them safe from the wild storm that crackled overhead. T'Challa was no meteorological expert, but based on what he knew of the weather, the system that raged over them shouldn't be possible. It took a lot to stir the dry, still air of Wakanda, let alone to generate a whole slew of weather phenomena at once. There was some unseen force at work here, and he intended to find out what it was.

He lifted his Kimoyo card, surveyed its cracked façade, and tucked it back into his pocket. There would be no calling for help, but he didn't worry. Yona assured him that she'd been in contact with Wakandan ground forces before they'd gone down. Someone would come for them, honing in on the half-submerged wreckage of their plane just a short distance away. They would provide medical care for the injured young woman, as well as transport home. In the meantime, all they could do was wait.

It didn't take long. After a few minutes, T'Challa heard a metallic crackle in the air. The hairs on his arm stood on end, and the scent of ozone filled his nostrils. Wrinkling his nose against the stench, he stepped out from beneath the shelter to look around. He didn't want to venture out too far into the open lest the lightning catch him in its grasp. But their rescuers might struggle to locate them if he didn't attract their attention. A storm of this strength would likely interfere with the delicate sensors of the Wakandan tracking equipment. He wasn't willing to risk the possibility. Anani needed medical care quickly to ensure that the leg would heal well.

Okoye followed on his heels, clutching her spear. He considered mentioning that its metal tip beckoned to the lightning as well as any rod, but he could not fault her caution. Something about this situation didn't sit right with him either. There were too many coincidences for his liking.

Together, they crept out of their hiding place toward the repetitive crackling noise. It sounded like a fire burning, and T'Challa's heart sank. A wildfire would decimate the land and endanger the livelihood of many of his people. If this strange lightning had started one, it had to be put out before it became uncontainable.

Okoye's wide and worried eyes met his, and he knew she'd

come to the same conclusion. Heedless of the continued danger from the ongoing storm, they hurried toward the noise as heavy snow fell on their heads and shoulders, quickly coating them in a blanket of flakes. For one brief moment, Okoye's eyes lifted to the sky in wonder at the miraculous snow, but then she returned her iron gaze to the ground before them, sweeping the area in a never-ending search for potential threats.

They circled the outcropping that sheltered their injured companion. Behind it, in a small copse of hardy desert trees, sat a huge globe of flickering green energy. It hissed and popped like a great bonfire, sending out glowing sparks like embers into the sky. At its highest point, the globe stood at least eight feet tall. Touching it would be hazardous; its left-hand wall had carved a giant gouge through one of the scrubby desert trees, and the remaining trunk bowed under the weight of its branches, which swayed wildly in the wind.

As they stood there, the globe cracked open. Through its bright green depths, he could see the dim outlines of some dark location, still and dead. They both crouched, ready for anything to come flying at them.

But nothing happened.

Okoye gestured him back.

"I will scout," she said, her jaw set against any arguments.

He nodded, summoning his mask up to protect his head once again. Normally, he waited for a threat to present itself before donning his Panther garb, but this situation warranted caution. He would not insult Okoye's considerable skills, however, by insisting that she could not handle this alone. She had earned her captain's insignia. It also didn't hurt that the portal stood just a leap away. If an enemy showed itself, he could engage in seconds.

Okoye scouted around the edge of the portal, unwilling to get too close lest a stray spark burn right through her. She held her spear at the ready, her grip on the burnished wood loose and relaxed. She had crossed to the opposite side of the magical doorway when the damaged tree finally gave way. The swaying branches fell to the ground with a crash, sending snow and sand swirling through the air.

As Okoye looked towards the downed foliage, a bolt of lightning lanced the air, impacting with the swirling circle of light. T'Challa's ears popped. The orb emitted a blinding flash of green light.

A figure appeared in the depths of the orb; its outline fuzzy at first but growing more distinct with every passing moment. It coalesced into a giant of a man, well over seven feet tall, in ornate armor. A barbute helmet topped with long, curving horns sat atop his head, the nose plate obscuring most of his face save his eyes and tight-clenched mouth. A braided beard hung down over his considerable chest, and in one gauntleted hand, he held a sword which would have been a two-hander for most people – if they could lift the enormous blade at all.

The warrior lifted his head to the snowy sky, taking a single moment to enjoy the feel of the flakes on his face. Then he looked them over, his weapon held at the ready. Behind him, the glowing portal crackled and hissed, casting a shimmer of sickly green light over his eyes.

T'Challa stepped closer to Okoye, moving with a deliberate slowness. As he crept forward, his eyes scanned the plate mail and sword, which were both in good repair despite obvious frequent use. A series of Asgardian runes ran along the pommel of the blade, their deep-etched outlines readable from a few feet away. After years of study, he could read the language, but the warrior's hand obscured half the runes. It didn't matter. He had what he needed to begin a negotiation and determine the interloper's intentions. Did he come as a refugee, or an advance scout for some otherworldly invasion party, or something else entirely?

"Asgardian," he said politely. "I am King T'Challa of Wakanda. I am friend and companion to Thor Odinson, and I greet you in peace. What are you called?"

The giant looked down at them both for a long moment of silence, the eerie green glow fading from his eyes as the energies of the portal released their hold on his body. Then, he said, "I am Heimdall the All-Seeing. Stand aside, king. I have no wish to harm a friend of Thor."

Okoye tensed, the tip of her spear slowly lowering to point at the armored man. T'Challa did not need to tell her to hold steady; she had been at his side long enough to know his desire to squeeze out as much information as possible before engaging in battle. Sometimes, needless bloodshed could be avoided that way. Something told him this would not be one of those times, but perhaps he could uncover some useful tidbit of knowledge.

"I do not wish harm upon you either, friend Heimdall. Perhaps we could negotiate," he said.

"Leave this place," Heimdall ordered. "Keep your people outside the area. Then we will have no quarrel."

T'Challa shook his head sadly. "I cannot. I am the steward of Wakanda. It is my duty to protect its lands and its people. All of them. I cannot leave some mysterious portal open within my borders, nor turn my back on a warrior armed for battle without any explanation for his appearance. Close the portal, and we will talk. I will hear you fairly. I give you my word on it."

Heimdall arched then, his armor creaking. His mouth stretched into a grimace, and the same green, crackling energy that made up the portal suffused his body. Every muscle tensed to its limits, and leather and metal squealed as his armor struggled to contain him. He let out a roar of pain.

"Go!" he yelled through gritted teeth. "Go now!"

Okoye glanced at her king, and he shook his head minutely. Her lips firmed, and she edged in front of him, clearly determined that if the portal – or the warrior – exploded, it would hit her first. Sometimes, she forgot that his armor would soak up such damage. It could get exasperating sometimes, but at least she cared.

Heimdall let out another deep bass bellow of pain, and his sword slowly came up. His muscles quivered with strain, like he resisted some unseen force that tried to wield his weapon despite his obvious reluctance. T'Challa activated the scanners that Shuri had installed in his suit, hoping that their readouts might give him some insight, but the portal threw out so much energy that it overwhelmed them.

When the attack came, it was fast. The sword moved with such speed that it nearly took Okoye by surprise despite the fact that she had been waiting at the ready. Asgardian steel swooped down at her head only to be met with the vibranium laced wood of a Wakandan spear.

Thok!

Okoye sank down as she went on the offensive, using her

attacker's height against him, twisting her body and moving past the backswing of the heavy sword. But Heimdall was a master swordsman, and he recovered quickly, using the momentum of his swing to bring the weapon around to bear once again.

But before he could strike, T'Challa joined the fray, leaping forward to grab the swordsman's hand. Clearly there was some unseen force at work here; otherwise, the Asgardian wouldn't have tried to warn them before attacking. If T'Challa could disarm and restrain Heimdall, they might be able to help him shake whatever compelled him to act against his nature.

The Panther attacked the weak point of the hand, trying to twist the weapon out of Heimdall's grip. On a lesser man, the move would have worked and, in fact, he'd done it a million times before. But even in the stiff gauntlets, Heimdall had a strength not possessed by mortal men. His grip was like iron, and the sword refused to budge.

The enormous warrior's free hand came sweeping down at T'Challa's head. He saw the blow coming, but there was nowhere to go. The strike knocked the breath from his body, sending him flying back into the copse of trees. Energy nipped at him, like a thousand needles piercing his body at once. He'd flown too close to the portal, and at this short distance, it pelted his skin despite the protection of the Panther suit. Now he understood Heimdall's gritted teeth and tense demeanor after he'd arrived here. The passage had hurt him.

He rolled free and launched himself back toward the fray. Okoye distracted the warrior with a flurry of blows from her quarterstaff, the wood moving so quickly that it blurred. Heimdall parried, making a slow and steady retreat as he watched for an opening to launch a counterattack. It came before T'Challa could rejoin the fray. The still-heavy winds skimmed along the ground, picking up sand and debris and flinging them into Okoye's face, almost as if the weather itself fought on the Asgardian's side. Temporarily blinded and teary with pain, she stumbled backwards, coughing heavily. Heimdall stepped forward, raising his blade to strike her down.

He was unnaturally quick. T'Challa would not make it in time. He lifted his arm, summoning up the stored power in his suit to push the warrior backwards with a blast of kinetic energy. But the suit hadn't yet had enough time to replenish itself after discharging most of its power during the landing from the plane. It let out a weak blast that failed to budge Heimdall more than an inch.

The sword swept down towards Okoye, who staggered backwards in a desperate attempt to avoid the attack she knew was coming but couldn't see. T'Challa threw himself forward, straining his superhuman speed to the limit, and did the only thing he could.

He threw himself into the path of the heavy sword and caught the blade between his gloved hands. It slipped, darting toward his face, before he could grip it fully. Heimdall tensed, using momentum to force the blade down. T'Challa strained, trying desperately to push it off to one side. But Heimdall had leverage and weight on him, and even T'Challa's superhuman strength couldn't keep the sharp Asgardian steel from inching ever closer to him. The Panther suit could protect him from many things, but he wasn't willing to pit it against this particular sword in the hands of this particular warrior.

They remained there, locked in a battle of muscle and

will. The sword edged closer, its tip hovering just a few short centimeters from T'Challa's eye. He shifted his grip to Heimdall's wrist, trying in vain to repel it, but the most he could do was delay the inevitable.

"Why are you doing this?" he gasped. "Wakanda and Asgard have no quarrel."

"I would choose otherwise, if I could," Heimdall replied with what seemed like sincere regret. "Now go to the halls of Valhalla and tell them to ready my place. I think I shall arrive there soon. I can take little more of this torment. Be at peace, king of Wakanda."

The giant warrior's muscles bulged, and his mouth drew back into a grimace of effort as he heaved the sword towards T'Challa.

A long length of Wakandan wood came sweeping through his field of vision as Okoye swung her staff in a wide and sweeping arc. The heavy wood impacted against the ornate helm with an ear-splitting crack, knocking the armored warrior off her king and onto the ground. The great sword fell to the ground in a puff of sand and snow. The helmet rolled free, exposing a face slack with shock and pain. She swung again, and Heimdall rolled, his body going limp as he lost consciousness. Her lips drew back from her teeth in a fierce snarl as she reversed the strike, whirling the staff up to point the butt end at his nose. One strike would shatter his skull, driving bone fragments up into his brain.

"Hold, Okoye," said T'Challa, pushing himself up off the ground.

She growled wordlessly, overcome with fear and fury. The end of the staff trembled. Okoye could face down any opponent with glee, but this fight had shaken her more than most. T'Challa thought he understood why. The Asgardian had nearly killed him, and her resulting fear had knocked her off kilter. She was no killer, but even Okoye had her limits, and she had been pushed to them.

T'Challa put a hand on her shoulder. He could feel the tense set of her shoulders through the sensitive microweave of his suit.

"Thank you for the save," he said. "Have you ever considered starting a Wakandan baseball league? Or cricket?"

The ridiculous question penetrated her tense anger like nothing else could have. She blinked, looking up at him in astonishment.

"You cannot be serious," she said.

"Why not?"

But she ignored the question, looking down at the unconscious figure at their feet. She frowned.

"I do not know much of Asgardians, but it is unsafe to assume that he will not recover quickly. We cannot leave him like this," she said.

He nodded. "Cuff him."

She produced a pair of Wakandan restraint cuffs from her belt and considered the huge figure sprawled on the ground. A faint rime of snow had begun to collect on his face.

"Will they hold him?" she asked. "I know Shuri says they can hold anyone, but…"

T'Challa nodded. "She assures me that they can hold the Hulk, if you could get close enough to put them on him. They will absorb Heimdall's energy and use it against him."

Okoye eyed the thin strips of metal. They didn't look

sufficient to restrain the huge warrior, but they didn't have much choice in the matter.

"Very well," she said. "I'll put them on."

A roar of massive engines heralded the arrival of the Wakandan Dragon Flyers. T'Challa tilted his head to watch the biomimetic rescue helicopters as they circled overhead, searching for a safe place to land. He would get Anani the medical help she needed and see to it that Heimdall was safely locked away in the brig until they could figure out what was happening to him. Then he would set a perimeter around the portal until Doctor Strange could tell him how to close it. As the first of the small aerodynamic aircraft touched down, he was already marching toward it, instructions on his lips.

He had work to do. First on the list: call Doctor Strange and give him a full debrief.

SIXTEEN

Ms Marvel leaned against a wall and tried to appear casual, but it was a losing battle. She couldn't stop fidgeting with her mask – was it slipping? – and her gloves – too tight! She thought she'd adjusted to the whole super hero gig pretty well; she'd channeled her inner Captain Marvel and stood up against some serious bad guys. But she still hadn't gotten the hang of walking around town in a mask. At the moment, she'd tucked herself into an alcove with a shadowy apartment door at her back, but the back of her neck still crawled with goosebumps. Pedestrians hurried past with their eyes locked on their phones, but that didn't help her shake her self-consciousness.

She tugged at her mask again. Maybe she should go for one of the full-face masks. Spider-Man didn't have to worry that his disguise would slide off when he swung around town like Tarzan on steroids. But she had no idea how to go about that. You couldn't exactly pick up a decent super hero mask at the mall, not unless you wanted to cosplay, and that wasn't the vibe she was looking for.

"I'm thinking we should start a club for Awkward Public Mask Wearers. Wanna join?"

Spider-Man's voice took her completely by surprise, and she nearly punched him right in the face when he dropped down to hang at the mouth of the alcove. He held onto a long strand of flexible webbing that extended up to anchor at some unseen point on the building above them. As she tried to get her breathing back under control, he let go with one hand, waving at her.

"You OK, kid?" he asked.

"Yeah. You surprised me, that's all."

"Sorry about that." He cartwheeled off the webbing, landing lightly on his feet. "So, I take it that's a no on the club?"

She tugged at her mask again, chuckling. "It would be an awfully small club. I can't think of anyone else who would join it. Can you?"

"Dang it. You're probably right. Most of the super heroes I know are members of Tony Stark's Rich Enough to Not Need a Secret Identity club."

"Or Star-Lord's Who Needs a Secret Identity When You Can Escape to Another Galaxy club?" she said, warming to the game.

"See, kid, you're getting the hang of this already. Nicely done."

Kamala grinned at him. Out of all the super heroes she'd had a chance to work with, Spider-Man was one of her favorites. Although he called her "kid" all the time, he didn't treat her like one.

"What are we supposed to be doing?" she asked. "Are the others coming?"

"Nope, it's just us. The doc wants us to look around for a magic portal. You got your magic detector thingy?"

"The Eye of Vouk? It's right here."

She pulled the artifact out of her collar, letting it dangle on its golden chain. The heavy pendant made a bulge in her shirt and thumped uncomfortably against her chest during gym class, but she carried it everywhere anyway. Worry curdled her stomach when she thought about leaving it at home. What if something happened, and she needed the Eye, and it was sitting at home on her dresser? Or what if her mom packed it up to take to the donation bin? Or what if another planet killer decided to try and destroy the Earth? If she hadn't had the Eye with her when that whole Kree thing went down, she wouldn't have identified the danger until it was too late. She couldn't risk it, so it went everywhere with her.

"Good. Although I'm not sure we'll need it. Strange got a call from T'Challa, and he's got a portal in Wakanda. It's a big green orb of glowing energy, and I think that'll stand out without the magic eye," said Spider-Man. "Even in New York."

She snickered. "OK, so where do you want to start?"

"Let's go round the corner to where Venom was dumping that glowing green glop. Strange said that T'Challa found some empty bins with green residue on them near the portal in Wakanda. Either it's all connected, or nuclear green is the preferred color palette of the modern super villain."

"Heh. Lead the way, then."

Her amusement faded as she followed him out of the alcove. Doctor Strange hadn't told her any of the details. He'd told her to meet Spider-Man and bring the Eye. Nothing else. Part of her understood the decision; she hadn't been at this hero thing for very long, and Spider-Man had been around forever. She had no problem following his lead. But she still wanted to be in the loop. To know that her judgment was trusted. Otherwise, she wasn't really a part of the Shadow Avengers. She was just its mascot.

She let out a heavy sigh as they hurried down the block. Although she was trying not to make a big deal out of it, Spidey's keen senses picked right up on it.

"Something on your mind?" he asked.

"No," she replied automatically. "I mean… maybe? I don't know."

"There's no pressure to share, but I'm here if you need to vent."

"It's just that this super hero gig is hard in ways I didn't expect." She paused, trying to put her misgivings into words. "I don't know how to explain it. It's silly to complain, but sometimes I want to do the right thing, but I don't know what that is."

"No need." His voice was gruff as he clapped her on the shoulder. "I know exactly what you mean."

She wasn't sure if that was true, but it made her feel better anyway. Less alone. She smiled at him, suffused with gratitude.

"Thanks," she said. "Don't tell anybody, but you just might be my second favorite super hero."

He let out a surprised bark of laughter. "That's some high praise. Second favorite…" He trailed off, shaking his head in amusement. Then he stopped so quickly that she stepped on his foot.

"Sorry!"

She followed his gaze down the street, expecting to see a

bright green portal, whatever *that* looked like. But instead, dense storm clouds hung low over the city, ending abruptly just a few blocks away. It looked like it was going to be one heck of a storm, but that was fine. She'd always liked the rain.

"Is there a problem?" she asked.

He hesitated.

"Not sure. Something about that storm has my hackles up. I'm probably just paranoid. And really, who could blame me?"

"Uh…"

"That was a joke. This way. The truck was parked just over here."

It turned out that the truck was still parked there. A bright orange sticker had been slapped onto the driver's side window, warning of an impending tow by city authorities, and a white paper ticket flapped under one windshield wiper. Ms Marvel circled the tanker, trying to piece together what had happened here. She could see the clear marks of massive fists in the metal, and she ran her hand over one of them, marveling at its size.

"See anything with the Eye?" asked Spider-Man.

"Oh. Yeah. Let me look."

She pulled out the artifact and concentrated. After the events with the Kree, she'd taken some lessons with Doctor Strange on how to use it. Although she still didn't entirely understand how it worked, that didn't matter. She held it up to her face, gazing through its faceted depths. The eye-shaped gem within overlaid her vision with a bright shimmer. Living beings stood out against the dim landscape, and magical residue – from spells or powerful magicians – blazed so bright that she had to squint when she looked at them. But she didn't see anything like that right now. Not quite.

"So, what's the verdict?"

She frowned. "I'm not sure. There are some bright streaks on the ground near that manhole cover, but I don't see anything that looks like a portal. Could those streaks mean something?"

He stroked his masked face. "That's where Venom dumped the goo. The question is whether the glop itself is magic or you're picking up on the residue from Loki's portal. Honestly, I'm not too sure what to make of all this. It kinda feels like we're looking for a needle in a haystack, only no one told us what kind of needle we need. Maybe we go back to Strange and ask him to portal us over to see the other... uh... portal."

"Yeah. It would help to know what it looks like when I use the Eye," she said. "Maybe this stuff on the ground matches it, but I can't tell for sure."

"Back to the Sanctum Sanctorum, then," Spidey suggested.

She nodded, and they turned toward the mouth of the alley. But before they could leave, a portal popped into existence overhead and two people stepped out through the opening, landing gracefully and blocking their exit. One wore a massive headdress with golden horns that arched gracefully overhead. The other was a giant black monstrosity, its glossy skin broken by the outline of a white spider that arched over its chest.

Venom. The other guy had to be Loki. Kamala hadn't met him, but he sure fit the description. That headdress would stand out in a crowd.

"I am afraid that your visit to the Sorcerer Supreme will have to wait," Loki said politely. "My companion and I would like to have words with you."

Kamala tensed. Spidey's story made her immediately distrust anything that came out of the Asgardian's mouth. This situation would likely turn ugly. She tucked the Eye into her costume where it would be safe and tried to ready herself for anything. Both Loki and Venom wore necklaces, too – bright green ones that probably gave them corrosive spit or something. Something about them gave her the willies. Adrenaline made her hands shake, but over her short time being a super hero, she'd come to realize that it was a normal reaction. It didn't make her any less capable.

But still, part of her pointed out that Captain Marvel's hands never shook, and it made her worry.

"What do you want?" she asked. "We don't want to hurt you."

Beside her, Peter shook his head, as if he sensed something she didn't.

In lieu of an answer, Venom launched himself into the air with a wordless snarl of fury. Peter was already halfway to meet him before Kamala could even think of making a move.

Loki shrugged. "Guess we won't be talking after all," he said. "Too bad." His eyes latched onto Ms Marvel, and a cold smile stretched his lips. "You should flee, little one. Before you get hurt."

SEVENTEEN

Luke Cage looked up over his shoulder as he waited for the light to turn green so he could cross the street. Heavy clouds inched down the block, promising one heck of a storm to come. The air positively crackled with energy. Normally, he didn't mind a little rain, but for some reason, this front set him on edge, and he'd learned to trust his instincts. Something would come of this storm, and when it did, he'd be ready.

As soon as the light turned he hurried across, pausing to help Mrs Hernandez with the rolling cart she used to take her shopping home. She thanked him in a string of rapid-fire Spanish, and he flashed his teeth in response without slowing. If he gave her the opportunity, she'd talk his ear off, and she didn't seem to mind that he only understood half of what came out of her mouth. She talked so fast that it was just a wall of sound without an individual word in sight.

He made his way quickly down the block, and within minutes, he'd arrived at his destination. The steps leading down to the below-street bar weren't much to look at as they needed some repairs and better lighting to ensure the safety of his future patrons. But the woman waiting for him had nothing to worry about when it came to muggers or street toughs. If anything, they should have been worried about her.

Jennifer Walters stepped forward to meet him, looking up the stairway. Light fell on She-Hulk's upturned face, making her green skin glow as if from within. She wagged a finger at him in mock exasperation.

"You're late," she said. "You do remember how much I bill per minute, don't you?"

"I was hoping for the ex-boyfriend discount. Lawyers give those, don't they?" He hugged her briefly, giving her a chaste kiss on the cheek.

She laughed. "You have that backwards. Ex-boyfriends pay more. How's Jessica and the kid?"

"Good. I'm supposed to invite you for dinner sometime soon. We'll get takeout."

"As long as Jessica isn't cooking, I'm in. That woman could burn water."

"Oh, she has." He gestured to the building. "Since I'm paying the ex-boyfriend rate, you want to get moving?"

She glanced down at her smartwatch, her muscles moving under the expensive suit that had been specially tailored to fit her superhuman build. Despite her tailor's efforts, one flex and that jacket would be toast. That was why Luke had always preferred t-shirts. They were generally forgiving in a fight.

"We'd better," she said. "I've got a two o'clock that I can't miss."

He nodded, pulling out the key. The lock was temperamental, and it took a few tries before he managed to open the door.

It swung free with a rusty creak, and he swept into a bow, gesturing for her to enter.

"After you," he said.

She arched a brow but chose not to comment on his display of manners. When she reached the threshold, she hesitated.

"Shouldn't your broker be giving us the tour? You didn't already buy the place, did you?" she asked.

"Nope. He had an emergency and gave me the keys. Man's desperate to sell it. For some reason, folks don't like the idea of buying a murder bar."

She shot him a look. "As far as they know, it's an arson bar. And it's going to stay that way, right?"

He held his hands up. "Same difference. The place has history, and it's scared away the buyers. If I decide to buy, I'll get it for a steal."

"Hm."

Jen pressed her lips together but held back her comments for the moment. Instead, she stepped inside, scanning the dimly lit room. Luke flicked the light switch, and a row of dusty bulbs flickered to life overhead. They did little to chase the shadows from the corners, but it would do.

The place had been called Staryymir, back when it was open. But it had closed its doors right after the mysterious fire and went on the market with surprising speed. The space was dominated by a long bar made of dark wood, which had probably been beautiful at one point. Now, a thick layer of grime caked its once-pristine surface. A row of shelves behind the bar was largely empty save for one vodka bottle on the end, a sliver of liquid at the bottom. An ancient TV had been bolted to the wall, the cords dangling freely underneath. Tables and chairs had once been evenly spaced throughout the bar, but most of them were gone now. A broken chair sat on its side in the middle of the floor, its dismembered leg a few feet away.

"Huh," said Luke. "That's odd."

"What?"

"I took all the broken pieces out last time I was here. Favor to the broker. I figured it wouldn't hurt me to get on his good side." He frowned. "I know I got it all."

"Cheap furniture, I guess."

"I don't like the idea of some young punk sneaking in here and busting things up." He folded his arms, glowering. "I don't like it at all."

"Don't blame you." Jennifer approached the bar, frowning thoughtfully. "Where did it happen?" she asked.

"Right here." Luke stepped up beside her and leaned over to blow on the surface of the bar. Dust billowed in the air, exposing the scorched wood beneath. "There's burn marks all along the back of the bar, and the wall behind it bubbled from the heat. They're lucky the liquor didn't catch. The whole place would have gone up like a torch."

"Yeah, well, that whole thing was a nightmare. Somebody had to luck out."

"Too bad the bartender wasn't on that list." Luke sighed. "I've come to terms with the inevitability of my own death, but being burned alive still gives me the willies."

She tilted her head to give him a long look, her green eyes missing nothing. Then she went to the one remaining table and dusted it off with a sweep of her hand.

"Sit," she ordered, coughing a little.

He joined her, settling with wary caution on the flimsy

wooden chair. It creaked and protested but held his weight, as did Jennifer's. After a moment of tense readiness, they both relaxed. Or at least She-Hulk did.

"What's going on?" she asked. "You're acting odd."

"What do you mean, odd?"

She ticked her points off on her fingers. "All of a sudden, you hare off and decide to buy a murder bar–"

"Arson bar."

"Whatever. You join Strange's band of merry men. Now you're getting all maudlin. You're not acting like yourself. So here I am, taking off my lawyer hat and putting on my friend hat. What's going on?"

"I want to diversify. Build up a chain of bars so that if one of them gets burned down or shot up, I've still got cash coming in. I need to take care of my family, Jen. You know that's been hard for me with my history. I'm not saying I shouldn't pay for my past choices, but my family sure as hell shouldn't."

"I get that," she said. "But this place is a dump. You're setting yourself up to fail."

His brown eyes flashed. "I'm an expert at making something out of nothing. Don't forget that."

"I didn't. I'm glad to see that you didn't either."

He let his breath out in a long, exasperated sigh. "Lawyers," he said.

"It's why I make the big bucks. So, what's up with the death talk? Is that a parent thing? Having a kid makes you contemplate your own mortality?"

"Come on, Jen. You and I might be physical powerhouses, but we aren't brutes. I expect other people to write me off as a Neanderthal, but not you."

"Touché. You want to talk about what's worrying you then?"

"I would if I knew what it was. I just got a feeling, and I've learned to trust them. I sent Jessica and Danielle out of town. Got them a trip to some fancy doll store. Jessica's going to have a week of manicures and high tea and pink frilly dresses. She'll do it, but she'll probably kill me later."

"At least they're safe."

"Yeah."

She paused, thoughtfully drumming her nails on the table. "I haven't heard anything that could explain your creepy crawlies, but I'll ask around. What does Strange say?"

"He's edgy, too. But he's so distracted by this Dormammu thing that it's blinded him to any other dangers." Luke hesitated. "You should join up. The Shadow Avengers could use your level head."

"Strange already invited me. I turned him down."

Luke blinked. "Why?"

"I'm already tapped out on other things. But if you need me, you know I'll be there. I just won't be taking orders from that egomaniac sorcerer," she said.

"He's not that bad. The man's got a tough job."

"Sure, but I've never taken well to people who assume I'm stupid just because I'm big and green."

"Not sure that's personal, Jen. Strange thinks everyone's an idiot compared to him. Most of the time, the man's got a point."

She grinned. "Well, he does with you. I still think you're a moron to buy this dump, but if you want to do it, I'll handle the paperwork for you. Free of charge."

"I thought ex-boyfriends pay more."

"Friends are free. But don't tell anybody, will you? If the word gets out, everyone will want to be my friend, and I don't really like people very much."

He snickered. "Deal. I'll talk to the broker, and we'll draw up the stuff and send it over."

"Pay me in takeout once your girls get home, and we'll call it even. I liked the Indian place we had last time." She paused. "And I'll be in touch if I hear anything. Keep me posted?"

He walked her to the door, flicking off the lights.

"Definitely. You taking the subway?"

"I make the big bucks now, my friend. I'm hopping a cab. I'll share if you have far to go."

"That works. I've got some errands to run. I'm gonna want new locks on this place as soon as it's mine, and I figure it doesn't hurt to add some on our apartment and the bar, too."

"You're getting paranoid in your old age."

He shrugged, letting her out and locking the door behind them. As they began to climb the crumbling stairway up to street level, a car alarm went off. The incessant beeping was quickly followed by a series of crunching impacts.

They exchanged a wordless glance and hurried up the stairs to be greeted by a gruesome sight. Chunks of hail the size of softballs pelted the ground and punched through windshields. A waiting cab sat right outside the building with its engine running, the driver unconscious and bloody. A giant ball of hail had smashed into his face, leaving it a gory, pulpy mess. On the sidewalk next to the stairs lay Mrs Hernandez, clutching her shoulder. Her pull cart sat on its side next to her, groceries strewn all over the pavement. The hail continued to pelt the old woman, and she whimpered.

"Help me," she said, stretching out an arm toward them with a hiss of pain.

"Sweet Christmas," said Luke, surveying the mess. People huddled in cars and beneath awnings, but both offered flimsy protection at best. As if to illustrate his point, another giant ball of ice punched through the back window of the cab, shattering the glass. The sound jolted him into action. "I'll get Mrs Hernandez – the old lady over there. You start pulling people into the bar. Otherwise, we're gonna have fatalities on our hands."

Jen nodded, kicking off her sensible heels and throwing her arms up to protect her head. "You stay safe," she ordered. Then she charged up into the hail, making a beeline for the cab. One mighty wrench of her arm pulled the vehicle's door right off its hinges. A ball of ice impacted her shoulder, making her snarl in pain, but she didn't even pause. She threw the door into the street where it landed with a crash and a screech of metal, and hauled the limp figure of the driver up and onto her shoulders. Then she ran for the stairway, the unconscious man dangling in her grip.

Not to be outdone, Luke crouched over Mrs Hernandez, blocking the hail with his body. Ice pelted his unbreakable skin with significant force, but he didn't budge an inch. He was a mountain. A glacier. It would take more than a hunk of frozen water to stagger Luke Cage.

"Can you stand?" he asked the old woman in gentle tones.

"*No se*," she said, gesturing to her shoulder. "Broken."

He'd assumed as much. Maybe worse. The old woman's arm looked misshapen beneath the loose sleeves of her flowered housedress, and her lips were white with pain. Her skin felt clammy to the touch. Shock was setting in.

She needed a hospital, but it wasn't safe to get her there, and the freak hailstorm didn't show any signs of stopping.

"I am going to lift you," he said. "It will hurt."

He slid his arms beneath her before she could protest and picked her up as gently as he could. The old woman went paler if such a thing were possible, and she reverted back to her machine-gun Spanish. He hurried down the stairs and into the shelter of the bar, and finally, as he was settling her into a corner, he made out enough to catch her meaning. She couldn't afford to replace the groceries.

"I'll get your food," he promised. "Try not to move."

"*Vete con Dios,*" she said, patting him on the hand. "*Mi héroe.*"

The compliment should have made him feel better as he climbed the stairs back up to the street and began to collect the spilled groceries, his back hunched against the storm. But worry suffused him instead. He had been waiting for something bad to happen. Something told him this was it. He squared his shoulders, grabbed a bag, and began to put apples in it.

No one would hurt the people in his neighborhood. If they tried, they'd have to go through him.

EIGHTEEN

Venom hit Spider-Man with the force of a freight train. Spidey rolled with the strike, and the two of them tumbled over the dirty concrete, exchanging furious blows the entire time. Kamala would have been worried – the symbiote was so much bigger than Spider-Man – but the red suited web-slinger seemed to take the attack in stride. He pried Venom's hands from his throat and said, "If we're gonna get up close and personal, shouldn't you buy me dinner first?"

She turned her attention back to Loki. He waited patiently, his hands clasped behind his back. Did he intend to wait until she made the first move? If she didn't try to hit him, could they avoid this whole fight thing altogether? This seemed like a major breach of super hero and super villain protocol. They weren't supposed to meet in a dimly lit alleyway for a nice chat.

Maybe he wanted something. If she could get him talking, maybe she could figure out what it was.

"What did we do to make you guys want to take our blocks off?" she blurted.

It wasn't the subtlest of approaches. But Loki didn't seem to mind. He shrugged.

"I have no quarrel with you, young one. My symbiotic friend here is another matter entirely, I am afraid," he said.

"He seems to have anger management problems," she agreed.

"Indeed."

"We could stop them?" she said, her uncertainty turning what was intended to be a suggestion into a question instead.

"I am afraid not. I have tasks I must complete. It would be wise for you to step aside. I have no wish to harm a child."

She lifted her chin. "I'm not a child. And I'm not afraid of you." That last bit might not have been entirely truthful, but he didn't need to know that. "You're not going to scare me off."

Those words rattled around in her skull. They felt important for reasons she didn't entirely understand at first. She'd said them because they seemed like the kind of thing a super hero should say in a situation like this. If Loki tried to intimidate Captain Marvel, she would have told him to go suck eggs, in a very dignified yet firm way. Kamala wanted to be just like that. She was still working on the delivery, though. These things took time.

But she'd accidentally stumbled onto something important, and after a moment of mental scrambling, she realized what it was. Although Venom had anger issues, Loki obviously didn't share them. If he was trying to scare her off, it was because there was something he didn't want her to see. Something they had left behind. Some clue or important artifact.

Her heart leaped. She almost shouted out her revelation just in case Spider-Man hadn't worked through it himself but decided against it at the last minute. Loki thought she was a stupid little girl. It would be better not to alert him to the fact that she'd figured him out. If she paid enough attention, she ought to be able to discover what he didn't want her to see.

"If you will not leave, you are unwise." He sighed. "I suppose I ought not be surprised. I am not unfamiliar with youthful exuberance."

"Do you always talk like a walking thesaurus?" she asked.

He shrugged.

"Fine then. I'm going to help Spider-Man," she said.

She made it two steps before his hand closed on her arm, the long fingers curling over her sleeve with a surprisingly strong grip. She'd never liked it when strangers touched her. For some reason, a lot of adults seemed to think that cute young girls were up for literal grabs, and they toyed with her hair or patted her on the head without even knowing her name. She'd been raised to be polite, so she'd tried to extricate herself from those situations without making a big deal out of them. But over the past few months, she'd begun to think that maybe that wasn't enough. Maybe she deserved to speak up for herself and to not be manhandled by random people on the street.

The Asgardian wasn't exactly a rando, but the point remained the same.

Without even thinking, she embiggened, her body stretching until she stood eye-to-eye with him. Activating her powers made her feel like she'd just gotten a double shot of adrenaline mixed with an energy drink. Every cell in her body hummed with power. With ease, she reached over and pried his fingers off her.

He withdrew his hand without comment, his eyes

narrowing as he began to take her seriously. That should have worried her, and of course it did; she wasn't stupid. But she couldn't help but feel a little relieved that finally he'd stopped underestimating her. At the far end of the alley, Spider-Man and Venom kept exchanging blows, but Loki had assumed that she'd just walk away because he ordered her to. He couldn't have been more wrong.

He grabbed her again, by the wrist this time, moving with an inhuman speed she couldn't hope to evade. This time he squeezed, forcing her to work to dislodge him. She looked down at the mottled skin of his wrist. Something didn't look right. A rash or something? At least it didn't look like poison ivy. Before she could get a closer look, he yanked her off balance, his bright green eyes watching her intently. Waiting for her response.

If he wanted a response, she'd give him one. She allowed her arm to lengthen, stretching like taffy instead of tugging her off her feet like he'd intended. The lack of expected resistance made him stumble, as he pulled against a force that was no longer there. She was ready for it, smacking him upside the head with her other hand. It wasn't a strike intended to hurt. She wanted to make a point.

Her message appeared to be received as intended. He grinned, an almost feral baring of teeth that clearly communicated violent glee. For the first time, she saw him as a villain. He'd been so polite. So restrained. She'd begun to think that maybe he wasn't so bad after all but apparently, he could be provoked.

He swung at her, his long green coat billowing out around him, obscuring the details of his movement. She ducked under the oncoming blow, but he kept coming at a pace she couldn't possibly hope to match, sweeping his leg around in a wide circle that would knock her off her feet. Her back arched in a liquid swoop, the ligaments releasing her into an impossible backbend, and when he hit her ankles, she managed to launch all her weight onto her hands, flipping away from him.

"Nicely done," he said, admiration clear in his voice.

"What are you trying to hide?" she demanded. "Are you trying to keep us away from the truck? Is there something important inside?"

He blinked, glancing toward the vehicle.

"I don't know what you're talking about," he said.

"That truck is empty now. There's no reason for you to come back here unless you forgot something. I'm pretty sure it isn't your house keys."

"Do you intend to unravel my motivations? This should be a diverting entertainment," he said. "I–"

He broke off, his body wracked by a sudden ferocious bout of coughing. It staggered him. He doubled over, covering his mouth as convulsive spasms wracked his slim frame. His necklace swung so hard that it nearly smacked him in the face.

Maybe she'd been wrong. Maybe Loki hadn't been delaying or manipulating her after all. Maybe he hadn't attacked her from the get-go because he was sick. Those marks on his wrist. That cough. They didn't seem good. But what kind of illness could fell a *god*? She was pretty sure they didn't catch the common cold.

"Get down!"

Spider-Man's frantic shout pierced her frenzied thoughts. She ducked without a moment's consideration, and barely made it fast enough. Venom's bulk flew overhead, so close that his claws caught a few strands of her hair and ripped them free. The symbiote crashed into the side of the truck, denting the metal. He scrambled to his feet, the wide chest heaving as he struggled to draw air. But the damage only seemed to enrage the beast further. He tensed, readying for another charge.

Kamala crouched in place, waiting to see what happened next. Spidey was holding his own, but something had to break in this frustrating stalemate of an encounter. When it did, she'd be ready.

Before Venom could pounce, Loki grabbed him. The enraged symbiote swiveled to face his captor, his arm lashing out to plant a stinging backhand to the side of the Asgardian's head. Loki dodged, but as he did, another bout of coughing wracked his body. The blow clipped him, spinning him around and knocking him to the ground.

Kamala didn't know what to do. She'd gotten into this hero business to protect the weak and do some good in the world, but what was the right thing to do when one villain fought another? Should she try to stop them? Just let them go at it? Take bets?

Luckily, she didn't have to decide. Instead of pressing his advantage, Venom crouched, putting his hands to his head and howling in what sounded like pain. She thought there were words in there, but they were so twisted with agony that she couldn't make them out.

Loki staggered to his feet and grabbed the symbiote by the arm. But instead of continuing the confrontation, the Asgardian leaned on the gargantuan creature, using his bulk to hold himself upright.

"Go," he gasped. "Go now."

"I'm not going anywhere," Kamala replied in confusion. Venom arched, still wracked by an inexplicable pain.

"Give in," said Loki, grasping the pendant that hung from his neck. "It'll only get worse if you don't."

"No way," said Ms Marvel.

"Ah, but I wasn't talking to you," said Loki, his expression mournful.

That gave Kamala pause. Who else could he be talking to? And what was wrong with Venom anyway?

Loki sighed heavily, holding out his hand. His fingers were outstretched, and for one insane moment, Kamala wondered if he wanted a high five.

"Not so fast!" exclaimed Spider-Man, dropping down next to Kamala to land in a light crouch. "We have some questions for you."

"So many questions," Ms Marvel agreed.

A ball of green magical energy came shooting out at them from Loki's palm, hissing as it flew.

"Look out!" yelled Spidey.

Kamala didn't need any such urging. She launched herself out of the way. Who knew what that thing would do to her if it hit? It could freeze her in place or turn her into a chicken. Or both. Loki was the god of chaos, after all. Chickens didn't seem out of the realm of possibility.

She rolled, the ball of magic sailing harmlessly past her to impact on the side of the truck. Steam began to curl from the metal as it ate its way through. If it had hit her, it would have been worse than her chicken idea. Much worse.

CLUNK!

A chunk of ice sailed out of the sky, impacting against the

truck mere inches from Loki's ear. The Asgardian's eyes widened, but his ironclad self-control kept him from making the slightest twitch. Smaller hailstones began to patter against the ground, pinging off the sides of the truck. One of them bounced off Kamala's eyebrow, leaving stinging pain in its wake. She clapped her hand to her head, feeling the trickle of wet, sticky blood.

Dazed, she reminded herself that she'd been in the middle of a fight, and Loki wouldn't miss this opportunity to knock her block off while she was distracted by the freak hailstorm. But when she whirled around to hold her hands up in a defensive stance, he wasn't even looking at her. He'd tilted his head up to bask in the hail like it was the most beautiful of sunshiny days. Ice balls the size of coins bounced off his upturned cheeks, but he didn't even seem to notice.

"Finally," he breathed.

"What's going on?" demanded Ms Marvel. "Do you two… need help?"

But before the God of Mischief could respond, Spider-Man came hurtling toward her with a shout of warning. She ducked her head, trying to shield herself from whatever unseen threat he protected her from. Milliseconds later, he grabbed her by the waist, flinging them both down onto the dingy pavement. Her face nearly landed in a pile of mummified and unidentifiable food, but she wasn't about to complain.

A piece of ice almost as big as her head slammed into the ground where she'd been standing only moments before. It would have smashed her into smithereens, and she turned wide and grateful eyes to her fellow Avenger.

"Thanks," she gasped.

He saluted. "Don't mention it." Then the opaque lenses in

his mask narrowed as something over her shoulder caught his attention. "Hey! Where are you going?" he shouted.

She swiveled to see a bright swirl of green glowing energy hanging in the air. It stood at least seven feet tall, crackling with ozone. Big chunks of hail pattered down into it at an angle and failed to come out the other side.

A portal. Kamala wondered where it led, but if the other side was visible, she couldn't see it from this angle.

Loki stood in front of the magic doorway, his shoulders hunched against another cough. "My apologies, Avenger," he said. "But I am needed elsewhere."

"Wait!" Kamala blurted. "You're sick."

His eyes met hers for a moment of complete understanding. In them, she saw an awareness of his looming end, and a furious, impotent anger. Although she'd been fighting for her life against him just moments earlier, the urge – no, the need – to help him took her over with an almost physical pain. Or maybe that was the hail.

"I know," said Loki sadly.

"Let us help you!"

But her words fell on deaf ears. Loki turned away as Spider-Man scrambled to his feet. The Asgardian entered the portal, dragging Venom along with him, and although the steady clatter of the hail and the repetitive bleat of alarms in the distance swallowed any noise that it might have made, she could feel the air on her arms stand on end as he stepped through the magical gateway. Spidey dashed toward him, desperate to catch his prey before the doorway closed. Kamala's heart leaped. What if he went through the portal, and it closed behind them before she could follow? How would she find him then?

She reached out toward the portal, her Terrigen-mutated cells elongating. Her arms grew to double and then triple their original length. Maybe this was a bad idea. Maybe she'd grab onto the portal, and then it would snap shut and chop her hands off. But she couldn't stand here and do nothing.

But they both failed. The portal snapped shut as soon as Loki and Venom passed through, air rushing back to fill the empty space with such speed that it registered to Kamala's overtaxed senses as a clap of thunder. Spider-Man flew through the empty space, twisting his body in midair to land in an agile crouch on the dented side of the truck. He hung there sideways as Ms Marvel sucked her arms back in, returning them to their usual size.

"Was it me or was that really weird?" he asked.

"Oh, it was weird all right," said Kamala. "What do we do now?"

Spider-Man would know. He'd fought a million super villains. He had to have run across one of these portals before, and he would know what to do. Heck, maybe he'd planted a tracker on Venom while they were fighting. Kamala took a mental note, although she'd never be able to put this excellent plan into motion. They didn't exactly sell tracking devices at the school spirit store.

But Spidey surprised her. Instead of whipping out another of his impressive devices and taking off on one of his webs to fight the good fight, he pulled out his Kimoyo card.

"We're going to check in. This is fishier than an all-you-can-eat seafood buffet, and I want to know if Strange has any guidance for us," he said. "I'm fine with the kicking and the punching, but magic is not exactly my forte." He paused as the Kimoyo card made the connection. "Hey, Doc. Got a few updates for you. But first, I gotta ask: should this freak hailstorm have us worried?"

The conversation was short. After Spidey made his report, Strange asked a few questions and promised answers "soon." Ms Marvel hoped that would be soon enough because she shared Spider-Man's restlessness. The moment he hung up, she launched into her litany of questions.

"What do you think's going on? What should we do now? We have to do something, don't you think?" she asked.

Instead of responding, Spidey tilted his head, listening. From out on the street, she could hear the distant and thready calls for help. It didn't take a genius IQ to figure out the cause. The hail kept thundering down, causing mass destruction.

"We're going to help those people," she said, answering her own question. "Aren't we?"

Beneath his mask, his face twisted, and although she couldn't see his mouth, she knew he was smiling at her.

"You learn fast, kid," he said. "There's something unnatural about this weather, and we'll get to the bottom of that once Strange has some guidance for us. But first, there are people who need us. You ready?"

She hunched her shoulders against the hail and nodded.

Together, they hurried out of the alleyway, dodging the increasingly large chunks of ice that plummeted from the sky. People were in trouble, and they would help because that was what heroes did.

NINETEEN

The hot, dry air of Wakanda smacked Doctor Strange in the face as he stepped through the magical portal he'd opened between the Sanctum Sanctorum and Shuri's lab. Since the formation of the Shadow Avengers, he'd become accustomed to visiting. The royal family of Wakanda had a level of intelligence that rivalled his own, and they'd spent many an enjoyable evening in heated debate as they upgraded the Wakandan sensors to pick up a variety of magical energy types. That work had provided some of the insight he'd needed to create the Lantern of Morphesti, which he now carried with him, tucked into a pocket dimension in the depths of his costume.

After all, Stephen Strange liked to travel light.

A row of uniformed Dora Milaje stood in wait for him, in what passed for parade rest here. As soon as his boots touched the polished tile floor, they moved as if on some silent cue, bringing their spears to bear on him. He'd been trying for weeks to pick up on the signal that allowed them to move in such perfect unison, but so far, he'd come up empty, and now wasn't the time to indulge in such idle musings.

He didn't take offense at their caution, either. Over the years, he'd managed to come out on top of major confrontations, but he'd had some losses along the way. It would happen again, and people would be injured as a result of his faults. He carried this knowledge around with him every day; it settled over his shoulders like the Cloak of Levitation and tried to crush him beneath its weight. But if he did nothing, everyone would die.

It was a numbers game. He played it because there was no other choice. His mastery over the flow of time had given him a level of insight that no one should ever have to bear. But somehow, it had also brought him peace. There were no timelines in which everyone lived happily ever after. It was one thing to know this logically and another to see it. As a surgeon, he had never lost a patient, and it had gone to his head. As the Sorcerer Supreme, he understood on a cosmic level that loss was inevitable, and even necessary for life to flourish. Sometimes he railed against that fact, as he had over the past few weeks, but now he was back to himself again.

But he chose not to accept any more loss than necessary, and to surround himself with capable people who would help him win the numbers game as much as it could be won. So, he welcomed the caution of the Wakandans. No one would step from a portal wearing his face and wreak havoc on the lab. Not without going through the guards first.

Okoye stepped forward, her dark eyes glittering as she pointed a scanner toward him. He could feel its cold touch on him even though he couldn't see the beam.

"He is clear," she said in her musical Wakandan accent.

The guards returned to parade rest, and she allowed herself a smile.

"Doctor Strange. Please accompany me. We have been waiting for you."

"One moment," Strange responded. "With your permission, I would like to bring my companion and confidant, Wong. I may need his capable hands, but I did not want to invite him into your inner sanctum without permission."

"The rumors of your wisdom are based in fact, I see," she responded. "Wong is known to us. If he will submit to our scans, he is welcome in our halls."

"Of course."

The guards returned once more to their ready stance, and the sorcerer turned back to the still-open portal and beckoned. After a moment, Wong stepped through, his bald pate glistening with sweat. He leaned heavily on a tall walking stick, doing his utmost to project the image of an old man brought down by age and infirmity.

"It's about time," he muttered.

"The proprieties must be observed, especially here," responded Strange, unruffled.

As they spoke, Okoye ran her scanner and gave the all clear. She tucked the device back into her belt and gave the retainer a little bow.

"Welcome, Wong," she said. "Wakanda appreciates your assistance and guidance in this concerning matter."

"But of course," said Wong. "It is my great honor to do so."

"Perhaps," she said, leading the way across the antechamber towards the doors to the lab proper, "we could persuade you to spar with us before you leave. I see you brought your stick."

"Ah, but I am not what I once was. Too many years, and too many pastries," Wong responded, patting his belly.

"How do your New Yorkers say it? You are full of it, yes?" asked Okoye.

Wong threw his head back and laughed uproariously, and she smiled again, opening the doors to the lab. As her eyes fell upon the unconscious figure of Heimdall strapped to Shuri's evaluation table, the smile fell. A shimmering containment bubble surrounded the Asgardian, its translucent surface coating everything inside it with a faint blue tint. The Wakandan princess herself stood just outside the bubble, reviewing a readout of diagnostics that hung projected in the air before her face. She turned to see them, with relief evident in every line of her body. Shuri's small stature and youthful exuberance stood in deep contrast to her formidable intelligence and deadly inventions. With the power of the Panther at his disposal, few people could keep up with T'Challa. But his sister could give him a run for his money. Still, she was usually playful and lighthearted. If she looked this grave, the situation was serious indeed.

The urgency of the problem at hand overrode the usual niceties. Strange strode forward without waiting for an invitation, taking quick stock of the situation. The Asgardian warrior lay quietly, his chest rising and falling with gentle breaths. But a full complement of restraints crossed his body and secured his limbs, and there were more guards in the space than usual. They carried an air of tense wariness, ready to pounce at any moment.

"Was Heimdall violent when you brought him in?" he asked.

"Not at first," replied Shuri. "After my brother and I restrained him, he was obedient but silent. We couldn't get a word from him other than a thank you when we gave him water. He came to the lab without incident and allowed me to begin the scans, but then he became so agitated that I worried he might hurt himself. I was forced to sedate him for his own safety."

"Interesting." Strange joined her by the patient's side, glancing through the readouts. Row upon row of complex medical information hung in the air before him, a testament to Shuri's thoroughness. Huge swaths of it would have confounded the world's greatest medical minds, but they lacked the perspective that Shuri and Strange possessed. He understood her records easily, and he admired her for their meticulous quality.

But the readouts concerned him. Some of the anomalies in the scans could be attributed to Heimdall's Asgardian physiology, but a few numbers stood out to him. He raised a finger toward one line, bringing Shuri's attention to it. "His magical resonance is at such a high level that it's a wonder it hasn't torn him apart. A human would not be able to withstand such energies. Only his Asgardian physiology is keeping him alive. Perhaps his violence was borne from pain rather than fury?"

"I proposed the same hypothesis myself. And look. Here are the readouts from the rescue crew who picked them up approximately one hour ago. They were working with limited equipment, but they performed the basics."

With a gesture, Shuri opened the new file and stood back to allow him to read it. He could sense her tense eagerness, but she held it back with effort, allowing him to make his own assessment. It was such a pleasure to work with professionals. If Tony Stark had been here, he'd be impatiently rattling off all the salient findings rather than letting the doctor make his own conclusions. Over the years, Strange had tried to point out multiple times that faster wasn't always better, but Tony deflected all attempts at course correction with a smokescreen of sarcastic quips. Stephen didn't hold with violence, but at some point, he might just punch Tony in the face.

His assessment didn't take long; the differences between the two readouts were blazingly obvious. Heimdall's condition had deteriorated at frightening speed. Only the magical readouts remained strong and steady. Frowning in thought, he turned to Shuri.

"Have you determined the cause of his condition, or may I provide a consultation on this matter?" he asked.

"I don't know yet," she responded. "But I am not sure it would be safe for you to scan him."

"Why not?"

"He didn't become violent until we mentioned your name. A burst of green magical energy emitted from his chest and appeared to cause him significant pain. We're unable to remove the armor, but my scans suggest that the energy is generated by something he's wearing over his heart. Some small device or magical artifact. He appeared to struggle against its effects, but his condition deteriorated rapidly. He developed physical symptoms right before my eyes: coughing, fever, and generalized weakness, but he still proved to be a formidable opponent. It took some effort for the Dora Milaje to restrain him so I could administer the sedative."

Strange frowned. "Did the magic come from him, or from elsewhere?"

"I think it has an exterior source, perhaps related to whatever he's wearing under that armor, but I cannot tell you more without exposing him to further damage, and he can't take much more. It didn't cut off until I closed the bubble around him."

"Therefore, I can't examine him without opening him to that influence." The Sorcerer Supreme stroked his goatee in thought. "This situation has some disturbing parallels to Spider-Man's report on Loki. I fear this may not be the last Asgardian we see who is under harmful magical influence and atypically hostile."

"That is a sobering thought," said Shuri. "What course of action do you recommend?"

"I would like to see the portal. If Heimdall is magically linked to it as I suspect, it should provide more clarity on next steps. It would take a great deal of energy to control such a powerful being. If I can unravel how it was accomplished, we could potentially free him."

"Okoye can take you there," she said readily. "My brother has already returned to the area to set up a perimeter, lest other hostiles come through it into our lands. So he will be there to provide any assistance you may need."

"Excellent." Strange hesitated. "Although I would welcome your insight on the portal itself. Perhaps Wong and Okoye could remain here to monitor Heimdall, while we travel to the portal? Your input could be invaluable in unraveling this mystery."

Okoye stepped up next to Wong. The two of them made no arguments and put on no airs. But their aura of calm capability spoke for itself. After a moment's consideration, Shuri nodded.

"Of course," she said. "In the event of an emergency, you

could return us both here within seconds, could you not? I do not wish to waste any more time than is necessary."

"I could."

"Then let us go." Shuri shivered. "Any magic that could steal a man's will from them is something I would like to rid from my lab – and Wakanda as a whole – as soon as possible. We must make haste before things get worse."

Wong clucked his tongue as she rushed about the room, collecting gadgets and gizmos in preparation for the trip.

"She *is* young," he commented. "Otherwise, she'd know not to say things like that out loud. It only invites trouble."

Normally, Stephen didn't hold with such superstitions, but as he stared down at Heimdall's unconscious figure behind the protective force field, he couldn't help but agree.

TWENTY

Venom hadn't intended to be thrust through the portal. In fact, he hadn't even realized there *was* a portal. Last thing he knew for certain, he'd been in the middle of a fight. He'd flown backwards after a particularly brutal two-footed kick to the breadbox, struggling for breath. He landed badly, rolling in painful skips as the symbiote worked overtime to absorb the damage, his claws leaving furrows in the soft ground. Rolling upright, he snarled, looking for his enemy. He'd rip Spider-Man's head from his scrawny body.

Then the pain had hit, Loki's voice had echoed around him that he couldn't do anything about the agony, and everything went white. Now that it had finally eased, all he could see was trees.

Where was he?

Before he could begin to reason this out, the air flashed with an energy that would have made all his hair stand on end in his human form. But as with most other things, the symbiote absorbed it easily. He shivered once, and then it was gone.

Loki appeared out of thin air. The Asgardian staggered, grabbing onto a nearby tree and using it to hold himself up. He was injured or sick, or both. Venom could press the advantage now and get the information he needed to remove this slave's collar from his neck.

But before he made his move, he paused. The pendant had punished him for striking Loki before. Eddie knew that it would happen again, even though his Other still chomped at the bit, eager to rend flesh and do damage. But he stuffed the urge down deep despite the symbiote's silent begging. The black symbiotic bulk turned liquid and flowed back into his pores in a process that defied all science.

In a moment, Eddie Brock was himself again. As much as he could be these days.

He straightened from the animalistic crouch that he'd been in and approached Loki. His efforts at squeezing info out of Osborn may have come up disappointingly empty, but perhaps this time would be different. Loki was hurt, and he wouldn't be at the top of his game. Maybe he'd give something away.

So instead of punching the Asgardian right in his smarmy mouth, Eddie offered a hand. "There's a bench over there if you want to sit," he suggested.

Loki looked up at him with obvious suspicion, but then his eyes lit on the pendant that dangled from Eddie's neck. The Asgardian nodded, holding out a hand.

"Thank you," he said.

"Don't mention it."

Eddie led the way to the aforementioned seat, his mind working overtime the entire way. He noted the way that Loki struggled to support his own weight on shaky legs. The moist smell of greenery. The absence of traffic noise. The lingering ozone smell in the air, quickly dissipating. He had made a living out of making a story from seemingly disparate sources of information, and he would put that skill to work here.

"What park are we in?" he asked, making an educated guess.

"Everwood," responded Loki. "Just outside the city limits. I thought it wise to have a bolt hole for the purposes of evading detection. The Sorcerer Supreme will be scanning the streets for us, but he won't look this far out."

"And if some brat comes looking for his ball, what do we do about that? No offense, but in that getup, you stand out."

Loki shook his head, a ghost of a smile flitting over his lips as he settled more comfortably onto the bench. A sigh of relief escaped him. *Good*, thought Eddie. *The more relaxed you are, the more you'll spill.*

"This will not come to pass," said Loki. "The park is closed. For construction."

"How do you do construction on a park?" Eddie glanced around. "What are they going to do, build some trees?"

"I fail to understand many things that humans do, but that does not change the fact that people do them."

Eddie smirked. The guy had a sense of humor, but that didn't make up for the fact that he'd thrown that chain over Eddie's neck. The pendant dangled beneath his shirt, next to his skin, and he wanted nothing more than to smash it right here and now, but even the thought filled him with fear. His fists clenched in a moment of anger, but he forced them to release. His emotions were making it tough to keep himself under control. Too bad that realizing it didn't make it any easier.

"Well, at least it's not hailing. That sucked," he said.

"Not out here, no. And the hail is a relief, my symbiotic friend. If not for the portal that accompanies the hail – or other weather phenomenon – you and I would be writhing in pain right now."

"I don't get it."

"Clearly, no."

"Then why don't you enlighten me?" An explanation flashed through Eddie's mind, a lightning strike of insight. If he hadn't been so worked up, he probably would have figured it out sooner. But he'd been too busy chafing at the bit. "You're in the same boat I am, aren't you? Osborn is controlling you through that necklace."

"Not Osborn, no." Loki sighed. "But otherwise, your logic is sound."

"Did they make you sick, too? How long have I got before I'm coughing up a lung?"

"You won't." Loki coughed again, producing a wet and painful sound. "As far as I can tell, my symptoms are a product of interdimensional travel."

"I'm not following."

"I'm not surprised."

Eddie tried not to take Loki's obvious superiority personally. Maybe the guy was a genius where he came from, but if he acted like that on the streets of New York, he'd get his face stomped. Then again, maybe that was the idea. Maybe he was trying to pick a fight. If so, Eddie wasn't about to take the bait.

"Explain it to me," he said. "Seems to me that you and I got the short end of the stick here. I'm willing to call a temporary truce if it means getting this thing off my neck."

"Nice thought, my symbiotic companion, but it won't happen."

"Why not?"

Loki took a moment to marshal his thoughts before he replied.

"I suppose you had best know some things lest you get us into trouble." He caught Eddie's indignant eye and shook his head slightly, his long dark hair rustling. "This is no insult. I stumbled into this thing just as you did."

"Fair enough."

Eddie laced his fingers behind his head and leaned back against the tree, trying to look casual. But his nerves jangled. Finally, he would learn what was happening here. What had happened to him. Tense alertness filled him to the core; even his Other was listening, and it hadn't been the listening type lately. If ever.

"I first got into this mess purely by accident. I was home, going about my own business–"

"Home, as in Asgard?" Eddie interrupted.

"Yes, but not your Asgard." Loki sighed. "There is no time for a metaphysics lesson, so let us simply say that there are multiple realities, all attached to each other. In each, there is a Loki. There is a Venom and an Eddie Brock. Each one diverges from the others at some point."

"In some realities, I don't have the symbiote?"

"Precisely."

Eddie's stomach plummeted at the thought. Sometimes he had nightmares about losing his Other. In them, he ended up alone. Homeless. Stripped of everything that had made him special.

It's OK, Eddie, said the symbiote, its voice echoing in his mind. *I won't leave you.*

Me either, bud, he thought. I promise.

"So, there's another Loki – our Loki – walking around right now," he said aloud, trying to keep his mind on the matter at hand. "Here, on this planet."

"You understand, then. Dormammu came to my reality. Mighty sorcerer. Delusions of…" He broke off, his forehead beading with sweat. "Never mind. You get the picture."

"Yeah, I get it. So, he's the one who put the pendant on you. He pulls the strings?"

"He is the Master," said Loki, coughing. "Most of the time, my will is my own, but when he calls, I must answer. Again, most of the time, as you've discovered, fighting against other pendant wearers produces an undesirable effect. I have been trying to determine what gets Dormammu's attention so that I might avoid it, but there's little pattern to be found. I suspect his attention is split between a variety of thralls, both here and in my universe. This takes a substantial amount of magic, in addition to the power necessary to open the interdimensional portals on his end. It's impossible to say when he is listening and when he is not, so it's best to behave. Thank Odin he is spread too thin to control us directly."

"What's the point of all this? The guy's got a sadistic streak, or what?"

"You still haven't got it, have you, Eddie? This is no game. It's an invasion. We are unwilling soldiers." Loki leaned forward, his eyes glittering. "The Master intends to take over your world, and there is nothing we can do to stop him."

PART TWO
FRACTURED WILLS, FRACTURED WORLDS

TWENTY-ONE

Luke kicked the door to the bar with one work-booted foot. Hail pelted his back at an increasing speed, balls of ice pinging off slabs of muscle. He grunted as a particularly large one tried to punch a hole through his lats which didn't move. In his arms, an unconscious dog walker in skintight exercise gear shifted as awareness began to trickle in. She still had the leash attached to her waist, and at the end of it, a tiny ball of fluff yapped in incessant panic. He'd tried to pick it up, but it scurried away every time he approached it, and he didn't have the time to play tag with a dog. The storm showed no sign of lessening. If anything, it had become worse.

At first, things hadn't been so bad. He and Jen had gone up to the street to find that only a few people needed their help, like Mrs Hernandez. Most folks had taken a hit or two and then sought shelter, and they tended to each other under awnings and inside overcrowded shops. NYC might have had an uncaring rep, but when the chips were down, the residents took care of their own.

Then the hail intensified, and instead of the occasional large ball of ice amidst the small patter of chips, the sky began to spit out huge hunks of frozen water at an increasing rate. They punched through windows and canvas awnings, left dents on car hoods, and clanged off railings. The glass in the grocery across the street from the bar shattered, pelting the crowd inside with shards. The two heroes had supervised the evacuation, shielding bleeding civilians and crying children with their bodies as they hurried across the street to the relatively safe sanctuary of the basement structure. Within minutes, the place was packed.

Luke had gone to all of the surrounding buildings and helped anybody who wanted it. On his way back, he'd seen the dog walker. She'd rolled halfway under a cab in the hopes of taking shelter before an ice ball knocked her out cold. At least she ought to be the last one.

He kicked the door again, and after a moment, Jen opened it.

"You good?" she asked. "All clear, or do I need to go out again?"

"It's clear. Everyone else on the street has enough space to shelter away from the windows. They know where we are if they need help. I'll stick my head out every five minutes or so and check on things until this storm's over."

"Gotcha." Jen looked down at the woman in his arms, and the dog that was trying to gnaw a hole in Luke's boot. "Want me to take her? The last thing you need is another pretty woman with a hero crush on you. Jessica has a lot of virtues, but patience isn't one of them."

He grunted again. "I wish people understood that we save

them because it's the right thing to do, and not because we're trying to make a move on them."

"Tell me about it. I tried a dating app once." She shuddered. "Never again. I'll die single if I have to."

He shifted the dog walker to her arms and surveyed the room. So far, so good. People sat in small groups on the dusty floor, helping each other out however they could. Complete strangers held ripped cloth to bloody cuts, pulled Band-Aids from purses, and offered whatever small luxuries they happened to have with them. Mrs Hernandez made her unsteady way around the room, offering her groceries to anyone who needed a snack, heedless of the pain that she had to have been in, or the fact that it would leave her without food for the week.

Jen set the dog walker down next to a teenage girl with dried blood streaking her temple. The girl squealed at the sight of the dog, scooping the little poofy thing into her arms while her mother took over first aid without being asked. She-Hulk gave the woman a grateful smile and a pat on the shoulder before turning back to Luke.

"We're all tucked in for now," she said. "But it won't hold."

"You think?"

"The suit in the corner," she said quietly, indicating a clean-cut young man in a three-piece suit who still wore a dazed expression as a Black grandpa dabbed blood from his split lip. "While we were helping the injured, he insisted that he had somewhere important to be, and ran out into the storm with nothing to protect him but an umbrella and an overinflated sense of self-importance."

"Tell me how you really feel," he murmured.

"Oh, I will. He's quiet now, but I'll bet you a million dollars that he'll be back at it as soon as he collects his wits. I know the type."

"He can get himself brained by a chunk of ice if he wants to, but if he talks anybody else into his nonsense, I won't be having that," Luke said, scowling.

"Exactly."

"I think the storeroom is pretty empty, but let me see if there's anything useful in there to distract folks with. Too bad the bar isn't stocked. I could offer them all a free round."

She nodded. "I'll do another lap and make sure nobody needs anything. But I think we're good. We've got one broken arm and a bunch of probable concussions, but nothing we can't handle in the short term. Once we can get out, I can call my car service and take the worst cases to the hospital. I imagine it'll be hard to get a cab once the hail stops, and I'm sure they closed the subways. It'll be a while before they can clear the tracks."

"Sounds like a plan." He paused. "Thanks, Jen. It's good to work with you again."

"I don't say this about many people, because I'm an introvert who doesn't like anyone on principle, but you, too."

Her teeth flashed in a grin, and she turned away before he could respond. Chuckling, he pushed through the door with a broken sign that proclaimed "PLOYEES NLY." Dust billowed in the hallway beyond, making him sneeze. Two sets of footprints were clear on the grimy floor, and as a matter of habit, he followed them down the hallway where they ended at the door marked "Bathroom." He hoped it was operational, but he'd better check to make sure the water was running before he offered it to the folks huddled in the bar.

He hesitated at the bathroom door for a moment before deciding to check out the storeroom first. Safety before comfort. They'd been lucky so far, but he knew from experience that luck wasn't infinite. At some point, someone on the street would take a ball of ice to the head and be killed. Luke didn't want the blood on his hands. He'd had enough of that to last a hundred lifetimes already.

Unfortunately, the storage room had been all but cleared out. A bag of moldering garbage sat in one corner, buzzing with flies. Empty plastic bags and cardboard boxes littered the space. One open crate of vodka sat in the corner, the clear bottles caked in layers of grime. Luke looked down at it in exasperation. Shots of straight vodka wouldn't do for his purposes. He wanted to give people a little distraction, not make them belligerently drunk. That would be a step in the wrong direction for certain.

There was nowhere to hide the liquor without drawing attention to it. The empty storeroom gave him no options, and if he carried it up to the bar, folks would ask for a drink. No way could he stash it up there without someone noticing. Maybe he could stash the booze in the locked bathroom cabinet with the cleaning supplies.

He nudged open the bathroom door with his elbow, trying to keep the bottles from jingling. The door flew back, slamming into his nose and making his eyes water, kicked by some unseen attacker on the other side with inhuman force.

Dazed, Luke Cage staggered backwards, trying to clear his vision. He clutched the box to him reflexively, blinking furiously. But he didn't need his eyesight to understand that his unidentified enemy held a sword to his throat.

"Move," they said in a low, feminine voice, "and I'll slit your bloody throat."

TWENTY-TWO

"Down there!" yelled Ms Marvel, pointing down the street as the hail continued to fall from the sky with a punishing intensity. "I think there are kids on that school bus!"

Peter Parker needed no further encouragement. He ran down the street, forgoing the webs even though they'd get him there faster. But he couldn't dodge the largest chunks of hail in midair, not without changing his trajectory and losing more seconds than he'd saved. The bus would keep the kids safe for now, but he wouldn't be able to forgive himself if he arrived seconds too late. He never had.

Ms Marvel kept pace with him. He wasn't surprised by this; she'd been smack in the middle of that Kree situation just a few months earlier and came out of the deal with Doctor Strange's respect. He'd worked with her in minor skirmishes since then, and despite her young age, she'd carried herself with calm assurance. Besides, as Peter himself knew very well, superhuman abilities could force a kid to grow up fast. It would be hypocritical of him to write someone off as inept just because they weren't old enough to vote yet.

When they reached the bus, they worked well together, calming the worried children and providing basic first aid to the half-conscious driver. When the hail hit, the driver had tried to shield her charges from the worst of it by backing into a narrow alleyway, trusting that the looming buildings would block most of it. The plan had worked, although it left her sitting exposed in front of the enormous windshield, and she'd paid the price. But when Peter lifted her out of her seat, the first words the bleary woman spoke were to ask about the kids.

"They're OK," he reassured her. "We're moving them inside where it's safe."

The kids were scared, but they scooped up balls of ice in their hands and marveled at them as Ms Marvel led them to safety in a nearby real estate office, arching her body over them and flattening out to provide a shield against the tumult. The children watched her with wordless awe, following her instructions without needing to be told twice. She stopped at the doorway, protecting them until they got inside. The real estate receptionist held the door, ushering them all inside to a back room where one of the agents turned the TV on to cartoons.

"Thanks for taking them in," said Peter, settling the driver down on a handy couch. "Can you take it from here? I'd like to go back out and see if anyone else needs help."

"Don't you worry about a thing, Spidey," said the agent, a thin and glamorous Indian woman. "My sister works at the elementary school these kids go to. I'll get in touch with her."

He flashed her a grateful thumbs up and helped Ms Marvel get the last of the students situated before hurrying to the door.

A few of the kids broke out into an excited chant as he left, and the words, "Spidey! Spidey! Spidey!" took him out the door.

A wave of guilt overtook him, and he paused on the front step. Hail pinged against the ground at his feet, missing him by centimeters.

"They should be chanting your name, too," he said. "I could go back and tell them…"

Ms Marvel laughed. "Don't worry about it. I'm fine with flying under the radar. Besides, I bet there's a drawback to being recognized all the time. Expectations, you know?"

"Oh, I know," Peter muttered. "With great power comes great responsibility. Tell me about it."

Her eyes narrowed behind her mask, and she set a hand on his shoulder.

"You OK?" she asked.

He shook himself out of the sudden fit of melancholy, turning his attention back to the task at hand. "Of course I am," he responded. "Let's go down towards the intersection and see if everyone's off the street over there."

"Sounds like a plan."

They began to move down the street. Ms Marvel stuck next to the buildings, using them to deflect most of the hail. They'd quickly learned to stick to the north side of the street, since the hail slanted in that direction.

His Spider-Sense and augmented reflexes kept him safe from the dangerous projectiles, so he darted to and fro across the street, looking under cars and into shadowy alcoves to make sure no unconscious pedestrians huddled there. He tried to move as quickly as possible, but thoroughness took time.

As he straightened up after checking under a long row of parked cars with damaged windows and duct tape on their bumpers, he noticed Ms Marvel looking around with the Eye of Vouk, frowning in thought. She hadn't lost sight of their mission despite the hail, and he was grateful for it. Her competence allowed him to concentrate on the rescue efforts.

"Anything yet?" he called to her.

"I don't think so," she said. "But this hail is weird. It registers on the Eye."

"I'm not sure it takes a magic artifact to tell us that monster hail out of a clear blue sky is weird. I kinda figured that out myself," said Peter, joking. But she didn't seem to get that. Her face fell, and he rushed to explain. "Sorry! Sorry. I kid around too much. It drives people nuts. My aunt used to swat me with a dish towel for it all the time."

"Maybe I should start carrying one," she said, relaxing.

"You can try." He grinned. "So, what does it mean that the Eye registers the hail?"

"It's magical somehow. The Eye helps me see magic, and there's this haze all over everything. But in places that are sheltered from the hail, it's not there. So that's got to be it."

"What does that mean for our portal search? Are you going to be able to see it, if the hail's fogging up the sensors, so to speak?"

"I'm still learning how to use this thing, but I think so." She paused thoughtfully. "Stronger magic looks brighter in the Eye, and a portal would take a lot of magic in one place to keep it open. Whereas the hail is a lot of magic spread across a large area, so it's dimmer, if that makes sense. And if it's strong enough, the thing hums so loud you can hear it."

"I get that. You've been studying this a lot, huh?"

"Doctor Strange has been giving me homework. It's a lot more interesting than American history, but still. The last thing I need is more homework."

He grinned. "Come on, homework's fun." He would have continued to tease her, except that he caught movement in the corners of his peripheral vision. Someone darted from doorway to doorway down the street, hunched over against the hail. Whoever it was, they were nuts. Did they want to get beaned by a hunk of ice and get a concussion for their trouble?

"We got a live one," he said, pointing.

"Wow. What's he gonna do when he runs out of canopies to hide under, dodge the hail?"

"I give him thirty seconds before he's out cold."

Together, they rushed down the street to intercept the reckless pedestrian. Ms Marvel tucked the Eye of Vouk away in her costume, and Peter edged in front of her just a bit. Old protective habits were hard to break.

When he got close enough to get a glimpse of the guy's face, he reached out and pushed her fully behind him. He would have recognized that grizzled jawline anywhere. He'd punched it quite a few times, but usually it was hidden behind slabs of symbiotic biomass.

Eddie Brock.

The reporter stopped a few yards up the street, taking shelter under a steel awning. The hail hit it with a rapid rat-a-tat that sounded like gunshots. He took his hands out of his pockets and held them out to the side as if he promised peace. But Peter wasn't going to fall for that again. Eddie always lied, and for a long time, that had taken Peter by surprise. But he'd learned his lesson. Some people couldn't be saved because they didn't want to be, and he just had to accept that and move on.

"What's going on?" asked Ms Marvel, trying to edge out from behind him.

"That's Venom," Peter whispered to her. They'd been at each other's throats for years, but they'd eventually come to a tentative détente about one thing: they didn't out each other's secret identities to the general public. If Peter shouted Eddie's identity to the rooftops, Eddie would immediately retaliate, and vice versa. So, they both kept mum. But Peter had no problem with warning Ms Marvel, who had only interacted with Eddie when the symbiote took over. She needed to know who she was dealing with, since he couldn't count on Eddie to play things straight with her. Which brought up a question: why wasn't Eddie wearing his symbiote suit and leaping into combat with the slavering anger of a hostile alien like he did just a little while ago?

"What's up?" Peter called. "You miss having my fist in your face?"

"I just want to talk," said Eddie.

"I've heard that a million times before. Usually before you stab me in the back. No go," replied Peter.

"I need your help."

That gave Peter pause. Turning down a request for help went against everything he stood for, but the bad guys knew that. They'd tried to use it against him before. This time, he could see the trap coming from a mile away, and he had the kid to protect. She could hold her own, but Venom was no run of the mill opponent. If she got hurt, it would be at least partly Peter's fault.

He hesitated, torn between two options, neither of which were particularly good. But Ms Marvel didn't have the same baggage he did, for better or for worse. She stepped out from behind him with a determined tilt to her head.

"We're going to hear him out," she said. He tried to butt in and explain their history, but she cut him off with a shake of her gloved finger. "I get it," she said. "I'm not stupid. But if we don't listen, we'll both always wonder if we did the right thing."

She was right. He probably would have come to the same conclusion with enough time, but still, it shamed him to have her call him out like that. He hung his head for a moment and sent out a silent wish into the universe that this would all turn out OK for the kid if not for him. She was a good person, and it seemed like the good people in his life always got hurt. He'd do anything to keep it from happening again.

"Yeah," he said. "You're right."

"I want to talk to her," Eddie called. "She doesn't have her head up her behind like some do-gooders we know."

Peter took a deep breath, which failed to calm him. Ms Marvel stared up at him with the confidence of a much older person, and he had to trust her. He stepped aside, but he didn't relax. He kept his web shooters at the ready, his arms curled into a stance that looked casual, but put him in the perfect position to cover Eddie in sticky webs at a moment's notice. If he tried to hurt Ms Marvel, he would regret it.

Ms Marvel turned to face him and held out her hand. "I'm Ms Marvel. It's nice to meet you."

"Can't shake your hand. But I appreciate the sentiment," replied Eddie. "I'm Eddie Brock. What are you doing with a judgmental jerk like Spidey here?"

"We're working," she replied, unruffled. "What do you need help with? Is it about the storm?"

He looked up. The awning above still pinged and clanged. The constant racket grated on Peter's enhanced senses and he was pretty sure Eddie felt it, too, based on the tense set of his shoulders.

"Kind of," said Eddie. "But it's bigger than that. I got information that you and your little club might be interested in."

"How much will it cost us?" asked Peter, unable to restrain himself.

Eddie ignored him, addressing Ms Marvel directly. "I'm still putting the pieces together, but I thought you should know that this hail isn't just a freak storm. It's the fallout from a spell. A big one."

"The portals?" asked Ms Marvel.

It was obviously a guess, but the shot hit true. Eddie flinched.

"Yeah," he said. "How did you know?"

"Well," said Ms Marvel, "I've got–"

She reached into her costume to pull out the Eye of Vouk. For all of her bravery and newfound composure, she hadn't learned that there are some secrets you just don't spill to people like Eddie Brock. Peter interrupted before she could get herself in too deep.

"What does it mean?" he asked. "You said you wanted our help, so get to the point."

Eddie's mouth tightened, but he refrained from commenting. "The portals are just the beginning," he said with a grimace. "They're coming, and it's going to be bad."

"The beginning of what?" asked Ms Marvel.

"An invasion," said Spider-Man, the pieces clicking together with a finality that made his stomach sink. "He's talking about an invasion."

TWENTY-THREE

Luke froze with the sword at his throat, blinking his eyes free of tears. His vision cleared quickly, bolstered by his super human biology, but he wasn't willing to make a move until he could fully assess the situation. The strike had rocked his world, if only for a moment, and that meant that his assailant was no ordinary joe. He would give the situation the respect – and time – it deserved.

His clearing vision revealed a woman so tall that she could nearly look him straight in the eye. She wore ornate bluish silver armor, clearly well cared for but with obvious signs of use. The longsword that still rested a breath away from his jugular gleamed from a recent polishing. Under different circumstances, Luke would have inquired about the weapon; the cold metal against his skin had a unique texture that he'd never felt before. Although he'd never been a swordsman himself, it was wise to learn about these things in case you found one of them at your throat.

Whoever she was, she hadn't come here looking for him. An

experienced warrior like her wouldn't leap into an altercation without studying her opponent, and she would have learned that threatening to cut his throat was an exercise in futility. So, he'd taken her by surprise. That was good. He could work with that.

He slowly and carefully set the box of liquor on the ground and said, "I mean you no harm."

An amused smile flickered over her features, and she took him in once more, her eyes roaming over him. As she did, her smile grew wider.

"Of course you don't. I'm sure it has nothing to do with the sword at your neck, either," she said in a low, pleasant voice.

She'd written him off as a muscle-bound lunk. Luke couldn't exactly blame her. He knew the type quite well himself: gym addicts who thought mass equaled strength, sacrificing flexibility and usefulness in exchange for the perfect bodybuilder form. A lot of them liked to push people around. One of Jessica's favorite hobbies was to teach them a lesson. He didn't hold with needless violence, but he had to admit that their shocked expressions when the small dark-haired woman began to toss them in the air like pizza dough were awfully amusing.

"The sword doesn't bother me," he said. "Who are you, and why are you in my bar?"

That last bit wasn't exactly true. It wasn't his bar yet, and lying made him uncomfortable these days. He'd done enough of it in his life to reach his fill. The warrior woman picked up on his discomfort and arched a brow. Whoever she was, she found him quite amusing, and she wanted him to know it.

"You're very relaxed. I can tell," she said.

"OK, let me prove it then. If I can get your sword off my neck without spilling a drop of my blood, you'll tell me who you are and what you're doing here."

"I'd like to see you try. That sword–"

He struck while she was mid-sentence. He brought his arm up into a forceful block, striking the flat of the blade aside with the hard ridge of bone that ran up the outside of his forearm. Although he had the element of surprise on his side, she resisted reflexively, and the tip of the sword dipped toward his exposed skin. If not for his unbreakable flesh, he would have lost the bet. It would have only grazed him, but that would have been enough. As it was, the razor-sharp blade slid off him. It tickled a little.

Her eyes narrowed, and for the first time, she began to take him seriously as an opponent. Now he would have to be on high alert. She couldn't hurt him, but there was a whole room upstairs full of innocent people, and depending on her morals, she might consider them acceptable casualties. He wasn't about to allow that. Not in his neighborhood, and definitely not in his bar-to-be.

"Who are you?" she demanded.

He shook his head. "That wasn't the deal. You're in my territory. You answer first, and then I'll do the same."

Her lips drew back from her teeth in a wordless snarl, and for one heart-stopping moment, he thought she might throw all caution to the wind and go for his throat. But then she mastered herself, lowering the sword in a wordless salute.

"I suppose such skill deserves my respect, but I cannot spare the time to sit down for a tea party," she said. "I am called Valkyrie, and I have no quarrel with you, whoever you are. I teleported into…" She glanced over her shoulder at the filthy bathroom beyond. "That."

"Uck." He made a wordless sound of disgust as he put it all together. A swirling green globe of magic hung in the air above the toilet. In his extensive experience as an Avenger, magic portals never meant anything good. Maybe Jen was right; this bar had bad juju, even for portal-summoned intruders. She must have come in through the portal and dropped straight into the bowl. "I'm sorry."

"The water has gotten into one boot," she continued with weary disgust.

Their eyes met in a moment of mutual revulsion, and Luke relaxed infinitesimally. Anyone would be a little touchy after teleporting into a toilet by mistake.

The more he thought about it, the more amusing the whole thing was. He couldn't help it. He snickered. Her eyes narrowed, and she drew her shoulders up in a prideful stance before she saw the humor in it, too.

"By Odin's beard," she said. "What awful luck."

"I can't argue with you." He offered a hand. "Luke Cage. I'm in the process of buying the toilet you just stepped in. Once it's mine, I intend to tear it all out and sterilize the place. Twice."

"That is a good plan." She inclined her head and shook his hand. Her grip was firm, but she didn't squeeze hard in an attempt to prove a point. He had the impression of coiled strength held at bay. It was a good thing they hadn't fought in earnest. They would have destroyed the place. "I apologize for trespassing in your luxurious bathroom facilities. My Master's people set up my portal at the convergence of the ley lines here. I would have chosen a less fragrant location if given the chance. I will see myself out."

He let the joke about his toilet pass this time, because an interesting thought began to occur to him. He held out a hand to restrain her as she tried to push past him.

"One question before you go," he said. "Will that portal close itself, or should I get a friend to close it?"

"You know someone with the magical abilities to do such a thing? I have always been under the impression that most humans wouldn't know real magic if it bit them in the hindquarters."

"I'm not most humans." He smiled. "I take it by your comment that you aren't either. I'm going to guess Asgardian?"

"Nicely done."

"I've worked with Thor on and off. Good man."

"Sometimes," she allowed.

"Well, I can get my friend Doctor Strange to close the portal. I'm assuming you didn't end up where you intended, so if you need a hand…"

He trailed off. Up until this moment, she'd been relaxing more and more, but now she'd gone tense and strained. Her hand gripped the pommel of her sword, shaking visibly. Alarmed, Luke scanned the small bathroom and up and down the hallway, attuned to any signs of threat. But he sensed nothing.

"Did I say something wrong?" he asked, his forehead furrowed in worry. "Are you OK?"

She shook her head hard and thrust a hand into his sternum, driving him backwards out into the hall.

"I don't want to hurt you," she said. "You seem like a decent person. But that name has caught the Master's attention, and I cannot resist long. Go now, before I lose control."

"What name? Strange's? Do you need help?" he demanded, ignoring her orders and stepping toward her once more.

"Are you stupid? Go!"

Her lips drew back from gritted teeth, and every muscle in her face and neck strained against some unseen force. Flickers of eldritch green light began to shine in her eyes. Luke's gaze went from her to the still-glowing portal and back again. Whatever sorcery controlled the portal still had a grip on her. Something told him that whoever was on the other side didn't mean well. She'd mentioned a Master.

Could it be Dormammu? If so, Strange would never let him live it down after all of his skepticism.

"There are innocent people in this building," he said. "If you lose it here, they'll get hurt. Hold on."

She gripped her sword so tight that he wouldn't have been surprised to see the mark of her hand imprinted in the metal. He looked around, thinking fast. He couldn't take her up the stairway and into the midst of all those people if she was about to go nuclear. Although he didn't know what would happen once she lost control, it probably wouldn't be good, and the green flickers in her eyes grew stronger with every passing second. But the basement level bar didn't have a back entrance.

He had no way to see her safely out onto the street. A row of thin, barred windows ran across one side of the storage room, about two-thirds of the way up the wall. They led up to the street, but a child would have struggled to fit through them, let alone a man of his build or a woman in full plate armor. He grabbed onto the bars and tore them free with a wrench of metal. A quick punch shattered the glass of both windows in quick succession. Then he grabbed onto the thin strip of brick between them and heaved, slabs of muscles along his arms straining to their max.

A small voice deep down inside wondered if maybe he was overreacting. Doing structural damage to the bar he intended to buy didn't seem like the smartest choice he'd ever made, especially since he didn't know what would happen when Valkyrie lost her struggle against the magical influence streaming from the portal. Maybe she'd just run, and then he would have torn a hole in the wall for nothing. But if he took the risk and somebody got hurt, he'd never forgive himself. Something told him she wouldn't either. She was fighting this thing with everything she had, letting out wordless grunts of pain, and he wasn't going to let her face the aftermath alone.

Brick crackled, pieces crumbling to dust in his grip. He shifted his hands as a chunk came free, trying to tear loose the strip between the windows. The resulting hole ought to be enough to get them both out of here.

"No!" she said, the word coming out choked. "Go now. It's too late. Go."

He heard the unmistakable rasp of steel being drawn, and the heavy thump of her booted feet on the concrete floor as she rushed him. The warrior maiden hit him with the force of a bullet train, but he was ready for her. They grappled. She was stronger than she looked, and no one would have pegged her for a weakling. The heavy sword swung down at him, and it took all of his considerable strength to hold it aloft.

"I'm trying to help you," he spat out between gritted teeth.

"I cannot stop," she said. "It is not my choice."

With a heave of effort, he diverted the strike, pushing her arm off to the side so the blade fell inches from his exposed arm. Before she could bring the weapon around to bear again, he stepped in close, grabbing her around the waist. She twisted in his grip like a snake, his hands sliding over the smooth armor. But she wasn't going to get away that easily. He squeezed, pinning her in place, ignoring the crunch of the hilt against his face. If not for his altered physiology, she would have broken his nose.

"Sweet Christmas," he said. "I've had enough of this."

He threw himself at the gap in the wall, carrying her along with him.

TWENTY-FOUR

Kamala Khan couldn't decide if the quivering sensation in her belly was excitement or nerves. She led the two web-slingers down the block to a café and righted one of the tables. If they sat against the wall, the building would keep most of the hail off. Although she'd brokered some peace for the moment, it might not hold, and she didn't want to go inside and have Spidey and Venom bust the place up in a fight.

Eddie stuck close to her the entire time. So close that she almost hit him with a chair when she turned around with it. He backed off a fraction of an inch at the most. Certainly not enough space to put the chair down. So she held it and wondered at his clinginess. When she thought it through, she realized he'd been orbiting around her, keeping her between him and Spider-Man at all times. Maybe he figured Spidey wouldn't hit a teenager. Or a girl. Or anyone who didn't deserve it. Or perhaps he was trying to keep his own temper at bay.

Spider-Man wasn't any calmer. She couldn't see his

expression, of course, but tension was written in every line of his body. It worried her. He'd always been the kind of guy who would crack a joke at the moment when it seemed like all hope was lost. Now he might as well have carried around a neon sign that said, "About to explode at any moment."

Maybe Eddie was right to keep her in the middle. Hopefully she could keep World War III from popping off in the middle of a little French café.

At least now she knew one thing. That flippy feeling in her belly was definitely nerves.

She gestured toward the table.

"Sit," she ordered.

They did. She took a seat, too, scooting close to the wall to shield herself from the hail. She'd never seen a storm like this. Usually, hail spat from the sky for a couple of minutes tops, and then it was over. But this one showed no signs of stopping.

"I'm not sure I get this. Can you explain it to me again?" she asked Eddie.

He scooted his chair a little closer to hers and nodded. His eyes didn't even flicker toward Spider-Man. Not once. It was probably better that way.

"I'll give it a try, but there's no telling how much I'll get out," he said. "Like I said before, Loki tells me this is all related. The weird weather. The portals. They're all a part of Osborn's plan to open a gateway for a guy they call the Master."

"That's not very creative," said Kamala.

"His real name is…" Eddie hesitated. "Let me spell it out for you." He traced the letters out in the drifts of snowy hail covering the table: D-O-R-M-A-M-M-U. "He's strong enough to take an Asgardian god and make a slave out of him."

Spider-Man tensed, his hands gripping the edge of the ornate iron-wrought table. "Are you sure? How do we know you're not making this up?"

Eddie smiled, bitterness practically dripping from his mouth.

"You'd like to think that, wouldn't you?" he asked. "Because otherwise, you'd have to acknowledge the fact that maybe you've been wrong about me this whole time. And oh, no, Spider-Man can't be wrong. It would be bad for his rep."

"I know what I saw, and you and Loki seemed awfully buddy buddy."

"Loki does not want to be here any more than I do." Eddie put his hand to his chest, over his heart. "But I am trying to protect this city."

"Yeah, that's convincing. I know you, Brock."

"You think I'd confide in you after all we've been through? As if you'd listen to me."

"Now wait a minute," said Kamala, but it was like they didn't even hear her. They glared at each other, their voices growing louder as their tempers took hold.

"You've proven time and time again what kind of monster you are, Eddie. Your actions speak for themselves," Spidey snapped.

"And yours don't? You're going to let our mess stand in the way and potentially doom millions of people because you can't stand to play nice with me. Priceless."

"That would only make sense if I believed a single word that was coming out of your mouth," said Spidey. "But I'm not stupid. When a guy like you conveniently shows up with all the answers, I know what's really going on."

Kamala couldn't take it anymore. She reached out, her arms lengthening to cross the last few inches, and slapped them both across the face.

For a moment, there was nothing but stunned silence at the table, broken by the ping of hail bouncing off the metal furniture. Her heart began to beat in double time, and her palms were instantly drenched in sweat. She'd just slapped Spider-Man and Venom. What in the heck had gotten into her? She wasn't the slapping type. Or the assertive type, really. Maybe her time hanging out with the Kree had changed her after all. Too bad it was probably going to get her killed.

No one spoke for a long moment, and Kamala swallowed, her throat gone suddenly dry. She was supposed to be the peacekeeper here, and she'd failed. Now she was afraid to do anything for fear of making it worse.

Without a word, Spider-Man stood up from the table and took a few steps away. Although he didn't comment, his turned back made his opinion clear. Now, in addition to being terrified, Kamala felt like an awful person. Maybe she should have slapped herself.

Eddie stayed at the table, though. His eyes remained glued to Spidey's back, but he scooted toward her. When he spoke, his voice was pitched for her alone.

"The Master wants to take over the world," he said. "Loki says that the guy's kidnapping a bunch of Asgardians from their dimension and sending them here to our planet, our dimension. Apparently, they're better at surviving the trip, but I gotta say that with every passing minute, Loki looks worse. The Master is controlling them with these green pendants. Sometimes he listens through them, too, so you got to be careful what you say when you're around them. But Loki thinks he can't control more than one at once, or something like that. Still, we've got to keep this conversation short. We've lucked out so far, but I don't know how long it will last."

"Good to know," murmured Ms Marvel.

But it wasn't good. She glanced at his neck. Hadn't he been wearing one of those pendants before? She thought she remembered seeing a necklace on him earlier, but she couldn't be certain. At the time, she'd been more concerned with fighting than with jewelry. But if he was wearing one, what did it mean that he hadn't mentioned it? Was he too afraid of getting Dormammu's notice, or just too embarrassed to admit to Spider-Man that he'd gotten in too deep? That felt right to her, so she wouldn't out him for now, but she'd have to keep an eye out. They were building trust, and she didn't want to push in the event it might break.

"You think? I think none of this looks good, personally. The more Asgardians the Master sends over, the stronger the link between Earth and his base will get. Eventually, it'll be strong enough to let him through. Maybe we're not always on the same team, but none of us want that."

Kamala nodded. "I'm sorry I slapped you. I didn't know what else to do."

He let out a huff of amusement, rubbing his chin. "We deserved it. Spidey probably knows it, too, although he's got a stick shoved too far up his – ahem. I mean, he'll never admit it."

"I can hear you," said Spider-Man. "I'm standing right here."

"Of course you can. I'm not stupid." Eddie stood up. "I don't expect you to believe me. But look into it. If the situation wasn't dire, would I sit here across from the guy who has ruined my life a hundred times over and play nice? Tell your sorcerer and see what he says. That's all I'm asking."

"Yeah, and what do you get out of it?" asked Spidey.

"I save my city, and I keep on breathing. I need to know how to shut those portals down and how to free the slaves."

Kamala froze, the word ringing in her ears. Slaves. If Loki – and even Eddie – were enslaved, it was no wonder he was reaching out for help. She wondered if she should ask outright, as she knew that after all their sordid history, Spider-Man would need proof before he believed it, but she didn't blame Venom for his caution. After everything she'd been through with the Kree, she knew things weren't always what they seemed.

"We'll check it out," she promised fervently.

Eddie's hand fell on her shoulder, and he squeezed once before letting go. Based on his expression, the gesture shocked him as much as it did her.

"Thanks," he said. "I'm going to try to find out more. I'll let you know whenever I have something good."

"How? You want to set up a date? Meet here for a latte?" asked Spider-Man.

"I could give you my cell number," Kamala suggested.

The mundane suggestion seemed to take both of the web-slingers by surprise. Maybe they were just old. Kamala darted into the café, the bell jingling, and came back out with her number jotted on a strip of cash register paper.

"Here." She glanced back into the café. "They think we're nuts."

"They aren't wrong," said both of the web-slingers simultaneously. They stared at each other for a long moment of mutual shock, and Kamala had to suppress the urge to laugh. Maybe she didn't know either of them very well, but she could tell they were more alike than either of them wanted to admit.

"No," she agreed, just to break the tension. "They're not wrong."

TWENTY-FIVE

The remaining brick wall shattered as Luke Cage and Valkyrie flew through it. Momentum carried the two warriors across the icy sidewalk and dropped them off the curb into the street. It was a good thing that the hail had brought all the traffic to a standstill, because otherwise they would have been flattened by a cab or a city bus in no time. But no one so much as honked at them, because everyone had taken refuge inside.

That left them free to struggle for supremacy out there on the dirty pavement while ice balls flew at them at irregular intervals. Valkyrie had the agility of a cat, and she managed to worm her way to the top, sitting on Luke's torso and raining blows down on his head. Although the Unbreakable Man didn't feel pain, he couldn't help but be impressed. She packed one heck of a punch. Her green, glowing eyes glared down at him.

"I'm sorry!" she cried, striking his jaw with such force that it knocked his head over to one side. "I can't stop."

"What's wrong?" he asked, deflecting a follow up blow. "How can I help?"

"That name. The Master doesn't like that name."

What name? Luke caught her hand in his fist as he thought back to what had happened moments before she'd lost control. They'd been talking as polite as you please. Then he'd mentioned the portals. And Doctor Strange. The magical force on the other side of the portal had lashed out at the mention of the Sorcerer Supreme. This fact only served to reinforce Luke's theory about the villain's identity, and he didn't like that one bit.

He needed to get the Master to release Valkyrie from his control once again. The Asgardian didn't look good. Sweat streamed from her brow, and her lips had gone pale with exertion. But she still tore her hand free, swinging at him with blistering speed. Even his arms got tired when he slugged it out like that, and she was in full armor. If she kept this up much longer, she'd burn out entirely.

"Look," he said. "You win. I surrender."

He hadn't been fighting back much, anyway. It didn't seem right to knock out a woman who was clearly not in control of herself and regretted every single blow. Besides, it wasn't like they hurt.

Regardless, the ruse didn't work. Her eyes dimmed for a moment, but then the glow came back in force. She kept on swinging.

She grunted in effort, and for a moment, her fist hesitated. Then *wham*! It rocketed into his jaw again.

"I'm sorry!" she repeated. The words came out ragged with exhaustion. Then she coughed in his face and apologized for that, too.

Surrender wasn't enough. This Master wanted to know

that he was out of commission for good. Luke had never been much of an actor – it seemed much too close to lying to him – but he knew he could sell this one. He waited until she landed a particularly good blow and let his head go with it. He even added a tortured groan to the mix before letting his body go limp and his eyes flutter closed.

She hit him once more before pausing. He didn't dare open his eyes to see what she was doing. She coughed again. He tried not to breathe, desperate not to give away the ruse.

After a long moment, she scrambled off him. He felt the brush of her hair against his face as she tested his breath. He held it. She stayed there a long time, until bright stars burst behind his closed eyes and his chest strained with the need to take in air.

"No, no, no," she exclaimed. "Breathe, damn it!"

He opened his eyes just as she'd begun to lean over to attempt a resuscitation. He knew he had to help Valkyrie. He wouldn't be able to live with himself later if he didn't, and he couldn't imagine admitting that failure to Jessica. It had taken work to earn her good opinion. Sometimes he still wondered if he deserved it. Old habits die hard.

"Oh!" exclaimed Valkyrie, scrambling backwards, her cheeks flushed. The green glow had faded from her eyes. "I thought you were dead."

"Yeah, that was kind of the point. You better now?"

She nodded.

"I think we need to talk. If I avoid any names, you think we can do that?" he asked.

"I'm not sure. I don't think he's always listening, but I can't tell for certain. We can try," she said. "As long as you're prepared to accept the consequences."

"That's all any of us can do." He stood, offering her his hand. After a thoughtful moment, she accepted it, and he helped her up. Then he paused in consideration. "Not in the bar, though. I don't want to risk bringing you around all those people just in case that puppet master of yours takes over again."

She nodded.

"Where, then?"

He considered. Even though his girls were gone, he couldn't possibly bring her back to his apartment. He didn't want the Master to know where he lived. But he wasn't ready to cart her off to the Sanctum Sanctorum either. Not only was it too far to reach without the aid of public transportation, but he didn't trust Strange not to strong-arm him again. Luke was willing to believe that Dormammu was the mysterious Master if that turned out to be true, but it might be someone else entirely, and he'd need evidence to convince Strange of that fact. He wanted more information before he made his report. They needed somewhere completely private, which was a tall order in the City That Never Sleeps. A ball of hail bounced off his cheek, narrowly missing his eye. That gave him an idea.

"I know," he said. "Follow me."

TWENTY-SIX

Ice clattered down the empty stairwell and echoed through the cavernous tunnels of the subway. Luke had been a city man all his life, and in all those years, he'd only ever been in an unoccupied subway a handful of times. All of them had been emergencies in which innocent people had died. He held no illusions about this one, either. Heroes of all stripes would give their all. Regular people would step up to the plate to help their fellow man. But still, there would be losses.

The empty subway platform haunted him with the possibility of failure. That someday, their collective best wouldn't be enough. If that happened, there was the distinct possibility that the Unbreakable Man would be one of the only people left in the entire world. The thought chilled him to the bone.

Valkyrie glanced around the deserted space. The platform was under construction with its entrance blocked off by a plywood door that Luke had torn from its hinges. Sizable drifts of hail had built up against the entrance and sifted down to coat the stairs once he'd opened the space. Construction equipment cluttered the area, but it seemed the actual work had barely begun. The digital displays that listed the next trains had gone dark, and only the red blaze of the emergency lights illuminated the space, coating everything in a ruddy haze. The power was out, but even if it came back soon, the subways couldn't run until the tracks had been cleared. No one would bother them here.

"It appears that we are alone," said the Asgardian, eyeing him with caution.

"We are," he agreed. "Now you can question me."

A faint smile crossed her face. He wasn't sure if he needed to keep up the illusion that he was her captive any longer, but it couldn't hurt. Whoever stood behind those portals and used their power to drive her to act against her will hadn't picked up on the ruse. They must not be listening very closely, and Luke didn't want to attract their attention by pushing too hard. This conversation must be approached very carefully if it was going to be successful.

"Yes, there are things I would like to know," she said. "You will tell me them. Perhaps you will not want to name names, but I will beat them out of you if I must."

Her icy blue eyes flashed in warning, and Luke heard it loud and clear. No names. If she had to add in a right hook or two to sell the story, it would be worth it. He leaned against a grimy tile column and nodded.

"Ask your questions," he said.

"Did you intercept my arrival on purpose, or was it an accident?"

"I didn't know you were there."

"That is quite a coincidence, is it not? That a man of your… skills would be positioned to intercept me?"

"Maybe the bar is a place of power. Places of power attract people of power."

"So, is it? A place of power."

"No clue."

"Then we are back to your lucky appearance. You were not sent there to intercept me?"

"No. Coincidences happen." He shrugged. "Now isn't the time to have a philosophical discussion, so I'll just say that I have faith. Sometimes they happen for good reason."

"But you don't deny that you are a man of extraordinary talents. What do you do?"

He nodded in approval. The question was nicely put, and open-ended enough that he could twist it to communicate whatever he wanted. He needed to offer help without seeming to do so, and without naming any names. Although the steady stream of half-truths made him uncomfortable, he relished the opportunity to use his mind in such a way. Although he could wade in with fists blazing, he liked using his head.

"I represent a collection of interests. We help people in trouble and protect the people of this city. If you've come here with trouble in mind, you'll have to go through us," he said.

She smacked him across the face. The blow was open-handed and barely registered. He nearly forgot to react to it in his need to see that she'd heard the most important part of that statement: the offer of help. Because Valkyrie was clearly in trouble. He knew it deep in his bones.

"You're lucky, hero," she scoffed, pulling a green, glowing pendant out of her armor with some effort. "If I had another of these pendants, I'd enslave you. They allow our Master to monitor you and communicate his instructions to you, as well as other slaves like me. I would enjoy watching him punish you when you try to resist." She shuddered, coughing lightly. "It is brutal. I do not recommend it."

He shrugged. "I'd just take it off."

"The backlash would likely kill you. I tried it myself, when he came to Asgard. He enslaved the people – my people – and held them captive to ensure our cooperation. Then he sent a few of us out into the world to spread his influence."

The explanation left a lot unsaid, but Luke could easily fill in the blanks. His heart went out to her, but he couldn't tell her that. Still, he met her eyes for a moment, trying to communicate his sympathy to her. If some megalomaniacal jerkwad came for his family, he'd punch them into the next century. But after a long moment of eye contact, she smiled sadly.

"The Asgard of my dimension has fallen," she said. "The Master's influence grows, and with every day that passes under his malign influence, I feel my power ebbing. There is nothing that can be done but to give way to him. You will see that in time."

"I will not. Doc – the guy I work with has some tricks of his own. We'll stand up to this Master of yours."

"It is already too late," she said. "The Master is too powerful."

"Yeah? I've never heard of him."

"His name…" she said, "is Dormammu."

There. Now he had it. It was time to call the Shadow Avengers in. Strange would be thrilled. Luke wouldn't have minded too much except that he'd lost his bet with Spidey. It was only a dollar, but he still disliked losing. It was the principle of the thing.

"Still not quaking in my boots." He cast a significant look at the stairway. "Did you hear that? I think someone's coming."

She glanced toward the empty stairs. Other than the hiss of hail from the street above, the place was cloaked in silence. After a moment's contemplation, she seemed to understand. She would search for the mystery intruder to buy him time to call in.

"I will go and check it out. Remain here. If you flee, I will hunt you down and make you pay. I'll enjoy it," she said, putting her hand to the hilt of her sword to underscore the mock threat.

"Yes, ma'am," he responded.

He needed to wait until she was out of earshot before pulling out his communicator. But halfway across the room, she froze in place. Confused, he scanned the platform once again. Was there really an intruder? But the only thing he could hear was the distant rustle of some small animal. Probably rats.

But she didn't go to investigate that either. Instead, she turned back around, heading toward him with purpose. Green light flickered in her eyes.

"Come with me," she said. "We are summoned. There is one final portal to open."

As she reached for him, he debated resisting. He could buy enough time to pull out his communicator and call the Shadow Avengers, but what then? That would only tip Dormammu off regarding their ruse. Once he knew where Dormammu hid, he could call in the cavalry.

So he nodded, allowing her to pull him up from the pillar and drag him toward the stairs.

"There's no need to manhandle me. I won't resist," he said.

She paused, looking at him with those crackling eyes. Then, after a moment, she nodded.

"No funny business, or I will end you," she promised.

"I wouldn't dream of it," he said, crossing his heart.

TWENTY-SEVEN

Stephen Strange stood in front of the glowing Wakandan portal, taking a moment to marshal his emotions. He'd known from the start that his duties as the Sorcerer Supreme would put him at odds with other mystics of significant skill. He'd faced down threats of such power that they nearly destroyed the entire universe. But this time, it felt different. This time, it was personal.

Dormammu's evil tendencies had cost him his chance of happiness with Clea. Of course, their relationship had devolved over more than that, but at the core, he felt certain that all their problems could be traced back to one simple fact: at some point, he would kill her uncle. Although Clea herself opposed Dormammu with every cell of her being, such a fact had to be difficult to deal with. It was only normal to want a healthy relationship with family, after all.

But this was his job. Billions of creatures throughout the universe relied on him to perform it to the best of his ability. That knowledge didn't ease the pain and anger he felt, however, staring at the portal and recognizing it as the first salvo in Dormammu's latest invasion attempt. He could not afford to indulge in those emotions. He had indulged enough over these past few weeks. So, he allowed himself a moment to experience them before tucking them carefully aside.

T'Challa and Shuri joined him as he contemplated the glowing orb of concentrated magical power. He had been standing here so long that snow coated his dark hair and outlined the soles of his shoes on the ground.

"What have you found?" asked T'Challa.

"It's Dormammu's work for certain." Strange held up the Lantern of Morphesti. "I've further calibrated this artifact to search for the portals. If any more of them open, we'll know about it."

"Very good. Do you have any insight on how to close it? I do not like such a thing to be open within my borders. It makes me twitchy."

"That is a default, my brother," murmured Shuri.

The king of Wakanda elbowed his sister, and the two of them fell into a companionable silence, waiting for the sorcerer's answer. Strange contemplated the portal once more. Something nagged at him…

"There's a magical vector here that I can't identify," he said. "I hesitate to shut it down before I understand it fully. What can you tell me, Shuri?"

"The ground beneath the portal is wet with some viscous substance," Shuri said. "I've sent it back to the lab for a full molecular analysis, but my initial readings and my instincts suggest that it's identical to the sample that Spider-Man got from the Oscorp truck."

"Perhaps this material primes the ground for the portals to open. Interesting," said Strange.

"My scouts found two empty barrels coated with a matching residue," added T'Challa. "I will be questioning everyone who has entered this sector to determine if we have a traitor."

"Good idea, although you might not find anything. Spider-Man reported that Loki and Venom vanished through a portal themselves. If they are the team that is opening the portals on this side, they could have teleported in, set up the portal, and then left before they attracted any attention."

"That is a relief. I hate to think that my people would get mixed up in any of this." T'Challa paused. "I will investigate regardless, in order to be certain."

"Of course." Strange considered this new information for a moment. "I understand that we're waiting on the full analysis, but what can you tell me about the substance? This information may provide the key to understanding how it all works together."

"Gladly," said Shuri.

She lifted her wrist controller and tapped a few buttons. Within seconds, a molecular diagram flickered to life in midair, outlined in glowing blue light. It spun slowly, offering a three hundred and sixty degree look at its structure. Each element was labeled and color coded, and it only took a moment for the doctor to determine what he was looking at. But he stood there in silence for a long time, frowning in thought.

"I'll admit that it's been a long time since I took biochemistry. Am I wrong that this molecule is unstable by default?"

"On the contrary, you are exactly correct. This is dormamine. It's a new compound recently patented by Oscorp. The paperwork claims that it's a chemical reagent designed for use in a lab setting, but the supporting documentation makes no sense."

"No?" asked Strange.

"It reads as if a PhD wrote it with the intent of using as many complicated words as possible to obscure the fact that their proposed application made no sense whatsoever," said T'Challa. "I am surprised it made it through the approval process."

"I assume it had help." The doctor nodded, surveying the portal once again. "Let me sum up. We have a portal that is at least partly fueled by dormamine, which was designed by Oscorp for reasons unknown. Dormamine was designed to be unstable, which tracks."

"Oh?" asked T'Challa. "How is that?"

"Portals require a certain amount of instability to operate. Greater distances between start and end points require more instability to rip a hole in the fabric of the two local realities and stitch them together."

"Interesting," said Shuri, tapping on her console again. "I hope you don't mind that I record this. It opens up some interesting avenues for research."

"If you publish, I expect first author credit," said Strange, his eyes twinkling in sudden humor.

"We will negotiate," she said, grinning.

"I am staying out of this," declared T'Challa, taking a deliberate step backwards.

"Wimp," said Shuri. "It sounds to me as if dormamine may have been specifically designed to open these portals."

Strange went with the change of subject easily, his brain

working overtime to unravel this mystery. For the first time in the past few weeks, he felt like his old self again, energized by the problem at hand and confident in his ability to handle it. Although he wouldn't admit such a thing out loud, he couldn't have been more relieved.

"Yes," he said. "Or its creation was influenced in that direction. Perhaps the researchers at Oscorp intended something else, but they were steered."

"Steered how?" asked T'Challa, all traces of his earlier humor gone.

"Magically, I suppose. Dormammu could do that, under the right circumstances. It makes perfect sense! Why didn't I see it before?"

"Please explain," said T'Challa. "I do not yet understand."

"Dormammu wants to come here. We know that. He played that funny business with Praeterus and blew up the planet, but I never understood the goal of that undertaking. At the time, we thought it a trial run for his attempt to do the same thing here. Now I believe we might have been wrong."

Doctor Strange began to pace, his cloak swirling around him as he unraveled this puzzle's tangled web of secrets.

"You see," he continued, "there is one other explanation for that behavior. Praeterus wasn't just a test subject. It also provided a resource Dormammu would desperately need to punch a hole from his dimension to ours. Remember: he is locked out of our corner of the Multiverse, and because we stand at the nexus of convergence, his lack of access has protected countless other realities from his malign influence. If he is to reign supreme over all realities, he must take our world. He must own Earth."

"In order to get here, he needs to destabilize the reality with a substance like dormamine, which is unstable at its core," said T'Challa, working it out on his own.

"But how does Praeterus fit in? Is dormamine a byproduct of its destruction?" asked Shuri.

"Exactly." Doctor Strange pulled the lantern out of its pocket dimension, producing it with a flourish. He spun it around for a moment, showing it off like a game show host displaying the grand prize for the audience to admire. "Allow me to introduce you to the Lantern of Morphesti. This shutter displays a map that can direct us to general locations where Dormammu's magical influence has spread. And, if I have calibrated this one correctly, it can lead us to his portals. But this third shutter will illuminate magic – any magic. I thought it would be handy to be able to show the rest of the Shadow Avengers what I see."

"What about the fourth shutter?" asked Shuri, curious by default.

The doctor shook his head. "That is a matter for another time."

"Fair," she said.

He opened the third shutter, and the portal blazed into magical light. But the ground beneath it seethed with darkness, as if a black hole was being born right here in the snow and sand of Wakanda. After a moment's contemplation, Shuri looked away, her face tinged with sadness and anger. But T'Challa stared it down with the intent gaze of a hunter memorizing the face of its prey.

"That must be Dormammu's plan," said the Sorcerer Supreme. "Use the unstable remains of Praeterus mixed with his own destructive magic to punch a way through to our reality and send through a servant, leashed to his will through magical means. Loki. The God of Mischief has his own magic that would help him survive the trip."

"Don't forget that he also sent Heimdall. Perhaps their Asgardian physiology provides them some resistance. They often travel through the Bifrost, after all. But still, I can't imagine that being exposed to those destructive energies would be good for you. I would expect the travelers to have something akin to radiation sickness," observed T'Challa.

"Yes, of course," said Doctor Strange. "Ms Marvel said that Loki appeared to be ill, and he has been here the longest. But that won't stop Dormammu. The more Asgardians he sends through, the stronger the link between our worlds becomes. Eventually, it will become stable enough to allow him to come here himself."

The two Wakandans faced him, shoulder to shoulder, their expressions resolute. Stephen Strange was a formidable opponent, but he wouldn't want to stand against them. Together, they commanded a significant intellect, physical strength, and the superior technology of a nation they were prepared to give their lives to defend.

"Wakanda stands ready to oppose this threat," said T'Challa. "You have all of the resources I can provide. What do you need us to do?"

"We need to further secure Heimdall and the portal. I cannot yet close it without potentially triggering the end game, and we aren't ready for that. We must buy time to figure out where the final portal will open. These smaller portals are just the warm up. The final one will be instrumental in bringing Dormammu here."

"We will make it so," T'Challa promised.

"This portal is consuming a tremendous amount of energy, which is a testament to Dormammu's strength," said Strange quietly. "Especially since he is holding open more than one, in addition to magically controlling his slaves. But everyone has a limit, even him. As he expends more of his power to create the final portal and bring himself through, his control will wane. That is our opportunity to strike. If we miss it, all will be lost."

"We will not fail," said T'Challa, clasping his arm. "I have faith in the Shadow Avengers. And in you, my friend."

"Thank you," said Stephen Strange.

"Come, brother," urged Shuri. "We can chat later. There is no time to waste!"

The two Wakandans hurried off, leaving the Sorcerer Supreme to stare at the portal alone. He pursed his lips in thought. Their plan was a spectacular one, but it had just one problem.

He had no idea how to locate the final portal until it was already open.

TWENTY-EIGHT

"I think I've got something!"

Ms Marvel's excited shout cut through the never-ending litany of worries that ran through Peter Parker's mind. He had no doubt that Eddie Brock would betray them at the first possible opportunity. The girl would never see it coming. She still believed that people were fundamentally good, and although he shared the sentiment, it made her vulnerable in this particular situation. She didn't understand Eddie's history, or the bloodthirsty nature of the symbiote that drove him. He had to protect her, but he didn't want to be the one to burst her bubble.

When it popped, it would hurt. He knew that from experience.

She grinned at him from beneath her mask. The small scrap of fabric barely served to cover her face. If she wanted to protect her identity and the people she loved, she ought to go with a full face. He'd offer to make her one once this whole thing was over.

"Hey," she said, some of her excitement bleeding off into concern. "You OK?"

"Yeah. Of course." He set aside the anxiety for now and nodded. "What have you got?"

"There's some big magic going on over there." She glanced through the Eye of Vouk and pointed toward a tall brownstone caked in layers of soot and grime. "Underground. In the basement, maybe?"

"Got it. Maybe we should go pay a social visit."

Peter began to march across the street, grateful to finally have something to do. They'd been looking around for so long that he'd gotten used to the hail, and freak weather patterns weren't the kind of thing you wanted to take for granted. That probably had something to do with his feeling of low-grade unease more than anything.

Yeah, right. He believed in the power of positive thinking, but he wasn't delusional.

Ms Marvel scurried to keep up with him, lengthening her legs to match his long and determined strides.

"Are you sure?" she squeaked. "Shouldn't we, you know, case the joint?"

He laughed. It felt good. "Only if I can wear a trench coat and a fedora." He paused. "On second thought, never mind. I'd look like a creeper."

"But we don't know what we're marching into."

"We don't. But most of these basements don't have windows, and we've just spent the past bajillion hours walking around in circles. Criminals don't usually sit around waiting for you to show up. We've already given them enough of a head start. Wasting any more time is only gonna make things worse."

He left the rest unsaid. Someone who knew him better might have picked up on the edge in his voice or the tense set of his shoulders, but he hadn't worked with Ms Marvel long enough for her to read his moods. Even if she had, it wouldn't have mattered. As the senior member of this team, it was his responsibility to protect her. He took that seriously.

There were two stairways that led down beneath the street level. One of them had a sign hung at the entryway that advertised a tax service. The other was unmarked.

"Which one?" he asked.

She pointed toward the unmarked one, and they descended the dark stairs together. The hail had accumulated on them, creating cold drifts that swallowed their feet.

The moment his hand touched the knob, the door flung open to reveal a hulking figure backlit by a dim and flickering light. Although his Spider-Sense didn't make a peep, Peter was still keyed up, and he took aim with his web blasters before his mind caught up with what his eyes were seeing.

"Whoops. Sorry," he said, lowering his hand.

Jennifer Walters, the She-Hulk, wiggled a finger at him in warning.

"You shoot me with that thing, I'll rip it off and shove it up your–"

"Got a kid here," he interrupted, gesturing toward Ms Marvel.

Jen relaxed as she caught sight of her fellow hero, and she gave a respectful nod. "Good to see you. Somebody here has to have their head on straight. What's gotten your tights all in a bunch?" Jen edged into the doorframe, blocking the room within with her muscular figure. "Whatever you're up to, keep it on the down low. I've got a room full of civilians in here waiting out the storm." She paused to look up at the sky. "Which by the looks of it will never end."

"We're tracking a magical signal," said Ms Marvel, pitching her voice low. "It's somewhere down here." .

Jennifer scowled. "Trouble?"

"Probably. You notice anything?" asked Peter.

"Now that you mention it, Luke went downstairs a while ago to look for supplies, and he should have been back by now." Her green eyes glittered with determination. "If anything happened to him, I'm going to punch a hole in something. Just warning you."

"Lead the way," said Peter. "We've got your back."

TWENTY-NINE

"We have to do something," said Eddie Brock.

"Rather open-ended suggestion, don't you think?" responded Loki with a hint of humor.

Eddie snickered, stepping out into the empty street and waiting for the Asgardian to make his way off the curb. Loki's slim figure was hunched over in pain, and wet coughs froze him in place once every block or so. But he'd shrugged off Eddie's offers of help, and there wasn't a working cab in sight. No one was willing to drive in this storm, and Eddie couldn't blame them. If not for this slave collar around his neck, he'd be at home with a pizza and a blanket.

Loki eased himself down, cleared his throat with a wet rattle, and followed him across the street. At the end of the block, the Oscorp headquarters loomed overhead, a monstrosity of glass and steel that glittered in the weak light. So far, the safety glass had withstood the hailstones, much to Eddie's disappointment. Seeing the building in shambles would have been a small revenge, but he'd take any vengeance he could get at this point.

"You know what I mean," said Eddie, toying with the pendant around his neck. He was trying to get his point across without saying it aloud. The Master didn't seem to be able to read his thoughts, so he might be able to avoid punishment by approaching the subject of rebellion in as oblique a manner as possible. It was worth a try. "We can't go on like this. You keep this up, you'll be spitting bits of lung onto the pavement."

Loki passed him, his shuffling steps scattering hailstones as he made his painstaking way back up onto the sidewalk.

"My deterioration is inevitable," he said. "Pay it no mind."

"You're giving up and going emo now? Is that it?"

"I am not familiar with Midgardian verbiage, but I suspect I've just been insulted."

"Damn straight you've been insulted! You're supposed to be a god, aren't you? Well, god up, buddy, or you're going down and taking me with you."

Impotent fury gave heat and volume to Eddie's words. He would have smacked some sense into the Asgardian if he could have, but he couldn't. He could do nothing but lead the way to the doors of Oscorp and hold them open for his sick companion. As soon as the mental summons had come, the deep voice echoing in the chambers of his mind, he knew they went to their death. He'd fight it until the end, but without some kind of plan to rid themselves of the pendants he knew it was futile. His symbiote offered no protection against the pendant's punishments. Either he would follow instructions, or he'd die. But he wasn't ready to give up the ghost just yet.

He would have said Loki had given up entirely, except that somehow, his insults finally got through. The lanky God of Mischief grabbed him by the collar and slammed him up against the door hard enough to make his ears ring, his strength surprising given his sickly condition.

"Puerile mortal!" snarled Loki. "I walked the universe when your people lived in caves. I could crush you with a thought."

A corner of Eddie's mouth quirked up in satisfaction. Maybe he'd finally penetrated the layers of Loki's shame and defeat. Maybe they could finally get to work and figure out how to beat this thing.

"Yeah?" he said. "Why are you rolling over and showing your belly?"

Their argument had drawn attention. Before Loki could reply, he was interrupted by the irate shout of the security guard stationed in the middle of the lobby. The man was middle-aged, with the beginnings of a pot belly growing over a sheath of muscle. His hand hovered near his sidearm, ready for anything.

"Hey!" said the guard. "If you want to rip each other's arms off, take it outside. Otherwise, I'll have to put you there."

Eddie's grin widened. "I'd like to see you try that, friend," he said. Another wave of coughing seized Loki. Spittle sprayed Eddie's face, making him blink. He wiped it away with a moue of distaste. "Come on, man. Not cool."

The guard took a cautious step backwards.

"What's wrong with him?" he asked.

For a moment, Eddie considered lying. He could claim that Loki had some communicable disease and get the guard off his back, but that wouldn't get them up to the penthouse undisturbed. Besides, as annoying as the interruption was, the guy was just doing his job, and Eddie didn't hold with injuring innocent people. His fight was with the man upstairs.

So he took a deep breath to marshal his temper and responded calmly. "Just a nasty cold," he said. "And sorry about the argument. We'll drop it."

"Sure. Great. Maybe get out of my lobby while you're at it?" asked the guard.

"No can do. We've got an appointment with Mr Osborn."

"Names?"

"Just describe us. He'll know who we are."

Skepticism was written clearly all over the guard's face, but he went back to his booth, keeping one eye on them at all times, and phoned up. He returned with visitor's badges and an apology.

"Sorry about before," he said. "The weather's got me on edge. No one else can make it in and… anyway, no offense intended."

"None taken," said Loki smoothly.

"Go to the second elevator. The first one's on the fritz. I'll send you up to the penthouse."

They did as they were told, and as the elevator doors closed behind them, Eddie murmured, "I should have just snuck in again," crumpled his visitor's badge, and dropped it on the floor.

A few minutes later, they sat in Osborn's empty office, awaiting his arrival. All the mess from their earlier confrontation had been swept up, and a new glass and metal desk sat in the place of the one they'd destroyed. Eddie wondered if Osborn had a room full of identical desks, ready to be pulled out whenever things got a little too rough in here. If he hadn't already disliked the businessman, this would have sent him over the edge. What a waste of resources.

When the door at the back of the office suite opened and Osborn himself entered the room, Eddie's stomach sank. Osborn wore his Goblin armor, the overhead lights glinting off the sickly green metal. He'd been wearing one of his fancy suits when they'd been here earlier. The wardrobe change couldn't mean anything good.

"Gentlemen," he said. "Please, take a seat."

Loki obeyed, his breath rasping. The Asgardian's condition had deteriorated noticeably since Eddie had first seen him. Mottled splotches crawled up his skin beneath his collar, reaching for his face. Beads of sweat collected at his hairline. It made Eddie angry, and for the first time since the pendant had smacked them down, he felt his symbiote stir within him.

That won't be us, Eddie, it promised. *Not us.*

Eddie couldn't have agreed more. He just needed an opening, some hint of how he could get out of this. The only way to find it would be to rock the boat a little. So he remained standing, and Osborn arched a brow.

"Or don't sit," he said. "It doesn't matter to me. We shouldn't have long to wait."

"What are we waiting for?" asked Eddie.

"Instructions. There are a few suitable locations to open the final portal, and Dormammu is evaluating the ley lines to determine which will work best for our purposes. It must be tonight, while the planets are in alignment. Once we have a destination, my helicopter will take us there to begin the ceremony," said Osborn.

"And you get what out of this exactly?"

Osborn offered him a tight little smile. "Take a wild guess."

"I'm assuming he's offered you power. Money. The usual."

"If you already know the answer, then why do you ask?"

"Because I never pegged you as stupid. The Master's playing you like a trombone, and you've never been the type to fall for that. So, I'm trying to figure out what your game is."

Osborn settled down into the swivel chair behind his desk, cutting an incongruous sight in his armor. But he seemed relaxed anyway, completely unruffled by Eddie's conversational jabs. Loki sat across from him, his shoulders slumped, but his eyes bright as he followed along with the conversation.

"You should be well aware that I am anything but naive," he suggested.

"Sure, except for the part where you're wearing one of those pendants," said Eddie. "The first time we were here, I assumed you were using it to control or communicate with us. But that's not true, is it? Dormammu puts these on all his slaves. So, what does it mean if you've got one?"

Norman's jaw tightened.

"It's a calculated risk," he admitted, "but one with immeasurable payoff. But you've forgotten one thing, Brock. Dormammu needs me. Without my resources, he won't be able to open the portal. No portal, no takeover. Game over."

"That's true. But you've forgotten one thing. You're expensive. I'm cheap."

"Come again?"

"I've got everything I need to open the portal myself. What's stopping me from taking your chopper, which I'm assuming is already packed up with all the necessary supplies, and cutting you out of the process?" Eddie paused, waiting while this argument sank in. "But I won't do that because we're on the same side. We can take these things off. I'm sure you know how."

The mogul considered it for a moment, and Eddie's stomach flip-flopped in anticipation. But then Osborn shook his head.

"No deal," he said.

"He'll turn on you the minute he steps foot on Earth. And then it'll be too late for you to resist. Come on, man. You're not a flunky. Don't let Dormammu turn you into one."

Osborn's teeth flashed in a smile. "That kind of talk is only going to get you punished. Dormammu, punish him."

Eddie tensed, mentally berating himself for pushing too hard. He'd been doing so well, too. For a moment there, he thought he might have found a way out of this mess. But now Dormammu would kill him.

Nothing happened.

After a few seconds, Osborn's expression of malicious relish began to fade into uncertainty. Eddie could barely believe it. Either the Master wasn't listening, or he'd decided that Osborn was a liability. Regardless of the reason, Eddie had to take advantage of the opportunity while it lasted.

But he was too slow on the uptake. While he stood there frozen in astonishment, Osborn flew into action, lifting his gloved hands and firing off an acid-yellow electronic Goblin Blast. The crackling energy flung Eddie across the office suite. He transformed in midair, black symbiotic biomass crawling out of his pores and thickening his torso. He twisted like a cat, landing on all fours and sliding across the floor, his claws gouging furrows in the imported tile.

"We are Venom!" he roared. "And you will pay!"

Venom charged at the Green Goblin on all fours, tearing across the space in animalistic fury. He leaped up onto the desk, the impact shattering it for the second time that day. The

Goblin was already on the move, sliding his helmet on as he rolled out of the way. But Venom had momentum on his side, and he gave close pursuit, pouncing on his prey. He rained down a flurry of blows, which the Goblin dodged in a burst of superhuman speed. But one of Venom's punches struck true. Although his claws skittered off the armor, the strike rattled Osborn in the armor like dice in a cup, and he let out a pained groan.

Encouraged, Venom continued his assault, so engrossed in his need to tear his opponent limb from limb that he didn't notice the Goblin's hand worm its way up between them. Venom opened his mouth to shriek in triumph and fury, and the Goblin fired one of his pumpkin bombs right into the symbiote's mouth.

The small device hit the back of his throat and exploded with a concussive blast that would have torn the walls off a building. The symbiote absorbed the damage, but it screeched in pain, its system overtaxed to its limit by the sonic blast generated by the detonation. It had managed to keep his head from being blown off, but it didn't have the energy to do much more. Eddie could only watch as the Goblin flopped him over onto his back, spitting mocking laughter into his face.

The symbiote faded away, screaming in protest the entire time. It just didn't have the strength to continue after all the damage it had taken. It needed to heal, and that meant that Eddie was on his own on the ground with the Green Goblin sitting his chest. As far as situations went, this one didn't bode well.

"No one double-crosses me, boy," said the Green Goblin. "I am the betrayer, not the betrayed."

Venom's eyes fell on Loki, sitting on his leather chair in the middle of the ruined office. The Asgardian still hadn't moved.

Osborn leaned down, removing the mask to reveal a triumphant leer. The weight of the armor sat heavy on Eddie's chest, squeezing the air from his lungs. His ribs creaked, making him groan. He knew he needed to fight back, but the bomb had hurt him down to his very cells. The pain made every movement agony.

Still, he clenched his fist and struck. The weak attempt at a punch bounced off the Goblin armor. Osborn chuckled under his breath, the evil sound echoing around the room, chilling the blood in Eddie's veins.

"Oh, I'm going to enjoy this," said the Green Goblin. "But I suspect you won't."

He leaned forward, pressing harder on Eddie's chest. Something gave way inside his body with a snap, and the flare of pain brought clarity back to him. He had to fight back, but Osborn held all the physical advantages, and Venom wasn't in any shape to take over. Eddie had to use his mind, or they'd end up as goblin chow.

There was nothing within reach that he could use to turn the tables. A picture of Osborn receiving the key to the city sat a few centimeters past his extended arm. He reached for it, straining, and managed to snag it. The flimsy frame would do nothing against the state-of-the-art armor, so he flung it at Osborn's face, hoping to create enough of an opening to wiggle free. It bounced off the mogul's cheekbone, drawing blood and a snarl of pain.

Wham!

The Green Goblin smacked him across the face with a blow

that nearly took his head off. Stars whirled across his field of vision, and he tasted blood in his mouth. When they cleared, he saw Loki, still watching them. All but forgotten. Eddie met his gaze, his eyes watering.

"Maybe this is inevitable," Eddie gasped, "but don't you want to go down fighting?"

Loki fixed him with his glittering gaze and said nothing. His breath rattled in his chest. Eddie would have sworn aloud if he'd had the breath to do so. The Asgardian was just going to sit there and watch him die. Well, he wasn't going to give up. He took a deep breath, steeling himself for the pain to come. Maybe this situation was hopeless, but he would stand strong until the end.

We will, said the symbiote. *We stand together like always, Eddie.*

Sometimes Eddie wondered if the alien creature truly cared for him, or if it just protected him the way you'd protect your house: because you owned it. But at this moment, he knew. If he died today, at least it would be in the presence of a friend.

"Damn straight we do," he muttered aloud.

Osborn took him by the collar, lifting his head up from the floor and leaning down close.

"What did you say?" he asked. "Would you like to beg for mercy? I love it when people do that."

"I've got a better idea," said Spider-Man, his voice shocking Eddie down to his core. "How about I kick you in the head and web you to the wall, and then the rest of us go out for pizza?"

For perhaps the first time in his life, Eddie welcomed the web-slinger's presence. Of course, that wouldn't stop him from smacking Parker when he had a chance. The guy must have followed him here, mistrusting him even after Eddie had swallowed his pride and asked for help. Eddie wasn't surprised, but it still stung.

The Goblin tensed, his head whipping from side to side. But Spider-Man was nowhere in sight. At any moment, he'd drop down from an air vent or smash in through the window. The guy was annoying that way.

"Where are you? Come out here and face me like a man," snarled Osborn.

"You sure you're a man?" Spider-Man taunted him, his voice coming seemingly from nowhere. "You look like a kid in a Halloween costume."

"Not sure you can throw stones on that one," muttered Eddie.

"Shut up," said Osborn.

The super villain smacked him across the face again, but this strike held much less heat than the last one. Eddie went with it anyway, pretending to be knocked cold. Osborn was too distracted by Parker's appearance to notice. As soon as his back was turned, Eddie would strike. His symbiote surged, gathering its remaining strength. It would have to be enough.

"You can't hide forever," snarled the Goblin. "I'll find you. And then I'll kill you."

He rose to a crouch, allowing Eddie to fill his aching lungs. His chest flared with pain, but the symbiote was already at work. The pain abruptly dulled to a throbbing ache. Soon enough, it would be gone entirely, and then he would wring Osborn's scrawny neck. The thought of it made his veins thrum with adrenaline. The symbiote's excitement mixed with his, and all he could think of was the intense satisfaction that would come with wringing Osborn's neck until the light faded from his eyes.

"You couldn't find your own behind with a flashlight and a map," said Spider-Man.

Osborn snarled, standing up and glaring at the air vent.

"I'll tear out your insides and use them as a jump rope," he said.

Eddie struck. A huge gout of webbing erupted from his body and hit the Goblin with a splat, slamming him against the wall and immobilizing him in a heap of sticky strands. But the Goblin formula lent Osborn super human strength, and he'd tear free of such things easily, so Eddie kept it coming, piling the stuff on. Maybe if he was lucky, Osborn would suffocate in there.

Finally, he sagged down, his reserves all but spent. Spider-Man wouldn't even have to break a sweat to win a fight against him now. But at least he'd shown Osborn a thing or two. He leaned down to catch his breath, the pendant swinging into his field of vision.

"Hey," he said, straightening. "Funny how that Master of yours didn't come to your rescue. It's almost like he doesn't need you anymore, isn't it?"

Osborn didn't answer, but Eddie grinned anyway. Then he turned, his eyes sweeping the room.

"OK, you can come out now," he said. "No more hide and go seek."

But Parker didn't appear. Instead, Loki stood from his chair, hunching over for a moment until he gathered the strength to straighten.

"You haven't put it together yet, have you?" he said.

"Put what together?" Eddie asked, impatiently.

"I am the God of Mischief. Trickery is my specialty."

As exhausted and beaten as he was, Eddie could barely think. He fixed Loki with a blank expression.

"Oh, for heaven's sake," said Loki, rolling his eyes.

Then Spider-Man's voice said, "I'm your friendly neighborhood Spider-Man, and also the president of Loki's fan club."

"What the…?" said Eddie.

But as the truth became clear, his mouth stretched into a wide grin. Spider-Man would never say such a thing. He wasn't here. His voice had been nothing more than one of Loki's illusions.

"Not a bad impression," Eddie said. "Although you've got to work on the jokes."

Loki arched a brow in inquiry. "Truly? I tried to think like a five year-old, and I thought I did rather a good job of it. Then again, my younger days were ages ago."

"You have the right idea," admitted Eddie. "Spidey's right around elementary level when it comes to humor."

He scanned the room, trying to come up with his next steps. Osborn struggled against his bonds, unable to speak. Eddie had aimed for the torso – he didn't intend to kill the guy, not when he might be needed later. But webbing someone to the wall wasn't an accurate science. He spit out another gout of the sticky stuff from his hand, coating the mogul's legs. It would dissolve eventually, but by that time, he'd be long gone.

The first steps of a plan began to assemble in his mind, but he needed Loki's support to make it happen. The trickster god wouldn't be the most reliable ally, but he wasn't stupid. He would have to realize that supporting Eddie would maximize his chance of survival. Eddie didn't want to plot aloud, though. He wasn't sure about the limits to Dormammu's influence, but he knew for certain that the sorcerer could hear them. Could he also see?

There was one way to find out. One dangerous way.

He made his way through the wreckage of the desk and rummaged through the mess, scattering bits of broken glass everywhere. Finally, he found a gold-plated pen and a torn piece of what looked to be a very important official report.

Aloud, he said, "I'm going to open the portal. I figure my best chance of getting out of this alive is to make myself useful and hope that the Master will keep me on. You with me?"

But on the paper, he scrawled: "I refuse to be a slave. Help me pull a fast one on the Master?"

It was a dreadful risk. Loki had been on his side so far, but this was clearly a partnership of convenience. Once one of them decided it was no longer valuable, things would get ugly. All Loki had to do was read the note aloud. If Dormammu decided to, he could end Eddie right now, and there was nothing he could do about it. But he was counting on the fact that Loki was the trickster god, and this would be the ultimate deception. It would be against the God of Mischief's nature – as well as his own self-interest – to refuse.

After a long moment of consideration, Loki said, "I'm with you."

Osborn said something. His voice was muffled by the goo, but Eddie was fairly certain it was a swear word.

They waited for one heart-stopping moment, but nothing happened. Either Dormammu couldn't see through the link, or he hadn't been paying attention. Loki took the sheet of paper and began to tear it into long, thin strips, obliterating the message written there.

"Shall we go to the helicopter?" he asked.

"We need the coordinates," responded Eddie. "Dormammu? We'll take care of this portal thing for you, and we're cheaper than Osborn. Where are we going?"

For a long moment, he heard nothing, which was both good and bad. Then the voice came, echoing through the chambers of his mind. Usually, the symbiote's voice soothed him, like whispers from his innermost self. But Dormammu's voice hit him like a freight train to the brain.

"Wakanda. Don't disappoint me. I do not have time to coddle my hirelings," it said. "Weakness does not serve my purposes."

Eddie glanced at the pile of webbing still stuck to the wall. Osborn squirmed in his restraints but didn't seem to be getting anywhere. Any additional webbing at this point would be overkill.

"Yeah, I see that," he said. "Let's do this, Loki."

"Excellent."

The two unlikely allies made their way out the door, leaving the office in shambles and the boss stuck to the wall.

THIRTY

The moment she stepped into the back room Kamala knew something was wrong. A chill breeze whipped her hair back from her face, creating a sharp contrast with the stagnant heat generated by the crush of bodies in the bar area. Jennifer tensed as it wafted over her, clenching her fists and muttering to herself as she stalked down the hallway. Kamala followed. She couldn't make out the words, but based on the lawyer's tone of voice, that might have been for the best.

Although she'd steeled herself for the worst, the decimation in the storage area still shocked her. A gaping hole in the brick had been torn through the upper half of the exterior wall, and debris littered the floor underneath. With each gust of wind, hail hissed in through the hole, coating the mess in a layer of forgiving white. Something groaned deep inside the building overhead, and she looked up in sudden alertness. Was the ceiling about to fall on them? The hole – while impressive – didn't seem large enough to take down a building of this size, but she wasn't an engineer. Maybe the damage had taken out some important metal beam or something. It didn't seem too far-fetched.

But neither Spider-Man nor She-Hulk called for a full evacuation, and between the two of them, they must have been inside tons of damaged buildings. She'd follow their lead on this one, but the groaning made her nervous. Hopefully it would stop soon.

She hovered in the doorway, wanting to help but not knowing how. Jen paced back and forth with increasing agitation while Spider-Man inspected the damage. He crept over the heaped debris with such a light step that it barely shifted beneath his feet. If anyone could figure out what had happened here, it would be him. At first, she'd been deceived by his constant jokes, but it turned out that he could keep up academically with Doctor Strange and Black Panther. Sometimes she had no idea what they were talking about at the Shadow Avengers meetings and had been forced to nod and smile and hope no one asked her a question.

"Whoever attacked Luke, they're long gone," he declared.

"Where?" said Jen, her brows drawn down in fury. "And who?"

"I'm thinking this set of prints is Luke. They're the freshest. Then we've got some funny ridged prints, probably female. They come out of the bathroom only, so they belong to whomever came out of that portal, and then they get into a tussle with Luke, and the two of them go out the window. But if you look closely, there are two additional sets of footprints. One male in heavy motorcycle boots. Another male with thin feet and a light step. Those prints are buried, so they were here earlier."

"To open the portal, maybe?" asked Ms Marvel.

"Makes sense. I'm guessing Loki and Venom, but I haven't exactly been paying attention to their shoe sizes." Spidey shrugged. "Besides, what's important here is Luke. If he was able to, he would have called in, or at least shouted for you. So, we've got to assume that he's unable to communicate for some reason, and that doesn't bode well. Not sure we're going to be able to track them far, but it's worth a try. Ms Marvel, can you take a look outside?"

"On it," Kamala replied, thankful to have something to do.

She reached for the hole, her legs elongating to carry her over the mess on the floor and past the jagged edges. As soon as she could brace her hands on the icy ground outside, she snapped her limbs back in. Something had attacked Mr Cage, and she needed to be ready in case it waited for her. The back of her neck prickled as she looked up and down the street, but there were no bodies slumped in corners. No one leaped out at her. No footprints either. Someone must have walked away from this mess, but the wind had swallowed all signs of their passing.

In a fit of inspiration, Kamala pulled out the Eye of Vouk and peered through its crystalline depths. She saw nothing up and down the street, but when she looked toward the building, the Eye picked up faint smudges of magical residue on the edges of the hole. She leaned closer, trying to get a better look. It didn't help, but something caught her eye back in the basement. She slid in through the window and went to investigate.

"What is it?" demanded Jen.

"I'm not sure yet," she said, heading down the hallway.

The door to the bathroom was cracked open, and a faint

green glow shone around its edges. Kamala couldn't believe she hadn't noticed it before, but she'd been distracted by the absolute mess in the storage room. Apparently, she hadn't been the only one.

She reached out a hand and pushed the door open, ready for anything. But it still shocked her to see the green glowing orb of a portal hanging in midair above the mold-encrusted toilet.

"Oh jeez," she said, lowering the Eye. "Guys? I think we've got a problem."

Spider-Man was at her side in a flash, and She-Hulk wasn't far behind. The three of them crowded into the doorway. Jen growled in frustrated aggression, disappointed at the lack of something to smash. After a moment, Spidey put a hand up to his mask to cover his nose.

"We sure do," he said. "I'm not going near that toilet without a Hazmat suit."

"I meant the portal," said Kamala.

"Yeah, that, too. I'll call Strange. He's gonna want to see this, and we ought to pass along the info from Venom as well. That sludge on the ground beneath the toilet looks too much like the stuff Loki was pouring into the water system, and the stuff Panther reported in Wakanda, and… you get the picture. Loki and Venom were definitely here. They opened this and then another Asgardian came through and got into it with Luke."

"But Venom's trying to help us," protested Kamala, hoping that it was true.

"Maybe he's trying to stay undercover," said Spidey, but he didn't sound convinced.

"I'll finish looking around outside," said Jen. "I've got to do something, or I'll lose it."

"Are you OK?" asked Kamala, worried.

The green eyes softened just a little before growing flinty again. "Luke is my friend. I don't have many, and I can't afford to lose them," Jen responded.

"We'll find him," Kamala promised. "Or he'll come back as soon as he can. Maybe somebody got the jump on him, but as soon as he recovers, that person is gonna be in a world of hurt."

Jen offered her a tight smile and a nod of approval before returning to the hole in the wall. Spider-Man patted her on the shoulder as she stomped past. After she left, they returned to their examination of the portal.

"Any chance Mr Cage went in there?" asked Kamala.

After a moment's consideration, Spidey shook his head.

"No," he said, "the footprints are all wrong for that. A big man like Cage isn't going to leap through the portal. He's always deliberate with his movements, because he breaks things when he isn't. He tussled with whoever came out of that portal, and then they went through the wall."

"They must have tricked him."

"You think? Why's that?"

"A strong guy like Mr Cage isn't going down without a fight. If his attacker was strong enough to take him out, that fight would have made a lot of noise. Somebody would have heard it."

"They didn't hear the wall, though."

Spidey's voice was encouraging. His approval washed over her, and she realized that he'd already worked this all out in his head, but he was giving her a chance to do it herself. Not because he wanted to test her, and not to prove his superiority, but to give her a chance to learn how to figure things out on her own. He wanted to help her. It was like he wanted to be her super hero mentor or something.

His obvious support made her even more determined to do this right, and she thought through the problem deliberately. Part of her wanted to hurry out after Mr Cage, but Spidey didn't seem too rushed. So, she took the time to think it through.

"Well," she said slowly, "the impact with the wall was over with quick. If it was loud enough in the bar, they might not have heard it. All it would take is one door slamming at the exact right moment, and they could miss it. But a fight is different. More noise. The only way it wouldn't attract attention is if the fighters tried to keep it quiet. Like… maybe if they were trying to keep innocent people from coming to look?"

"Bingo."

"Then Mr Cage probably drew the fight away from people on purpose. That's why you didn't run outside and start searching for him." Excitement suffused Kamala's voice as it all clicked into place. "Somebody came out of the portal, and Mr Cage knew that was bad, so he led them away from the people in the bar. As soon as he wins the fight, he'll be back."

"Out of all the possibilities, that makes the most sense to me. I'm glad you came to the same conclusion."

"But why didn't Ms Walters?"

Spidey hitched a shoulder. "Emotions," he said. "She's worried about her friend, and she's not thinking clearly right now. Happens to all of us. I mean, we both wear masks in public to protect our friends and family. We can't exactly throw stones here."

"Oh, I didn't mean to. But maybe if we said something, it might make her feel better?"

"You can try." Kamala could hear the smile in his voice as he spoke. "Or just let her work through it on her own. I'd rather not patronize her. I always hate that when people do it to me."

Kamala nodded. He'd made a real point of not patronizing her just because she was new at this super hero gig, too. When she was older and led a group of her own, she'd remember this. Maybe she could help some newbie the way he was helping her. That would be cool, like paying it forward.

"So we bring in Doctor Strange and he'll deal with the portal while we wait for Mr Cage to come back?" she asked.

"Well, I've just thought of one more thing to check out. Could you call while I go?"

"What is it?"

Spider-Man hesitated, and Kamala's stomach sank.

"Look," she said. "Either you mean everything you just said, or you don't. But don't pretend to understand what it's like to be protected by more experienced super heroes and then turn around and do it to me. At least be honest about it."

After a moment, his shoulders slumped in defeat.

"You're right. Of course you're right. I have some overprotective tendencies, you know. I try my best, but sometimes they sneak in when I'm not paying attention. Gimme a sec, and I'll call."

He dialed in with the Kimoyo card and brought the Sorcerer Supreme up to date. Then Spidey said, "I've got an idea. It's a crazy one but hear me out. There's one guy who might be able to help us put the pieces together. He won't be happy to see me, but I don't think we've got a choice."

"Who?" asked Doctor Strange and Ms Marvel simultaneously.

"I think we need to go see Norman Osborn," said Spidey. "After all, Eddie mentioned him, and Loki was driving an Oscorp truck, remember?"

THIRTY-ONE

Peter led the way from building to building, looking over his shoulder as he swung from one web to the next to make sure that Ms Marvel kept up. She sprinted across the icy rooftops, stretching her legs to impossible lengths to bridge the gaps. They made excellent time, and within minutes, he stood atop the Oscorp high rise, staring down at the miniscule abandoned cars on the street below. It took a moment for Ms Marvel to climb up next to him. When she did, she was grinning.

"Remind me never to challenge you to a race!" she exclaimed.

He laughed. "Never gonna happen. You might win."

She flushed in pleasure, and his stomach sank. He'd always wanted more family, envying other kids who had siblings coming out their ears, and different relatives to visit for the long succession of family holidays. Aunt May and Uncle Ben had done their best, showing up for Parent's Night and Grandparent's Day, and Special Person Day, and all the others. He'd appreciated it, of course, but it couldn't stop him from wishing. He'd never had a sister, but something told him it felt like this. He wanted to protect her from everything, but to do so would be a grave insult. It was one thing to encourage her to engage in an intellectual discussion like he had at the bar, but he was leading her quite literally into the belly of the beast, and he knew full well how dangerous Norman Osborn's enmity could be. How could he live with himself if he made her a target, too? But he saw no way to avoid it now that she'd called him out. He couldn't make the decision for her no matter how much he wanted to.

But he could try to put it into perspective for her at the very least.

"Listen," he said, putting a hand on her shoulder, "the guy in there is serious. I'll joke about nearly anything, but I can't laugh about him. Not really. Osborn gives me the heebie-jeebies."

"OK, thanks," said Ms Marvel.

But Peter didn't let go, not yet. He had to make her see. She wasn't frightened enough yet.

"I'm not trying to insult your intelligence. I'm just saying that I've been fighting the Green Goblin for years, and I know how he ticks. Some villains are about as smart as a box of rocks. When you go up against them, you know you're just going to whale on each other until they go down. But with Osborn, things are never what they seem. He's probably a psychopath, or maybe a sociopath… or both. Can you be both?"

She shrugged wordlessly. The color had drained from her lips, and although the sight made guilt wash over Peter, he couldn't help but be glad. Scaring a teenager wasn't a great look, but he'd take that over the alternative any day.

"Anyway, don't take anything for granted in there. Any time Norman Osborn is involved, it's like swimming with a shark, but the shark is a genius and wears nearly indestructible armor."

She choked a little, and he patted her shoulder.

"OK, so what's the play here?" she asked.

"Loki and Venom were driving one of his trucks," Peter reminded her. "And Eddie mentioned him when we were talking. I should have asked about it, but I didn't think to do so at the time. There was so much going on. Osborn has teamed up with the Master, or perhaps he's a slave, too."

Ms Marvel mulled this over, nodding slowly as the full implications dawned on her.

"And you want to sic the shark on the evil sorcerer who wants to invade the world?" she asked.

"Bingo. It's risky, but we're at the point where risky is all we've got."

Her teeth flashed in a quick smile. "Let's go talk to the shark, then."

They made quick work of the security measures, and within minutes, they stood outside the closed door to his office. Peter paused there, alert for any potential dangers. But his Spider-Sense remained quiet, and his keen ears picked up nothing. He opened the door, stepping into the room and blocking the space with his body. If anything came at them, it would hit him first. But the only thing that hit him was a face full of powdered drywall.

The place had been demolished. The desk sat in shambles, and the walls sported giant holes that suggested bodies had impacted against them at high speeds. The floor was strewn with a mess of broken glass and mangled office supplies.

Ms Marvel peered over his shoulder.

"That can't be good," she said.

He held a finger to his masked lips. Osborn might be

watching them at this very moment from somewhere in the depths of the spacious office suite. Now wasn't the time for idle chit-chat.

She nodded, and they entered the office together. It only took a few steps to bring Norman Osborn into view. He hung suspended from the wall in a mass of webbing. As they watched, the webs began to disintegrate, releasing his face and shoulders. The sticky stuff continued to dissolve, revealing bands of magical energy wrapped around Osborn's body. They continued to hold him in place when the last of the webs faded away. Osborn struggled, but to no avail.

If he was surprised to find them there, he didn't show it.

"Come to gloat at my expense, have you?" he asked.

"It wasn't in the original plans, but it's hard to pass up the opportunity," Peter admitted. "That's quite a pickle you've gotten yourself into."

Osborn's jaw tightened. "A minor glitch. I should have no problem in remedying it."

"You call this minor?" asked Ms Marvel, clearly astonished.

The Goblin's piercing gaze fell on her, and Peter's stomach did a slow flip-flop. He shouldn't have brought her here. Osborn would eat her alive. Figuratively, of course, but that was bad enough.

"Who's your friend?" asked Osborn. "We haven't been introduced."

"I'm Ms Marvel, and you really need to redecorate in here."

Osborn chuckled, the sound sending chills down Peter's spine. The villain wriggled a little, testing his bonds, but the magical loops that secured him to the wall had been wrapped tight. He couldn't so much as scratch his nose.

"We're not here for a social call," Peter said. "We're here to find out about the portals."

"What portals?" asked Osborn in the kind of mock innocent tones that made the lie as obvious as possible.

"Not in the mood to talk? Fine. Let me see if I can fill things in myself." Peter glanced around, even though the story had been clear from the moment he'd seen the space. It all slotted together nicely with the intelligence he'd received from Doctor Strange. "Venom and Loki came here. You've been working with them, letting them use your trucks, and probably synthesizing the green liquid they've been using to open the portals. Too bad they turned on you."

"How do you know all that?" murmured Ms Marvel.

"My webs don't dissolve like that. Those are symbiote work for sure. And Loki is a magic user, which explains his current predicament. They bound him together; it's the only possibility that makes sense." Peter returned his attention to the man hanging on the wall. "Am I right?"

"What do you want, cookies and a Boy Scout patch?" asked Osborn.

"I'll take that as a yes. Where'd they go, Norman?"

At this, Norman Osborn threw his head back and laughed. The low, mocking noise filled the room, echoing through Peter's skull, reminding him of all the times they'd fought. The numerous times one or both of them had nearly died. All the hairs on his body stood on end. That laughter was evil made audible, and sometimes it haunted his dreams.

Next to him, Ms Marvel had gone stock still, like a deer watching a semi as it charged down the road on a collision course. Peter found her hand and squeezed it. She returned the gesture but didn't take her eyes off Osborn, not even for one minute.

Good. She was learning.

"You don't expect me to answer that question, do you?" asked Osborn. "Why would I help you?"

"Because you know I'm not going to let you down off that wall, and every moment you waste increases the possibility that they'll get away with it. They betrayed you, Norman, and you can't do a thing about it unless you tell me where they went and what they're up to. Do you want to let them get away with stabbing you in the back, scot-free?"

Norman's body jerked against its restraints, what would have been a convulsive, angry gesture cut short by his bonds. His face twisted in fury, but after a moment's struggle, he relaxed. The fury disappeared, replaced by a cold calculation.

"You don't have the guts to do anything about it, Boy Scout," he spat.

"If it means protecting innocent people, you know I do," said Peter.

Osborn considered this, then nodded.

"Fine. I'll answer your questions," he said.

"Where are they going?"

"I don't know. I had everything ready, but I hadn't gotten word on the location for the final ceremony."

"You expect me to believe that?" asked Peter. "You're a planner. We both know that."

"Some things can't be planned. A portal of this magnitude requires a specific set of circumstances to open fully. The convergence of magical energies must be precise, and only a few locations are powerful enough to support it."

This was Strange's department, but Peter had picked up enough to understand the basics.

"Like ley lines," he said.

"Precisely. But the lines fluctuate slightly. They ebb. They shift. So, there are a few potential locations, and the selection wasn't made until the last possible moment to maximize the chances of success. I've had my people in place at each of the locations for the past few days. Once I knew which one we were using, it was just a portal away."

"Your Master told Venom and Loki which one he chose, but not you? That's cold."

"Partners require payment," said Norman. "He might try to get out of his end of the deal, but I intend to see that he keeps his promise. He won't be on this world forever once it's conquered, and once he's gone, it'll be mine. That's worth playing nice in the short term."

Peter's stomach plummeted. He had no desire to contemplate the specifics of such a deal. They wouldn't be good. But he kept his voice light, betraying none of his dread.

"Good luck with that. So, this final portal will bring him here? Where are the potential sites?"

Osborn offered him a thin smile. "You don't expect me to spoon-feed you everything, do you, Spider-Man? You're a hero. Figure it out."

"That's fine. I wouldn't believe you anyway," said Peter. "But it all seems a little too easy to me. Open up a few portals, and that's it? Why hasn't he done this before?"

"Easy? I'd like to see you harness the energy of a dying planet, distill the destructive magic emitted from it, turn it into a physical substance, and merge it with the magic of a sorcerer who can't even enter this universe. Then pick the ley line with the correct resonance to amplify that during a once-in-a-lifetime planetary alignment and open a door between realities. Go ahead. I'll watch."

"That's… a delicate process," said Peter.

His mind whirled. Norman Osborn didn't give away information for free. He was telling Peter all of this for a reason. Could he be hedging his bets? Giving Peter the ammunition to stop the ceremony from happening, in the event that Osborn couldn't be there to share in the triumph? It was tempting to believe that, but Peter had learned from experience that he couldn't be too cautious when dealing with Osborn. Some of this could be a lie, but it dovetailed well with the information that Doctor Strange had put together.

"It would be easy to disrupt," admitted Norman. "Each progressive portal gets a little bigger. The next one will likely bring multiple Asgardians over. Their physiology allows them to survive the jump, although the destructive forces necessary to open the gate still do their damage. He needs their magic to open the portal from this end."

"So that's it? You're turning on him now that you're no longer the captain of his invasion team?" asked Peter.

"You know me, Spider-Man. I always have a backup plan." Norman gave him a thin-lipped smile that made shivers run up and down Peter's spine. "Now toddle along. Even you should be able to stop them before they let Dormammu through."

"Thanks for the vote of confidence," muttered Peter. "That's it. I think we're done here."

He started for the door, but stopped a moment later when

he realized Ms Marvel wasn't following him. She stared at Osborn, chewing on her lower lip in thought.

"What about the pendants?" she asked. "I can see the chain around your neck. How do we know that you're not just telling us what Dormammu wants you to?"

"His influence is fairly obvious to the naked eye." Osborn shrugged, or tried to. "The fact that I'm not screaming right now means his attention is elsewhere. Certain things draw his attention and focus, so I beg you not to say the name of a certain pompous magic man. It won't go well for any of us."

"So, if you avoided getting his attention, you could help us," suggested Ms Marvel.

"But you never know when his eye will fall upon you again. He's spinning a lot of plates as the ceremony draws closer, but there are no guarantees." Norman shook his head. "Nice try, but it isn't worth it for me. I can still benefit from this situation, and I've told you all I'll say."

"If you find out where the ceremony is, you should tell us," she said.

"And why is that?" Norman countered.

"Because if I was an evil sorcerer, the first thing I'd do when I took over a planet is go after the big guys with the power to resist me. Especially when they know all my secrets. I don't know you well, Mr Osborn, but something tells me you wouldn't be thrilled to be a slave along with the rest of us, despite what promises you've been made. More than likely, Dormammu has his own backup plan to deal with the likes of you."

There was a long moment of silence, and then the Green Goblin inclined his head to her.

"Touché," he said. "I like this one. You should bring her around more often."

"Over my dead body," said Peter.

"That would be nice," replied Norman Osborn.

THIRTY-TWO

Stephen Strange paced back and forth across the lobby of the Sanctum Sanctorum, his boots squeaking on the freshly polished floors. On a lesser man, this would have been an expression of nervousness, but he was used to working under pressure that would break most people. In fact, he thrived on it. His mind whirled in multiple directions at once, assessing potential roads of action, following the threads of future possibilities with the mental agility of a chess master searching for all the plays that would get him to checkmate and win the game.

Wong made his slow way down the hall with a laden tea tray and stopped to watch for a moment. Strange lifted a hand but didn't slow his pacing. It helped him think, and if he was going to go toe-to-toe with Dormammu, he'd take all the help he could get.

"You're going to wear a hole in the carpet," Wong observed, not unkindly.

Strange paused and looked down. "This carpet has been here since time immemorial. If I can wear through it in half an hour, I'm more powerful than I thought."

"Still, you're making me dizzy. Come. Sit."

The old man gestured, and after a moment, Strange relented. He had exhausted the possibilities and planned for all likely potentials. At this point, he could do nothing else but wait until it was time for action. He followed Wong into the study and accepted the steaming cup with a nod of gratitude.

Wong settled opposite him; his hands curled over the delicate china as if trying to soak in the heat of the liquid inside. But his eyes were keen as he looked over the Sorcerer Supreme. Long ago, the walls had been firmly up between them, and Wong had been the servant while Stephen was the master. But those walls had dissolved, which meant that he was about to be lectured again.

"I overheard your call. You are worried for your friend," said Wong. "Luke Cage is missing?"

Strange blinked. That wasn't what he'd expected at all. A pang of misgiving went through him. Had he been blinded by his emotions? Had he truly planned for all eventualities? Or was this a sign that he had fallen short?

The teacup rattled ever so slightly against the saucer as he set it down, betraying the miniscule tremor that gripped him. Stephen Strange had performed the most difficult of surgeries without a hint of nerves. He had stood against villains that would swallow the universe if left unchecked. He did not shake. He did not falter. Not since he had left his darkest days behind him. But he had found himself again after the accident, and he refused to return to that weakened state once more.

"I am prepared for all eventualities," he said, hoping that it was true. "I trust Luke's judgment."

"But you are also a man. You have feelings, and denying

them will only give Dormammu an opening to exploit." Wong sighed. "We have been together now for many years, and I have accepted your lead and your wisdom without argument."

"Without *much* argument," Strange muttered.

Wong grinned. "As you say. But I am worried for you, Stephen. This time, things are different, and if you refuse to admit that to yourself, I worry about what it might mean."

"I will do my duty, Wong. That should be without question," Strange replied in a tight voice.

"You will do your duty to the office of the Sorcerer Supreme without question, and you will do it well. But you are still a man, and although you might try to deny your feelings, they still affect you. Feelings are what make us human. That denial could prove to be a weakness, but acceptance of them? That is humanity's greatest strength."

Strange had to admit that being questioned like this by someone who should have supported him unconditionally stung. But he hadn't become the Sorcerer Supreme by throwing temper tantrums. He forced himself to set his ego aside and listen. Wong didn't challenge him often, not about things that counted. He must feel strongly about this to speak so freely. So Strange swallowed his injured pride – or attempted to.

"You should write a self-help book," he said, in as neutral a tone as possible.

Wong shook his head in exasperation. "Just think on my words, please. Your friend is in danger. You'd hoped to stand with Clea against her uncle, and she isn't here. A weaker man would have broken under the strain already. But it is not a weakness to admit that you care."

The mention of Clea's name made hot words leap to

Strange's lips, and that more than anything convinced him that Wong might have a point. He fell into a pensive silence.

"I will think on your words, my friend," he said eventually. "Thank you for trusting me enough to say them."

"Don't get too used to it," Wong replied with a twinkle in his eye. "I'll be back to pestering you about the dishes tomorrow. I can't keep up with all the crockery you leave around the house. Honestly, with all your talents, why haven't you created an artifact that does them for you?"

Strange cracked a smile, imagining the Sanctum Sanctorum full of *Sorcerer's Apprentice* style brooms doing dishes and cleaning the carpets. One thing was for certain: even if Clea had chosen not to stand by his side, Wong would be there, and the man would never falter. That fact alone steeled Strange for the fight to come. Wong had a point – this was personal – but Strange wouldn't stand alone, and that made him stronger than any of his arcane powers.

"I would," he said, sipping his tea. "But then what would you complain about?"

Wong blustered and complained about that until the bell rang, announcing the arrival of the Shadow Avengers.

THIRTY-THREE

A green, glowing portal hovered above the subway platform, directly beneath a sign that read "Stay Back." The sign referred to the tracks, but Luke thought it seemed apt. He knew his plan was solid. So far, the ruse seemed to be working. Posing as Valkyrie's prisoner, he would learn what he could about this "final portal" she'd mentioned and then turn on his locator or call if he could do so without her hearing.

Although he strongly felt that this was the only possible road to success, he still hesitated in front of the portal. Valkyrie had opened it with a flash of magic from her pendant, but no green ooze. He was a bit out of his depth when it came to magic, but he suspected that the ooze was what separated Dormammu's special portals, like the one in his bar's bathroom, from the garden variety teleporter. This one ought to take them to the site Dormammu had selected to host his arrival. Only a stupid man would step through such a thing without a single misgiving, and Luke wasn't dumb. It could be a trap. Dormammu might know that he'd been fooled. Valkyrie could double-cross him.

These things weren't likely, but he couldn't discount them. So, he approached the magical gateway with caution, all his senses alert for anything out of the ordinary.

"Move!" Valkyrie demanded, shoving him in the back.

She seemed to be enjoying her role in this ruse, and he paused for a moment to give her an exasperated glance over his shoulder. He didn't like being shoved around any more than was absolutely necessary. To her credit, she flushed bright red and gave him an apologetic look in return. So, he gritted his teeth and said nothing.

He'd learned the hard way that it was better to make up your mind and go when it came to facing the unknown. Caution had its moments, but some things were best gotten over with as quickly as possible. He took a deep breath, held it, and stepped through.

Cold goo surrounded him on all sides, clinging to him in a sickening manner. As soon as he was fully immersed in its depths, his sense of proprioception told him he moved at great speed, but the gunk clogged his eyes and ears, leaving him with no way to anticipate the movement. His stomach roiled as he flipped and jerked around. It felt like he'd been tossed blindfolded into a running dryer full of Jell-O, which was then thrown off a cliff.

In short, he wouldn't recommend it.

Then the portal spat him out on the other side. Disorientation still gripped him firmly, and he could do nothing for a moment but stand there and try not to fall over. But finally, his vision cleared, and he was able to straighten up without feeling queasy.

Valkyrie stood by his side, staring at him with concern. She appeared completely unruffled by the journey, and her blue eyes creased with worry as she put a hand on his shoulder.

"Are you quite well?" she asked.

"Sweet Christmas," he answered. "That was awful."

She gave him a ghost of a smile. "And that was only across the planet. It's much worse to travel between universes. It feels a bit like going through a blender and then being reassembled on the other side. I don't recommend it."

"I believe you," he said fervently.

Together, they examined their surroundings. They stood in a small clearing in the middle of a verdant jungle. Birds chirped and whooped in the distance, and heavy leaves rustled with the gentle breeze. The air sat heavy on his skin, laden with moisture. The smell of green things filled his nose.

At first, he delighted in the sight. He'd never been able to afford fancy vacations, so the only time he got to visit exotic locations was when he was doing the super hero gig. Usually, some villain with a complex was trying to shoot his head off, so it was nice to get a few moments to appreciate his surroundings. But that feeling didn't last long. An eerie sensation ran over him, like some giant predator watched him from the shelter of the thick undergrowth. The area between his shoulder blades itched, and he had to resist the intense urge to look behind him. But that would only make him appear weak. Instead, he concentrated, opening all his senses and waiting for the inevitable attack.

"We expecting a welcoming committee?" he asked quietly.

She shook her head, her hand dropping down to rest on the hilt of her sword.

"Not that I know of," she responded. "But this is a wild

place. I'd react if someone trespassed on my hunting ground, too."

That made sense, and now that he knew what to look for, he scanned the foliage again. There! For just a moment, the sunlight glinted off a pair of slitted eyes. He stared directly at them, and a leopard came padding out of the jungle, belly down to the ground, moving in the slow slink of a predator stalking its prey.

Luke Cage was many things, but prey wasn't one of them. He bared his teeth in a silent growl, sinking down into an easy crouch. Next to him, he heard the metallic rasp as Valkyrie drew her sword. The leopard paused, its tail whipping to and fro as it considered them. Its nostrils flared, scenting the air. The moment stretched out, and Luke honestly couldn't say whether he wanted the giant cat to run off, or if he wanted a chance to test his skills against it. He could imagine Jessica's face if he told her he'd wrestled a leopard. She'd hit him over the head and scold him for his recklessness, but secretly, she'd be jealous.

The cat seemed to realize that they weren't going to be easy prey. In fact, they weren't prey at all. It tensed, gathering all of its strength into coiled muscles, and darted back into the underbrush. The leaves rustled, swallowing it, and the prickly feeling at the back of his neck slowly eased.

"Damn," he said. "I was looking forward to that."

Valkyrie snorted. "Come, prisoner," she said, gesturing. "We have some walking to do."

Now was the time. His hands were tied behind his back, furthering the illusion that he was a prisoner at the mercy of his captor. But he broke the bonds with a quick jerk of his wrists, turning his body so Valkyrie couldn't see, and worked his hand into his pocket. She kept her eyes steadily on his face. Either she hadn't noticed his subtle movements, or she was making a concerted effort *not* to notice. It didn't matter so long as he managed to activate his communicator.

He pushed the emergency button that would contact Strange directly and record their words for him. Hopefully the Sorcerer Supreme would listen and understand. Luke would have to direct the conversation to tell the Shadow Avengers what they needed to know.

"Is it far?" he asked, digging for information. "I didn't bring my good shoes."

"The temple to the god Sobek sits about a kilometer to the north," she said. "You will have to handle the blisters, or I will feed you to the leopards."

"You got friends to meet there? I didn't bring my party duds."

"Friends? No. But the Master has recruited other Asgardians. I do not know how many. We will meet them at the top of the temple stairs where the ley lines intersect. There, we will open the portal to let the Master through. I will need to cut your bonds in order to climb to the top, and I remind you not to flee. Although I do not wish you ill, I will stop you. I do not have a choice."

Luke didn't know if she had seen him activate the transmitter, or if she was play-acting for Dormammu's sake. Regardless of the reason, he was determined to take full advantage of it.

"The Shadow Avengers won't sit idly by while your Master takes over our world," he said. "They will stop him."

"They will try," she said sadly. "But he will enslave you all, just as he did in my universe, and in countless others before it."

The words hit him hard. In his darkest days, Luke had known despair. He'd stared at the walls of his cell and believed with every fiber of his being that he deserved to be locked up. That he was nothing but a monster that needed to be caged. When he thought back, he pitied that angry, stupid boy. He'd learned the value of determination, how to stand against insurmountable odds and emerge a victor. But he'd learned a few other things in the process. He'd learned to evaluate people with honest impartiality, tallying the odds of success with apparent ease. After all, it didn't make sense to start a fight you couldn't win, and when you ran with the Avengers, you were working in a whole new weight class. His caution had saved countless lives.

Now, he couldn't deny his misgivings. Valkyrie's despair spoke volumes. After all, if he understood the situation correctly, her universe had the same heroes theirs did, with a few differences. There, another Luke Cage must have been determined to save his family, and he must have failed. Or worse yet, he'd never gotten out of that cell to begin with.

The thought sobered him. Dormammu had done this many times before. He'd perfected his process in preparation to approach their reality, knowing that it would open the gates to countless other worlds ripe for the taking. He would anticipate resistance. After all, hadn't this seemed too easy? Luke hadn't questioned it too much before this moment because Valkyrie's grief and resignation were undoubtedly real. But based on everything Doctor Strange had said, Dormammu was too smart to leave such an obvious vulnerability.

There was only one possible explanation. He was luring the

Shadow Avengers into a trap. They would sneak in, believing they were undetected, and his Asgardian slaves would be waiting. If Luke had been in Dormammu's shoes, he would have played his less powerful pieces first. Not too weak, but weak enough that the Shadow Avengers would come here confident. Then, hit them with some big guns, stronger Asgardians who could go toe-to-toe with the group of them, holding them off long enough for Dormammu to make his appearance. Their resistance would be over before it began.

Doctor Strange might have already figured it out, but Luke couldn't chance it. He had to warn them. But he didn't want to tip his hand either. If Jessica had been on the other end, or the Defenders, or his Avengers team, they would have picked up on unspoken messages. But the Shadow Avengers were still gelling. He would have to hope that they'd hear the subtle undertones of what he was about to say.

"This is gonna be a snap," he said. "I thought your man was smarter than this."

Valkyrie recoiled. "That is dangerous talk," she warned.

"I just call it like I see it. From what I heard, I expected that Master of yours to be a devious opponent. But instead, he's all but advertised his intentions. I'm surprised he managed to take over your world, since we saw him coming a mile away."

Her fist cracked against his jaw. If he'd been able to feel pain, that one would have rocked his world. Maybe knocked out a tooth or two. Instead, all it did was hurt her knuckles, and he felt bad about that. But it meant that he'd convinced her, and if he'd done that, maybe Dormammu had bought his posturing, too. He could only hope that Strange knew him well enough to pick up on his true meaning.

"We fought with everything we had," she hissed. "But the Master set his eyes on Asgard, seeking to enslave us because we are uniquely suited to survive the trip. He is more powerful than you could ever imagine. Once he steps through the portal, your world is lost."

He nodded. "Yeah. Sorry," he said, putting a little extra emphasis on that last word. He regretted the pain his words had caused, atop everything else she'd been through. It must have been brutal for her to watch her world being destroyed, doing everything she could to stop it, and ultimately ending up as a slave for a being she must despise to her core.

Uncertainty flickered in her eyes, and she looked down toward his hands before she caught herself and lifted her gaze back up to his face lest she alert Dormammu to whatever he was doing. Even though she despaired, she still tried to give him a chance. He admired that.

The pendant around her neck flickered with green energy, and she winced, holding her hand to her chest.

"The Master calls. We must go," she said.

"Lead on," he responded.

Again, she seemed about to speak, but shook her head with obvious frustration. He regretted leaving her in the dark, but he was determined to make this work. He would defeat Dormammu and send Valkyrie back to her home, or die trying.

THIRTY-FOUR

After the communicator cut off, the Shadow Avengers sat in silence for a long moment. Doctor Strange drummed his fingers on the table, lost in thought. T'Challa stroked his chin, his fingers rasping against the stubble. Wong sipped his tea, unruffled by the timely call.

"Smart man," said Spider-Man.

Kamala had no idea what he was talking about, or how they could all be so calm when one of their own had been taken by the Master. She knew that Mr Cage could handle himself in a fight, and she understood that he'd chosen not to resist for reasons he'd explain later. But that didn't change the fact that he needed backup. What else was a team for if not to watch each other's backs?

She stood up, and everyone turned to look at her. Her cheeks flushed, but she didn't sit back down. Maybe she was the youngest one there, but they should have figured out by now that she wasn't about to sit by when she could make a difference.

"Well?" she asked. "What's the play? Do we wait for Dormammu to come here before we kick his butt, or do we go through one of those portals to his house and kick his butt?"

Doctor Strange's lips curled up into a faint smile. "I would not advise the latter," he said. "Portals of this nature are unsteady at best. There is no guarantee that you would be able to return to your rightful reality."

"Oh. Well, at least that makes it easy to choose. Why are we still sitting around?"

"Patience, young one," he said. "There is much to unpack here. Luke contacted us as he did for a reason, and what he didn't say is just as important as what he said. A moment of planning might save us much grief later."

"My thoughts exactly," said T'Challa. "Either his Asgardian captor is trying to help him as best as she can, or she is remarkably careless to spill so much information."

"Or Luke maneuvered her into it," suggested Spider-Man. "He's so big that people assume he's as dumb as a post. Luckily, I've never had that problem. I'm too thin and pasty to be anything but a nerd."

Doctor Strange nodded. "His warnings were subtle but clear. Our adversary has made it all too easy for us to find him, and there is too much riding on this conquest for him to be playing his hand so recklessly. We should expect significant opposition. This is likely a trap."

"I'm sorry if this is rude, but didn't we already know that?" asked Kamala.

Wong snickered.

"What do you mean?" asked T'Challa, mildly.

"He's a super villain. I know I haven't fought as many as you have, but they backstab. They lie. It kind of comes with the territory, right? So how is this any different?" she asked.

They all considered this for a long moment. Long enough to make her fidget. She knew how smart they all were. A few weeks ago, she'd been struggling with her math review sheet while she waited for the meeting to start; T'Challa had taught her how to do the problems and then told her a bunch of stuff about how he and his sister used algebraic equations just like these to create their weapons. She hadn't understood a word of it, but it had been cool, anyway. Besides, she'd gotten an A on the worksheet.

Given the fact that they were all geniuses, not to mention actual adults, she probably should have kept her mouth shut and followed their lead, but at some point, it took a leap of faith to get things done. She'd made one when Dormammu had tried to destroy Earth the first time, and it had paid off. So, she was going to stick with it until she came up with something better.

"She's got a point," said Spidey. "I'm not advocating that we charge in there like idiots, but I hope we wouldn't have done that anyway. At least some of us have common sense."

He winked at her, and she smiled gratefully back. At least Spidey had her back. She had the feeling he always would.

"You know," said Doctor Strange slowly, "something has been bothering me for some time. I have been agitated for reasons I did not entirely comprehend until this moment. I know that Dormammu has taken over many worlds before ours, and I assume that I am present in at least some of them. There are many Stephen Stranges in the Multiverse, after all, just as there are many copies of each of you. It is my destiny to oppose him here, in our reality, and I can only assume that I must carry the same charge in at least some alternate realities. It only stands to reason that I must have failed."

"We all did," added T'Challa.

"I have looked into the future many times, knowing that each time the options would change, hoping to steer us toward an eventual triumph. Although I cannot see all actions, I can pinpoint essential moments that must happen in order for us to succeed. Convincing you to join the Shadow Avengers was one of them, Ms Marvel," said the sorcerer.

"So I could call you out and feel really sick to my stomach?" Kamala asked uncertainly.

Spidey patted her on the shoulder.

"So you could remind me of the power of faith," said Stephen Strange. "You believe we can win, and you are eager to go out and make that happen. And for your faith in us, I thank you. I should have shared it from the beginning. After all, I handpicked you myself. But instead, I… allowed myself to be distracted by what I foresaw, rather than what was."

He sounded genuinely ashamed, and that horrified Kamala. After all, he was a doctor, and a sorcerer, and one of the smartest people she'd ever met. He'd saved the world more times than she could count. But maybe even the strongest heroes in the world sometimes needed a pep talk.

"I have no idea what I'm doing half the time," she admitted. "But I have to try. And maybe I don't understand what's at stake the way you all do, but I've got the basics. Dormammu has taken over a bunch of other worlds, so he knows what he's doing. But those times don't matter now. We're going to stop him this time. I just know it."

T'Challa slapped his hand on the table to emphasize her words. "That's enough planning for me. The temple Luke referred to stands at the very edge of Wakanda. It is a place of power that has been long abandoned by my people. Can you open a portal there, if I pinpoint it for you on the map?"

Doctor Strange nodded.

"Very good," said T'Challa. "Time is wasting. I will call up my guards to surround the area and handle any auxiliary troops. That should leave us to face the Asgardians alone." He turned to face Kamala, a faint smile on his face. "Does that meet with your approval?"

For a moment, she couldn't tell if he was joking or not. But he kept on waiting, and she had to say something.

"I have faith in us," she said, "but not getting stabbed in the back by some flunky is peachy in my book, too."

"I like how you think," responded the Black Panther.

THIRTY-FIVE

Eddie leaped off the helicopter, trying to keep his nerves under control. The flight had been surprisingly short, the entire craft vanishing through a portal over the Hudson River and blinking back into existence over a humid jungle. Running on the instructions they'd received via their pendants, the pilot had dropped them off with all their supplies atop a tall ziggurat made of sandy stone threaded with vines. The entire place was alive with noise and motion. Exotic birds fluttered through the trees, calling to each other in a raucous chorus. Some unseen animal croaked in protest as the chopper roared away.

Loki coughed. He had grown visibly weaker in the few hours that Eddie had known him. His body had begun to curl in on itself, his shoulders hunched, as if it might disappear altogether. Sweat beaded on his forehead, and his fingers trembled as he tapped the top of the palleted supply cache.

"Help me move these barrels," he wheezed.

Eddie hesitated. The Master had been communicating more frequently ever since they'd taken Osborn out of the picture, so it was in his best interest to follow orders like a good little flunky. If only he and Loki could talk things through, he might have felt more secure. Then again, given Loki's reputation, probably not. The God of Mischief lied like some people breathed. But that didn't change his dilemma. He could refuse to move the barrels. That blasted magical pendant would probably kill him, but he'd still gum up the ceremony and save the day. Loki wasn't strong enough to lift the barrels into position.

Then again, the trickster god was wily. If he wanted to, he could find some way to jury rig the supplies. Or magic them into place. Although his physical body continued to fall apart, his mojo seemed as strong as ever. Eddie would just have to save his heroic sacrifice for later.

Just wait, Eddie, said his Other.

The symbiote didn't often urge caution, so he was inclined to listen to it. It curled inside him, its energy gradually building up to full strength. It would be back to normal soon enough, and then they'd make their move. If he died in the aftermath, so be it, but he wanted to go to the afterlife knowing for certain that he'd ruined Dormammu's year. He wanted to go out fighting.

Parker would have a fit if Eddie died a hero's death. He grinned to himself thinking about it.

Loki arched a brow. "Did I say something funny?" he asked.

"No, no. Just thinking."

"You were not recruited for your brains," replied Loki, in sour tones.

"Yeah, well, I didn't sign up with a whiny Asgardian baby on purpose either, but we're stuck with each other."

Muttering to himself, Eddie pulled out the first drum and

hoisted it overhead. The contents sloshed menacingly, and he could only hope that the thing didn't give way and drench him in Dormammu's magical green soup. He wasn't sure what would happen, but he knew he didn't want to find out.

"Set it here," Loki ordered.

He pointed at the ground next to an ornate altar decorated with climbing crocodiles at each corner, but Eddie was too distracted by the green flicker of magic in his eyes to do as he was bid. Dormammu's magic washed over Loki, and Eddie's skin crawled as that alien gaze touched him. For one heart-stopping moment, he was sure that Dormammu could see his intentions and was just stringing him along for kicks and giggles, only to eviscerate him later. Maybe it was true, but what other choice did he have? He hoped Parker and his band of do-gooders would show up, but he couldn't count on them. Ms Marvel had believed him, but those pompous jerks probably wouldn't listen to her. They were too puffed up on their own self-importance to take advice from a teenager. So, he couldn't count on the cavalry. It was up to him.

Up to us, the symbiote corrected him. *We have bested many enemies. This one will be no different. We will rip Dormammu's head off and feast on his brains.*

At least one of them was confident. He tried to believe it, too, but he'd never been very good at optimism.

He wrestled the drums into place and straightened, wiping the sweat from his brow. His shirt stuck to his back, pasted there by the thick air.

"If we were going to lug around heavy objects, maybe we shouldn't have come to the jungle," he complained.

"It was the best location," said Loki. "You have no idea how much energy will go into opening a portal of this magnitude. It will be fueled by the destructive magic of a dying star and the energy of the ley lines that converge upon this site of power. It must be performed at the precise moment of planetary convergence, when the veil that separates your world from the rest of the Multiverse is at its thinnest. The slightest deviation from these elements could have catastrophic consequences."

"Not sure that's a bad thing," Eddie said.

Loki shrugged. "If you want to pulverize your entire planet, sure."

"Is that gonna happen? If things go bad?" Eddie's stomach plummeted as he spoke. He could handle his own death if he had to, but the whole point was to go out saving the world. Maybe then he'd feel like he'd made up for some of his worst mistakes. Balanced the scales a little. But if the whole planet went kablooey, that kind of ruined his whole plan.

"Many things could happen," Loki admitted. "Not all of them are awful."

He stiffened, and Eddie initially thought he was going to cough again. But when he straightened, the green glow of his eyes said it all. Dormammu had stepped in again, picking up Loki's strings and maneuvering him like a puppet.

"There is only one ending to this story," said Loki. "Resistance is futile. It has been in countless other worlds, and this one will be no different."

Loki nudged the valve on one of the barrels open. With excruciating slowness, green sludge began to leak out against the base of the altar. It seeped down between the cracks, coating the entire surface in glistening green slime. With painstaking care, the Asgardian made his way to the other barrel and repeated the process. Then he climbed atop the altar and slumped there, his breath rattling.

Eddie didn't know what to do. He could attack, but then Dormammu would release Loki and punish him. Not an improvement. He had to convince Dormammu that there was nothing to see here. No reason to micromanage. If the ceremony was as delicate as Loki had suggested, maybe he could throw some small wrench into the gears when no one was looking.

"We've got it covered, Dormammu," he said.

In response, Loki coughed, the glow fading from his eyes. Eddie played it cool despite his immense relief.

"Some God of Mischief you are," he said. "I could smear you into a pulp with one foot."

Loki smirked. "I distinctly recall that no such thing happened during our first meeting. In fact, I handed you your behind on a platter."

"That was then, and this is now, bucko. What have you done lately? Sure, you called up some illusions to fool Osborn, but you're still licking Dormammu's boots."

As soon as the words left his mouth, he knew he'd made a mistake. Loki froze, his eyes going to the pendant. Eddie's heart skipped a beat. He'd tried so hard to talk around his true feelings, but he'd gotten carried away at the worst possible time. Dormammu had just been listening in only moments before. Chances were good that he hadn't switched the channel yet, or whatever he did to listen in through the pendants. Within seconds, Dormammu would punish him. Maybe even kill him. Worse than that, if Dormammu was listening, he would now know that Loki and Venom had tried to trick him.

There was only one option. His hand closed over the pendant, which had remained strangely cool to the touch. The chain rattled, abnormally loud to his ears. With a convulsive jerk, he lifted it. It came up past his ears. To his forehead. But before it could clear the top of his head, it roared to life, coating his hands in green fire. All of a sudden, Dormammu's awareness filled his mind, coating his synapses in flame and agony. The symbiote howled in pain, curling down deep inside him in an attempt to get away. But there was nowhere to go. Every cell in his body screamed in agony.

"You will do my bidding!"

Dormammu's voice shook him to his core. All thoughts of resistance faded away, only to be replaced with a bone-deep certainty that resistance would do him no good. Dormammu was a god compared to him, and Eddie could only cower before his might and hope to be spared.

He had no choice but to obey.

"No," said Loki, stepping up to intercept him. "I've had enough of this. You may yet conquer the Multiverse, but my hands will not be your tool, and neither will his."

THIRTY-SIX

To his immense surprise, a wave of optimism ran over Stephen Strange as he stepped through the portal and into the Wakandan jungle. The conflicted misgivings that had plagued him for the past few weeks had finally dissipated, only to be replaced with his usual steely resolve. Given his past dealings with Dormammu as well as his mystical expertise, he had felt a certain crushing responsibility to lead the Shadow Avengers as they stood against him. But somehow, that had morphed into the sense that he had to anticipate everything, answer every question, and be prepared for every eventuality. Despite his best efforts, he couldn't control everything. That had rankled, but Ms Marvel had managed to put his head straight completely by accident. Based on the confused glances she kept shooting his way, she still didn't comprehend what had happened at the meeting, but that didn't matter. It felt as if a weight had been lifted from his shoulders, and he appreciated the clarity that came with it.

They all had a job to do, but he had allowed the stress and uncertainty of the situation to throw him back into old habits.

In the surgery suite, he had ruled as a god. Nothing happened without his go-ahead, and any mistakes made by a member of his team reflected on his leadership abilities. Leading heroes was different. It required a certain amount of trust in the abilities and decisions of his team. He had to cultivate a looser grip. For one bemused moment, he wondered if his career would have been even more successful if he'd approached his medicine in the same way. Certainly, there would have been fewer crying nurses involved.

He had allowed his worry and hurt to master him and slipped back into those old authoritarian habits as a result. Perhaps this had been part of Dormammu's plan, or maybe it had been an unfortunate coincidence. It didn't matter. He had recognized the error of his ways just in time, and now he could make their final stand without those distractions.

The Shadow Avengers filed out through the portal and stood arrayed behind him, surveying their surroundings. The tall stone steps of the temple loomed over the trees just a few hundred yards away. A pensive hush had fallen over the jungle, broken only by the rustle of leaves. The back of Strange's neck prickled as he surveyed the land. Someone watched them, and his instincts screamed at him to run.

Instead, he held his ground, scanning the foliage for signs of life. T'Challa stepped up next to him, donning the Panther mask and surveying the landscape.

"Dormammu's people have had time to plan," he said, quietly. "I would expect a full complement of guards. My people can neutralize them, but it will take time to ferret them out."

"We don't have that time to waste," replied Strange. "Perhaps I can be of assistance."

He crouched down, pulling the Lantern of Morphesti from the depths of his cloak. Magical light spilled out, drawing the outline of the world's continents onto the ground. The Sorcerer Supreme muttered a few words of an incantation, zooming in on their immediate location as the members of the Shadow Avengers arrayed themselves around him, protecting him from potential attackers while he was distracted by this important task.

As he had hoped, bright green lights dotted the immediate area around the temple, signifying the location of guards who were under Dormammu's magical influence. He gestured, drawing T'Challa's attention to the map.

"This ought to help," he said.

The panther cowl nodded. "Let me patch Shuri in so she can direct the Dora Milaje. Perhaps you could find us a path that will avoid the majority of the fighting while I handle those arrangements? We will be delayed if we are caught up in the battle."

Strange nodded in agreement as the Wakandan activated his Kimoyo card. He turned the volume down low, holding a conversation with his sister in whispers that would have been inaudible over the standard cell phone. But the two siblings seemed to have no problem hearing each other. T'Challa transmitted a picture of the map and cut off the transmission.

"Shuri and the Dora Milaje will handle the guards," he said. "Give them two minutes to get into position. Then we can make our move. Have you found an approach?"

"The only option I can find takes us through the water," said Strange, frowning. "This seems like a poor choice given our location. I assume that the temple of the crocodile god might attract crocodiles, even if it is no longer in use?"

"There is a reason those waters are not guarded," admitted T'Challa.

Spider-Man tore his attention from the trees to glance down at the map once. "Ms Marvel and I could take you all straight up to the top floor, but that gives anybody on top of the temple a potshot at us."

Strange shook his head. "No, if I was Dormammu, I'd concentrate my strongest firepower there. We can't be certain who we will face, but it would be reckless to give them a free strike at us."

"I thought the same thing," said Spidey. "But I like to feel important."

"Couldn't we just open another portal and go straight to the top?" asked Ms Marvel.

"I cannot risk it," replied Strange. "There are too many magical forces at work here. I dare not open another portal lest I destabilize the delicate balance of power and blow the place sky high."

"Oh. So, what do we do?" she persisted, her voice quivering slightly from nerves or excitement.

Strange considered for a moment. "We must get to the top and stop the portals from opening. Dormammu will be at his weakest as the final portal opens, which gives us an opportunity to wrest control of his slaves and work together to keep him from coming through. That means time is of the essence. Spider-Man and Ms Marvel, can you leap over the waters and climb the temple if the Panther and I remain behind?"

"Do you mean to use us as crocodile bait?" asked T'Challa, his voice dripping with amusement.

"Well… yes. Unless you have a better idea. We will catch up."

"On the contrary. I would be delighted. I haven't wrestled one of Sobek's crocodiles in years."

"I say this with all due respect, man, but you're nuts," said Spider-Man, shaking his head. "Croc wrestling is *not* a normal hobby."

"You will never know until you try, my friend," responded T'Challa. "Perhaps after we have resolved this situation, you will come visit and see for yourself."

"No, thank you! I like my fingers where they are."

Strange cut off their banter with a wave of his hand. He straightened, holding the Lantern of Morphesti toward the still-open portal, where Wong waited in silence.

"Take this," Strange ordered. "It will show you the battle. If we are defeated, you must take it to Clea and convince her to act. She cannot hide from her uncle forever. Besides, she owes me."

A flicker of a smile ran over Wong's features. "You could not pay me enough to tell her that last bit. But I will do as you request. Stay safe, and don't do anything too stupid."

"He's going to wrestle crocodiles on purpose," said Spider-Man. "I think his stupidity meter is broken."

"On the contrary," said the Sorcerer Supreme. He summoned the magical energy that thrummed through his veins, his feet lifting a few inches from the floor. His hair crackled with static. His skin prickled with the magical potential that infused every cell of his being. When he spoke, he had to hold back lest his voice ring out with power, alerting Dormammu to their exact location. The Dread Sorcerer would know they were coming, of course, but he didn't need to advertise. "I am a Master of the Mystic Arts. I do not wrestle."

He turned his attention toward the swamp as the war cries of the Dora Milaje filled the air. Distant gunfire answered their shouts, and a man's scream of agony, abruptly cut off, made all the birds in the nearby trees take wing. Doctor Strange did not pause. He began to float towards the swamp, energy arcing from the tips of his fingers.

"Avengers? *Assemble*," he said.

T'Challa joined him, loping over the ground with an easy stride that spoke volumes about his comfort in this wild place. But Spider-Man paused for a moment.

"Actually," he said. "We're splitting up. Shouldn't you say, 'Avengers, disassemble'?"

They all turned to stare at him.

"OK, I'm going, I'm going," he said, holding up his hands. "Sheesh. I thought it was funny."

The sound of fighting drew closer, and the foliage began to whipsaw back and forth, the leaves battered by stray bullets. They needed no further encouragement. Strange launched himself in the opposite direction, which would take him down the slope toward the water. T'Challa kept pace with him, the panther suit blending in with the dark leaves, turning him into an unseen predator.

The time for talk was over. Now, they would fight for their world, and for everything they had ever known.

THIRTY-SEVEN

Luke ascended the temple steps a few paces before Valkyrie, maintaining the ruse that she drove him before her as a reluctant prisoner. At first, he had remained on high alert, scanning their immediate surroundings in the hopes of seeing something that would help him. Some clue. Something he could use to stop Dormammu. But their enemies had chosen their site well. There were no handy weapon caches to plunder, no convenient alcoves where allies could hide. The only option was to rush to the top and hope for the best.

He saw no signs of the Shadow Avengers, although they had to be here by now. He could do nothing but trust in their judgement. They would show themselves when the time was right. In the meantime, he would maneuver himself into the best position to make a difference. The final portal would be opened on top of the ziggurat. That was where he would go.

The climb was brutal despite his superior physical condition. Each step stood nearly mid-thigh on him. They would have been up to Jessica's waist. Luckily, Valkyrie was tall for a woman. They leaped up the first few steps, drawing on their superhuman strength, but the process quickly drained them. Valkyrie wore a full set of armor, and her cheeks went red with heat and exertion. Although she didn't slow, Luke suggested that they take it a little easier so they'd be in better shape when they arrived at the summit. It was a measure of her fatigue that she agreed.

So they pulled themselves up onto each step and climbed to their feet, over and over again, their palms going brown with sweat and dust. The sun beat down on them with laser-like intensity, glinting off the silver armor and blinding Luke. No, wait. That flash of light came from overhead. Green tinged flickers drew his attention to the top of the stairway. There was no mistaking that color after all that he'd seen. It had begun.

"Hurry!" he urged, scrambling to his feet and taking the next step in a quick bound. The time for caution was over. He had to get up there before Dormammu summoned more enslaved Asgardians to oppose them. Valkyrie kept pace with him as he rushed up the remaining steps and reached the top of the temple, puffing with exertion. As she climbed to her feet, her sword rasped on its way out of its scabbard.

Beneath him, the jungle exploded with sound. War cries and gunshots filled the air. The tumult could only mean one thing: his allies were here, to his immense relief, but his heart still pounded. He could only hope they weren't too late.

Atop the temple stood a wide, flat space dotted with crumbling statues. At its center loomed a well-preserved altar, its corners decorated with friezes of curling crocodiles, and in its center was a statue of a crocodile that reared back on its hind legs, a spear clutched in its clawed hands. Its eyes glittered green as the sun caught the emeralds set into its face.

Suspended in the air over the statue was a growing circle of green energy. The portal. It had not fully opened yet, but it was only a matter of time.

On the other side of the portal, Venom and Loki struggled against each other. The symbiote had the upper hand. He sat astride the Asgardian, pummeling him with his fists as well as a second set of symbiotic hands that jutted from his body near his ribs. Venom's eyes glowed with a familiar green fire.

It didn't matter. They could punch each other in the face until kingdom come while he dealt with the growing portal. If only he knew how to close it. Magic wasn't his strong suit, and this particular portal didn't appear to have come with a handy on and off switch. He could message Strange for advice, but that would attract more attention than he wanted. Flying under the radar would give him his best chance of success.

He tapped Valkyrie on the shoulder and jerked his thumb toward the portal.

"Any idea how to work that thing?" he muttered.

She shook her head with what appeared to be sincere regret. He chose to believe it. After all, it represented her only way home. Taking charge of the portal would be in her best interest if she ever wanted to be free again.

He crept forward, avoiding sudden movements that would attract the attention of the combatants a few yards away. They were really going at it. Loki had reasserted his dominance, blasting Venom with a burst of magic that shook the ground. Neither of them had noticed the interlopers, but it was just a matter of time. Luke needed to take action, and quickly.

As he approached the altar, he ran through what he knew about the portals. From what he understood, they were complex magical constructs that required a number of different elements to function correctly. If he could interfere with just one of them, that might be enough to destabilize the entire structure. While he couldn't perform a magic spell to save his life, one of those elements was physical. Luke Cage could do physical all day, any day.

The altar glinted with green slime that reflected the growing portal above. If he could remove it, that might be enough to stop the portal from opening, or at the very least, delay it long enough for the magical cavalry to arrive.

He put his shoulder to the altar. Valkyrie stood over him, her sword in her hand, nervousness clear in her eyes. If Dormammu took control of her again, it would be over. Luke couldn't take down the altar and fight her at the same time. Although he was unbreakable, he had his limits, and he wasn't confident that he'd have enough juice to move all this stone after going one-on-one with a warrior of her caliber.

Her hand tightened on the grip of her sword. The other went to the pendant that hung around her neck, hovering there as if she was too afraid to make contact with it. She closed her eyes briefly, her face spasming with pain and regret. Then she opened them again. Released her hands. Put her shoulder to the altar next to his.

"I'll get you home," he said quietly. "I swear it."

She smiled sadly, her disbelief clear. But she thanked him anyway.

"On three?" she asked. He nodded, and she counted it off. "One... two... three."

They pushed. The thick rock groaned as the two powerful super heroes put all their strength into tearing the altar from its moorings. Pebbles and dust sifted onto the ground. A hairline fracture crept across the surface of the crocodile figure on the corner directly to the left of Luke's face. It was working! He gritted his teeth, summoning up every ounce of power he possessed. Muscles bulged along his arms. Veins stood out in his neck. He bellowed with effort. Beside him, Valkyrie dug her feet in, every muscle in her body straining to its limit.

"By Odin's beard. That's something you don't see every day," said Loki.

He sounded impressed as he studied them, his thin face streaked with dust and pinched with fatigue. He wiped sweat from his brow with a shaking hand. Venom was nowhere to be seen, and Luke now realized how quiet the area had become. Had Loki defeated the symbiote once and for all? It seemed unlikely given the Asgardian's weakened state, but the trickster was wily. Perhaps he'd sent Venom off to Siberia via a portal, but Luke knew the symbiote would be back. For the moment, Luke had bigger fish to fry. After they destroyed the altar, he would follow up.

The stone tore free with a massive ripping sound. The immense bulk of the altar shifted, broken loose from its moorings. Green sludge coated Luke's shoulder and arm, but he ignored it, pushing with all his might. Valkyrie followed suit.

The plan turned out to be a bad call. He'd hoped that Dormammu hadn't interfered because his attention was elsewhere, but maybe he'd let them break the altar because he knew the outcome wouldn't be in their favor. When the Master's furious magic pulsed through the magical liquid, it hit both of the heroes hard. Fiery pain engulfed his skin everywhere the liquid touched. It bypassed his unbreakable flesh, digging down deep within him to the pain centers of his body. It felt like he was being burned from within. He staggered backwards, his vision white with pain, the altar forgotten.

A voice came to him then, echoing in the chambers of his mind. It dripped with a power that would have driven him to his knees if he hadn't already fallen to them.

"Puny mortal," said Dormammu. "You are too late."

THIRTY-EIGHT

T'Challa followed the floating sorcerer through the jungle, his every sense alert for any signs of approach. He could still hear the distant sounds of combat, although the constant gunfire had begun to taper off. Shuri and the Dora Milaje had already made clear headway. Their hasty plan to draw off their attackers into the crocodile infested waters that dotted the area seemed to be working.

A short distance behind them, Spider-Man and Ms Marvel waited in the underbrush. They did their best to remain out of sight, but their bright costumes made it almost impossible for them to hide in the verdant green jungle. Besides, as agile as they might be, they weren't at home here like T'Challa and his people.

The temple loomed over them, its tall steps bare of ornament. The crocodile clan had been long gone before he was born, but he had studied it extensively, hoping to avert mistakes of the future by learning about the past. Unfortunately, the records he could find had left him with more questions than answers. Sobek, the crocodile god, was sister to Bast, who imbued him with the power of the Black Panther. But there had been some falling out between the siblings, the cause of which he could not determine, and the Wakandan people worshiped Sobek no more. His temple still stood, however, defying the ravages of time despite its long years of disuse, and he had ordered his people to steer clear out of respect for the holy place and his long gone ancestors who had worshiped here.

Over all of these years, the crocodiles had stayed, their swamps remaining verdant regardless of the weather. No drought had ever touched them, as if the hand of their god protected, preserving this sacred space in the hopes that one day he might return.

He was unsure of the welcome he would get here. Perhaps if Sobek had parted with Bast on good terms, he might pass through undisturbed. But he couldn't be sure that Sobek's power extended that far after all this time.

The scent of water filled his nose, but Doctor Strange didn't pause. He continued to advance, the air around him full of crackling magic, his feet floating high above the soft ground, borne aloft by the magical cloak around his neck. T'Challa summoned his Panther mask and launched himself forward, eager to take the lead and hopefully avert another fight.

Alas, that was not to be. The moment his foot touched the water, loud splashing alerted him to the approach of the aquatic reptiles. Good. If they paid attention to him, they wouldn't notice the others as they snuck past and made their way up the side of the ziggurat.

"I am the Black Panther," he declared. "Bast's hand on this earth. I greet you, servants of Sobek, in the spirit of brotherhood, and request safe passage through your lands."

"You think that'll work?" asked Doctor Strange.

"It can't hurt."

But either Sobek didn't appreciate the intrusion, or his power had ebbed too low. The eight-foot crocodile that thrashed out of the water to lunge for his feet did not seem to welcome him except as a potential lunch. The Black Panther leaped into action, stunning the massive beast with a blow to its snout and kicking it so hard that it flew from the water. But he had no time to celebrate his victory. Another croc grabbed him by the ankle, yanking him off his feet and rolling into a spin meant to disorient him before the kill. Water whirled around him, deeper than he'd initially realized. But his enhanced stamina gave him extra time without oxygen that normal mortals lacked. He twisted catlike in his attacker's grip, scrabbling for purchase as the reptile switched directions. Disorientation nearly took him over, but Bast supported her warrior, providing him with the innate directional sense that all cats possess. He thrashed toward the surface but was unable to break free.

Fine, then. He went on the offense instead, slashing at the beast's delicate underside. The claws of his panther suit raked at the exposed flesh, tearing great gouts that spewed dark blood. With a pained lurch, the crocodile released him, fleeing into the deep waters. T'Challa had no desire to pursue it, but made for the surface instead, gulping down the air with relief.

In his absence, Doctor Strange had acquitted himself well. One confused croc hovered in midair, suspended by a bubble of magic that spun in the wind. He held the jaws of a second one inches from his face, and T'Challa scrambled from the water, preparing to offer aid when the sorcerer spat a single phrase of magic.

"By the whirling winds of Watoomb!" he cried.

A jet of concentrated air shot from his hands, catching hold of both crocs and sending them sailing through the trees. T'Challa listened for the sound of their landing, but he could hear nothing.

"How far did you send them?" he asked.

"Not far. They are beasts, and only attacking out of instinct. It didn't feel right to kill them," replied Doctor Strange. "In a way, they are your subjects, too, aren't they?"

"Indeed. Thank you."

"My pleasure."

The two of them made their way toward the base of the temple, dripping with swamp water. T'Challa's suit dried quickly, its microfiber weave ejecting water to protect the delicate circuitry woven into its fibers. Strange's cloak fluttered and twisted, squeezing the water from itself as well as from the clothing beneath.

"Strange," said T'Challa. "No signs of the portal yet."

As soon as he spoke, the top of the temple flared with an eldritch green light. The sorcerer gave him a look of utter exasperation.

"My apologies," he said. "I shouldn't have tempted fate."

"No, you shouldn't," said Strange without heat. "Come. If I can get to the portal in time, we can still be victorious."

T'Challa needed no further encouragement. He took the first two steps in a single bound. The sorcerer floated up next to him, and they proceeded to climb into the heavens, racing against the clock.

THIRTY-NINE

Peter Parker wasted no time. As soon as the water at T'Challa's feet began to churn, he led Ms Marvel away through the swamp, trying to stick to dry land as much as possible. Crocodiles could sense disturbances in the water; he'd learned that from some late-night trivia show, and these might not be regular crocs. In order to reach the top of the temple in time, they had to pass through the water undetected.

The uneven ground didn't cooperate. Even with his light feet, he still slid into the water a few times, as did Ms Marvel. Once, the muck gave out so quickly beneath him that he made a splash when he landed, the sound ringing too loud to his ears. He paused, stricken, waiting to see if it would attract unwanted attention. But his Spider-Sense remained quiescent, and they continued on, reaching the foot of the ziggurat in what must have been a minute or two but felt like an eternity.

They didn't delay, climbing up the tall steps in tandem. Neither of them were particularly tall, forcing them to shimmy their way up each one, coating their bellies in a thick layer of fine tan dirt. It was an exhausting process. If this was like other ziggurats he'd seen on TV (and on rare occasion, fought villains on), it would likely have a set of more reasonably sized steps etched into one side, but they lacked the time to go searching for them. Which was too bad.

"I wish we could just zoom straight up there," Ms Marvel panted, echoing the gist if not the exact content of his thoughts.

"We've got to stay low. I think people will notice if we start flying through the air with the greatest of ease."

"Oh, I know," she responded. "But that doesn't mean I'm happy about it." She gave him a weary smile, her teeth flashing bright in her smudged face. It turned into a worried look at the exact same moment that his Spidey-Sense flared into life. "Look out!"

She smacked him to one side with a hand that was suddenly the size of a door. Although the blow was unexpected, he rolled with it, his innate agility turning what could have been a painful landing into a ready crouch. The hollow *piff* of a silenced weapon reached him before he spotted their attackers, and he dodged on pure instinct, jerking out of the way at impossible speeds as bullets zipped past him in quick succession.

A young man in brown camo with the Oscorp logo over his heart pointed the semi-automatic weapon at him, pattering the ground with bullets and showing a grim determination that would have served him well under different circumstances. But his ammunition wasn't endless.

Click!

The young guard shook the weapon as if that might make bullets magically appear in the empty cartridge. Then he turned a stricken look towards Peter, holding his hands out in the universal sign of surrender. His eyes were wide and nervous over the patchy beard he'd been attempting to grow. Probably trying to make himself look older. Tougher. It hadn't worked.

Kids. Peter wanted to sit this one down and lecture him on the wisdom of signing up to work for the bad guys and how to spot a bad guy at a thousand paces, but there was no time for either. He jerked his thumb down the ziggurat, indicating the direction the guard should flee.

"Leave the gun," he said.

The weapon clattered obediently to the ground, and the guard bolted. Peter probably ought to have shouted some kind of warning after him, something along the lines of "If I see you again, I won't be so kind," but he just couldn't do it. He'd done some stupid things when he was young, too. If not for the good people around him, he very easily could have blundered too far into something he couldn't take back later. The guard deserved a real chance to learn from his mistakes.

Speaking of kids, Ms Marvel had handled herself well. She'd used that giant fist of hers to smack a second guard around until he didn't know which way was up, and as Peter watched, she picked him up and threw him. He went sailing down the steps, landing with a distant splash. Her hand shrank back to normal size, and she dusted it off with satisfied finality.

"Nicely done," said Peter.

"You, too," she replied. "Any more of those guys out there?"

He paused to listen, but his ears told him nothing he didn't already know. Wait. That wasn't true. He picked up a low hum at the very edges of his hearing, one that set his teeth on edge. He scanned the area, looking for the source. When he found it, the sight made his stomach sink.

Wisps of bright green were barely visible at the top of the temple. They flickered intermittently into sight before vanishing again. He could only hope that they hadn't been there long, that the Shadow Avengers weren't too late to stop Dormammu from taking over the planet and subjugating everyone there.

He drew Ms Marvel's attention to it, and she looked for only a moment before her mouth firmed into a determined line. No words were necessary. They attacked the stairway once more. This time, Peter used his webs to pull himself up over two or three blocks at once, remaining low to the ground but covering a great deal of it in a small amount of time. His companion kept pace with him, stretching and shrinking her limbs to skim up the steep incline with minimal effort. If the portal was opening, stealth no longer served their purposes.

They reached the top in unison, landing at its edge. A sobering sight awaited them. A portal hung in the air over the temple, almost large enough to let a full-sized human adult through. It grew in size with every passing moment. Beneath it, Luke and a tall woman in full armor fought next to a cracked and shaky altar. Crackling green energy coated the altar and their bodies, sheening her eyes in green flame. Luke seemed to be resisting the evil influence so far. As Peter climbed to his feet, Luke tore the woman's sword from her grasp, roaring. He flung the weapon to the side as she flew at him, throwing him to the ground. Loki stood nearby, ready to interfere if the need arose. Venom's webs catapulted him forward out of nowhere, and he landed next to the Asgardian. Together, they spun to face the interlopers, their eyes glowing bright with the same energy that fueled the portal and restrained Luke.

That didn't bode well.

Peter dropped to a ready crouch. He knew how this would go. Venom would leap at him, his mouth open wide and his symbiotic tongue tasting the air, as if it could almost taste the violence to come. Peter would catch him. They'd plummet down the side of the ziggurat, the sharp edges of the steps digging painfully into ribs and shoulders as they struggled for dominance. Venom would thwap him with symbiotic tendrils; he'd shoot webs into his attacker's face. They'd each land a few blows that would rattle the other. It seemed like a foregone conclusion at this point. They'd fought so many times that he could replay any one of their encounters out, move-by-move, without missing a beat.

Venom lifted his hands up and shot a bolt of nuclear green energy from them. Peter's Spider-Sense went into overdrive, but shock locked him in place. The magical blast struck him square in the chest, sending him flying off the edge of the temple. Every muscle in his body tensed as the magic coursed through his veins, locking him in some kind of seizure. He fought for control, only dimly aware of the fact that he flew through the air, and eventually, he'd land. He couldn't move, couldn't even see, and his Spider-Sense bombarded him with warnings he could do nothing about.

He hit something, hard. Wood cracked, giving way slightly, and then he fell straight down, striking obstacle after obstacle on the way down. A tree. He'd hit a tree, and now the branches slowed his fall. Still, when the ground smacked him in the face, it hurt. He groaned, struggling to lift his head. The magic slowly began to ebb, and he struggled for breath against a body that no longer wanted to comply with his wishes.

His vision resolved into dim outlines and finally into wavy forms that made him sick to his stomach. Finally, his arms decided to cooperate, and he slid his hands down with excruciating slowness to support his weight. But when he tried to push himself up, his arms quivered like a baby deer trying to take its first steps. What in the heck had Venom hit him with?

Speak of the devil, the symbiote landed on the ground a few feet away, dropping into an animalistic crouch, muscles rippling. Venom surveyed him implacably, green fire still gathered around his eyes. Then, the symbiote leaped forward, landing atop him with bone-cracking force. Peter groaned again, struggling weakly, but he still didn't have all his parts in working order. Hopefully they'd come back online soon, or his goose was cooked.

Venom grabbed him by the collar, and Peter's hands scrabbled for purchase but didn't even have the strength to pry off a single finger. A symbiotic tendril emerged from the creature's back, brushing the hair back from Peter's forehead with an almost tender gesture. Then it struck, impacting against the side of his head and spreading, coating his skull in a thin layer of black biomass. It filled his ears and covered his eyes. But for some reason, it left his mouth alone. He gulped down air, trying to slow his racing heart. He'd never been much of a claustrophobe, but this situation would have given just about anybody the heebie-jeebies.

The symbiote's mental voice took him by surprise.

We are sorry, it said.

Peter recoiled, overcome with revulsion. The alien creature didn't understand human emotions. It would tell its hosts anything to get what it wanted. He knew that from experience, as much as he'd like to forget it.

Yeah, right, he thought. There was no need to speak aloud, not now, and that fact chilled him. Could the symbiote do this with anyone, or did it retain some link to him still, despite his desperate attempts to purge it from his body?

It is true. We will kill you someday, but it will be a fair contest. Your might against ours. But our will is not our own. We have no choice but to obey.

Dormammu, thought Peter.

We tried to resist, but…

Well, try harder! Two against one. You're no weakling.

He is too strong for us. His magic burns our essence and drains our strength. If we resist him, we will not survive.

Baloney. I know how strong you are. Eddie has given you a home. Acceptance. And this is how you repay him? He wouldn't want to die a slave. He deserves better than that.

You hate us. You hate Eddie.

Hate isn't the right word. Maybe we're not best buddies, but I don't want this any more than you do. Peter paused, thinking hard. The symbiote's body hadn't moved, and he presumed that Dormammu couldn't pick up on this unique mode of conversation, but their time ran short. The portal still opened. Run, he thought, in a fit of inspiration.

We are not cowards.

Dormammu's only got so much magic to throw around, but

he'll get stronger once he's here. Get as far away as you can
to break his hold over you. Opening that final portal is going
to take a lot of juice, so he won't want to spend too much to
bring you back. That makes you one fewer body he can use
against us. And if we fail, tell everyone you can find. Find every
Avenger you can and bring help.

Perhaps… but they won't believe me.

Tell them… Peter took a deep breath. He couldn't believe
he was saying this, but at some point, you had to put aside your
personal feelings for the greater good. If he didn't, he was part
of the problem. He couldn't let his emotions get in the way of
doing the right thing. Tell them you've got my support. Scout's
honor.

We could save the world, the symbiote said thoughtfully.
*Eddie's world. Eddie will approve. But we do not like to run from
a fight.*

I'm not your enemy right now. I don't like it either, but right
now, we don't have time to squabble. There won't be anything
left to fight over if we don't work together.

There was a long silence as the symbiote thought this over.

Yes, it responded. *You are a good person, Peter Parker.*

"Thanks," said Peter, shocked and more than a little touched.

It is a weakness. Someday it will undo you.

With that parting shot, the symbiote retreated from his
mind, releasing his head and withdrawing its mass. The black,
glistening fluid shimmered as it seeped into Eddie's pores,
leaving him in human form. It only took a few seconds for the
creature to communicate their conversation to its host, and as it
happened, emotions flickered over Eddie's face in what would
have been a comically predictable succession under different

circumstances. Shock, disbelief, anger, rejection, pleading, and finally acceptance came over him in turns.

"You are one lucky son of a gun," he said aloud.

Peter nodded. While he'd chatted with the symbiote, his body had recovered quickly, and he was fairly certain that he had control of himself. He could fight if he had to, but the odds remained stacked against him, and he refused to make the first move. If Eddie turned down his offer, it wouldn't be Peter's fault. He wouldn't even celebrate the fact that he'd been right. To his surprise, he found himself hoping for the first time in a long time that Eddie would do the right thing.

Their eyes met, and they shared a rare moment of unspoken accord. Tomorrow, things would return to normal. But today, they would join forces to save the world. Because no matter their differences, they shared one important thing in common. This was their town, their people, and no upstart sorcerer with a god complex was going to take them over.

Eddie nodded, and Peter nodded back. Then, the symbiote manifested once more, gathering all its strength in bulging thigh muscles, and sprang into the air. It sprinted into the verdant brush, loping like a jungle predator. Peter pushed himself up with more weakness than he liked, watching. His heart thumped; his hands went clammy with sweat. For the first time he could remember, he truly worried about Eddie Brock. Sure, he'd worried about what Eddie would *do* millions of times, but that was different. It had cost Eddie a lot to set aside their grudge. Peter knew that. Maybe it would even change things between them going forward. He didn't want to be naïve, but he could hope.

He pushed himself up onto shaky knees and looked up

the ziggurat. The steep steps blocked his view of what was happening up top, and Ms Marvel was nowhere in sight. But green wisps of magic still flickered in and out of sight. This thing wasn't over yet. He took the briefest of moments to collect himself and shot out a web, beginning the arduous climb to the top once more.

FORTY

Kamala screamed when Venom knocked Spider-Man off the top of the temple. Maybe that wasn't very heroic of her, but he was her friend! He'd listened to her and made her feel like her worries were valid. He'd made a special effort to include her. He'd respected her. She had to help him.

But the portal kept on growing, spitting magic into the air. The only other member of the Shadow Avengers in sight was Mr Cage, and he sprawled on the ground next to the broken altar, getting back to his feet to fight Valkyrie. Kamala had to choose, but the options were impossible. Both sucked rocks. She could stop the portal and save the world from Dormammu, but then who would come to the rescue the next time one of Spider-Man's enemies came calling? Or she could save Spidey and hope that they could handle Dormammu later. At least she wouldn't be alone.

She took a hesitant step toward the edge. A short distance away, Loki watched her with green, glowing eyes. His frail figure hunched in pain, but she'd seen him at work before. He didn't need muscles to smack her around with his magic. She thought she could go toe-to-toe with him, but it would hurt, and meanwhile, the seconds would tick away.

"Go ahead," Loki urged, gesturing in the direction that Spider-Man had fallen. "Find your injured comrade. I won't stop you."

Now that gave her pause. She shook her head.

"No, thanks. He can take care of himself."

The moment she spoke the words, she knew them to be true. Spider-Man was no wuss. He'd come swinging up here any minute now, making wisecracks and kicking bad guys in the face. It was how he rolled. He would have trusted in her abilities if the situation had been reversed. She had to give him the same courtesy.

She turned to face the Asgardian, rolling her neck and making it pop. She stretched out her hands. Rolled her shoulders. Made everything nice and loose in preparation for the fight to come.

"OK," she said. "Let's do this."

But Loki shook his head, obviously reluctant.

"I do not want to do this," he said. "You are not my enemy. But I must protect the altar. The Master commands me. It is essential to maintaining the portal for these last few moments until it is fully open."

"Fight against him, Loki," she urged. "He can't keep all those magical plates spinning forever."

He shook his head in disappointment, raising his hands. A bright ball of magical energy flared to life between his palms, and he released it with a convulsive motion, flinging it toward her. But Kamala had been waiting for this. She stretched, her legs growing to giraffe-like proportions, and the ball of magic sailed harmlessly beneath her. Without waiting for the next strike, she shrank down and rolled toward him, popping up with a hand that had embiggened to the size of a horse and caught him in the chin with a bone-shattering uppercut.

The Asgardian snarled in pain as he went flying. His eyes flared brighter, and magic gathered around his body, slowing his flight until he hovered in midair above her. He glowed like an avenging god, magic dripping from his fingertips. He tensed them again, but this time there was no ball of power to dodge. Instead, the ground turned to quicksand beneath her, swallowing her to the waist in an instant. But this didn't bother her. She merely grew giant-sized, swatting at him in midair. He darted out of the way, born aloft by his magic, but she kept on swinging. It was only a matter of time before she hit him, and at this size, she'd likely break him.

He swooped and dove, flinging bolts of magic at her that never even came close. They were locked in a stalemate.

Loki – under Dormammu's control – was stalling. The realization came to her in a burst of insight. He wanted her to focus on him. What was it that he'd said? He had to protect the altar for these last few moments before the portal opened. But here she was, focused on him while Dormammu carved his way into their world only a few feet away.

She risked a glance over her shoulder only to be dismayed by what she saw. The portal was almost blindingly bright. It would have caught her attention if she'd been facing it, but Loki had positioned himself well, forcing her to face the other direction to defend herself from his attacks. A dot of blackness had formed in the center of the portal, and although she didn't know precisely what that meant, it couldn't bode well. If she had to guess, she'd say it was opening.

It was now or never. She had to act, but what could she do? She didn't know magic, and Doctor Strange was nowhere in sight. Her only choice was to stall, but how?

Her train of thought distracted her, leaving an opening in her defense. A stray bolt of magic took her in the side of the head, hitting her with such power that it pulled her free of the quicksand and flung her with great force against the side of the altar. The rock quivered, raining dust down onto her face. Something had given way in her lower back, sending laser bolts of pain up her spine. She lay there for a moment, panting. Her body would heal itself given enough time, but she had none to waste. She had to do something.

The ground shook as the portal continued to open. The altar above her glowed green. Maybe that was just a reflection, or maybe the magic that fueled the portal came from deep within the ground beneath her…

Finally, the pieces clicked together. Loki had had no reason to tell her about the altar, or about the portal opening. Based on what she knew of him, he was too smart to let essential information like that slip from his mouth. He'd been trying to warn her in a way that didn't get Dormammu's attention. Maybe the sorcerer could make the God of Mischief fight, but he couldn't keep Loki from doing one of the things he did best – stabbing an adversary in the back. Just as Doctor Strange had predicted, Dormammu was spread too thin to notice. Even under the Master's control, Loki was trying to help them.

Hopefully she hadn't figured it out too late. She struggled to sit up, but she could go no further. Her legs had gone completely numb, and they refused to move when she tried. That worried her, but she could tend to her injuries later. She had a job to do, and she would only get one chance at it. She thrust her arms out with all the strength she possessed, embiggening them as they went. They hit the side of the altar like a freight train at full speed, pulverizing the rock into a million little pieces that went flying in all directions. One of them clipped Kamala on the eyebrow, stinging. There was a sound like a giant bell going off, and for a moment, she swore she could feel the magic dissipating into the ground beneath her as if sucked down a giant drain. The green glow faded from the ruined mess that had once been an altar to the crocodile god.

Kamala looked around, her breath ragged with excitement. She'd taken down the altar just like Loki had suggested. For a moment, she hoped that this had freed him from Dormammu's influence, but he lay slumped on the ground near the edge of the steps. That didn't seem like a good omen at all. She turned her attention to the portal that still hung over the ruined mess that used to be the altar.

Three figures stood outlined in the center of the portal, backlit by the magic that had brought them there. Somehow, their features remained in darkness, turning them into nothing but shadow shapes. Two were tall: one male and one female. Both of their figures were obscured by long cloaks, and what looked like pointy wings jutted out from the tops of their heads. The lithe woman who accompanied them wore a cloak, too, as well as the coolest headpiece Kamala had ever seen. It looked like spider legs pointing out from her head, reaching for the sky.

Maybe she'd done it? Doctor Strange had shown the Shadow Avengers sketches of Dormammu from his ancient books, and he'd looked nothing like this trio. Maybe by breaking the altar, she'd mucked up the portal enough that it had brought these three here by accident instead.

They landed in a bolt of lightning that shook the temple. Kamala stayed hunkered down against the ground, trying not to lose her lunch. Loki pushed himself up off the ground a short distance away. He met her eyes, his expression bleak.

"What?" she demanded. "What's wrong?"

"The fight is over," he said. "We have lost."

"No, it's not. Isn't there some saying about that? It isn't over until some lady sings, and I don't hear any singing."

But he didn't even react to her poor attempt at humor. He slumped down in place as if prepared to die right there. She scooted closer to him, shielding him with her body as he coughed weakly.

"You have spirit," he said, gasping for breath. "But it will do you no good."

The ground shook as the man leaped toward them, landing with a thunderous impact. Kamala turned, ready to do battle if necessary. She would protect Loki. Maybe he'd try to stab her in the back later, but she'd be ready for it. Heroes protect people, even when the chance of success seemed bleak. Carol Danvers had taught her that, and she wouldn't let Captain Marvel down. Besides, Loki had tried to help her, even though he didn't believe it would make any difference.

"Allow me to introduce our guests," said Loki, his voice weak from coughing. "Thor Odinson, Hela, and the Enchantress."

FORTY-ONE

Luke didn't like what he had to do next, but there was no avoiding it. He slammed his hand against the side of Valkyrie's helmet, putting all of his immense strength behind the blow. She went down with a finality that would have worried him if not for her obvious stamina, and the pulsing magical light faded from her eyes. He pushed to his feet with teeth gritted in determination. His head didn't feel quite right after the magical blast and the subsequent fight, but at least Dormammu's voice had faded from his mind as the ooze dripped off his skin. Bright flashes danced before his eyes at random intervals, and his muscles quivered and jumped like grease on a hot pan. Every once in a while, bright wisps of magic came off him like raindrops.

He took quick stock of the situation. Valkyrie knelt on the ground with a dazed expression. Ms Marvel stood alone and defiant against a powerful trio of Asgardians. Loki hung in his brother's grip like a dead thing, limp and boneless.

Above them, the portal sparked and hissed. A bright, clear light began to grow in its depths. An acrid scent reached

Luke's nostrils. Smoke. He could see it now, filtering in from the portal, like a window somewhere in its depths had been cracked.

This was it. The portal was opening. The Asgardians had paved the way.

He staggered toward Ms Marvel. For a moment, he marveled at how much the magic blast had rattled him, until he realized his problem had nothing to do with his head. A giant bolt of lightning stabbed at the side of the temple, blowing bits of rock into the sky. Luke was no meteorologist, but he was fairly sure normal lightning didn't do that. Perhaps it was Thor's work, or maybe the opening portal would bring with it extreme weather just like the others had. Either way, he needed to work fast before one of them got roasted.

The three Asgardians stood between him and the portal. Now he could see them better. All three stared down at him, eyes brimming with crackling magic, and those familiar pendants hung from their necks. But they still retained hints of the people inside. Thor stood with the proud bearing of a natural leader, his cloak whipping in the wind and Mjolnir clutched lightly in the hand that wasn't busy throttling his brother. Hela's gorgeous face was marred by her smirk, her mouth twisted with scorn. Enchantress's blonde hair whipped around in the wind as she stared imperiously down at him.

The odds weren't great, but he'd faced worse. If they wouldn't get out of his way, he'd have to go through them.

He launched himself at Thor's feet, taking the Asgardian by surprise and knocking him off balance. Loki went toppling to the ground, but Luke had no time to check on him. He rolled across the hard-packed dirt as Thor tried repeatedly to stomp his brains out. But those strikes had a pattern, and finally he had it. He grabbed onto Thor's ankle and yanked the armored man to the ground.

As they struggled for dominance, Luke cast a glance around the temple. Ms Marvel desperately dodged a quick series of magical strikes from both Hela and Enchantress. The two of them flung bright green bolts at her, just like the one that had knocked him off his feet. She needed help, but Valkyrie hung back, conflict written in every line of her body.

"Help her!" yelled Luke.

Valkyrie nodded, hefting her sword. Then she staggered. A wracking cough seized her, making her double over. She couldn't fight like that, not against such formidable foes. They would tear her to pieces.

He had to break free. He locked Thor's wrists in his own. The two heroes strained against each other, muscles bulging. Perhaps under different circumstances, Luke could have held his own, but that magical blast had drained him. Thor's hands inched toward his throat despite his best efforts.

They were losing, and he could think of nothing to do about it.

FORTY-TWO

Peter wasted no time. He hurtled up the side of the temple with no attempt at stealth. He needed to get there quickly, and if that meant someone would take potshots at him along the way, let them try. But no one bothered. There were still pockets of fighting down in the trees, and he could see Shuri off in the distance exchanging plasma blasts from her gauntlets with some unseen attacker in the underbrush. But the Dora Milaje had done their job well. They'd drawn off the guards and kept them from interfering with the battle atop the temple.

About halfway up, lightning began to stab at the ground out of what had previously been clear skies. Storm clouds moved in over the area in fast forward, cutting off the sun. His Spider-Sense flared, alerting him to danger, and he shot out a web off to one side, diverting his trajectory just in time to avoid a bolt that took out the bulk of two of the giant steps. The temple groaned as if it was alive and protesting the damage. Heck, maybe it was.

He climbed the last few steps, dodging another bolt, and landed lightly atop the temple. A quick glance told him everything he needed to know. Dormammu had summoned more Asgardian slaves. Ms Marvel was in trouble. The kid stood alone against two Asgardian sorceresses, and although she'd managed to escape with only minor singeing so far, it couldn't last. She needed a hand, and luckily, he had two.

He leaped toward the green-garbed Enchantress. She didn't see him until the last minute, and as soon as she turned her glowing eyes on him, he struck, hitting her with a blast of webbing that pulled her forward into his fist. He hit her with the force of a speeding rocket. She would have gone flying if the webs hadn't held her in place. He let the force of his movement take them both to the far side of the temple where stray magic wouldn't hit any of their allies.

"Two against one, and she's a teenager," he scolded, releasing her. "Who does that?"

"She chose to stand against us," replied the Asgardian, unruffled. "I faced her with the respect she deserved."

"Look, you don't have to do this," he said. "We can free you from Dormammu's influence. You're not lightweights; he can't control you all and open the final portal at the same time if you fight back. Let's set aside our differences and beat the crap out of him. With respect, if you want."

She laughed, the bitter amusement in her voice sending chills down his spine.

"You silly child," she said. "If the collective might of Asgard could not defeat him, you do not stand a chance. I will do what I must to survive, and if that means squashing you beneath my heel, I might as well enjoy it."

Peter's stomach sank. He'd hoped that he could talk some sense into her. After all, even Eddie Brock had seen the light.

But that approach seemed to be a no-go. He would have to take her down and hope that Strange arrived soon enough to close that portal. Because he had no idea how to handle it. Maybe if he had time to examine the thing, he could work something out that would destabilize the magical resonance, but the interaction of physical energy and magical power got complicated quickly. If he miscalculated, he could blow the whole continent sky high. It wasn't the kind of thing he was willing to attempt on the fly.

He'd just have to duke it out.

"That's pretty messed up," he said. "But what do you think he's going to do once he wins? Share? I'm pretty sure that's not his strong suit." A flicker of uncertainty crossed her face, and he pressed on, encouraged by her reaction. "This doesn't have to happen. My fight isn't with you."

"I will get my due," she said.

"Like Loki? Dormammu's been leading him around like a dog on a string, and it's only a matter of time before he does it to you, too."

She snarled in fury. Peter wasn't about to wait while she slung magic at him. The moment her hands tensed, he launched into action. Bright bolts of magic lanced the ground, and he darted back and forth, dodging each strike and moving progressively closer. She couldn't hold him off forever, and then he'd knock her out cold. Asgardian physiology was tough, but even if he couldn't lay her down with a punch, everyone needs air. He could bring her down as soon as he got close enough.

She began to back away as he drew closer, her eyes widening in worry. He kept on coming, implacable, her magical strikes falling just a moment too late to catch him. She bared her teeth, shooting them out faster, but still, he came on. The ground beneath him was pockmarked with divots and dotted with scorch marks, but she hadn't managed to touch a hair on his head.

His fingers grazed her shoulder. He darted to her side, grabbing for her neck. She'd probably start shooting wild as soon as he grabbed her, so he had to control her movement. If he angled her just right, those magic bolts of hers would go sailing off into the empty air.

A bolt of lightning split the air just a few feet away. Every hair on his body stood on end. White spots danced behind his eyes. His ears rang. But he could spare no time, so he grabbed her.

But she wasn't there. She vanished from beneath his fingers. He shook his head, trying to clear his thoughts. She'd teleported out from under him, he realized. Where had she gone?

A blast of magic caught him in the back, flinging him into the air. At least that answered his question.

FORTY-THREE

Kamala looked up at Hela's imposing figure. The Asgardian woman wore a tight-fitting bodysuit, a wicked-looking spidery headdress, and a smirk of complete amusement. She might have been totally evil, but Kamala had to admire her style.

"Little worm," said Hela. "You cannot hope to stand against the likes of me. I could kill you with a touch."

"Maybe not," Kamala replied. "But I'll do it anyway."

She just wished that she felt as confident as she sounded. Everything hurt. Her back still didn't feel right, and shooting pains radiated down one leg every time she took a step. Limping only communicated weakness, but she couldn't keep from doing it. The thought of embiggening the lower half of her body made her shudder. She would heal the damage eventually, but in the meantime it was gonna hurt.

But what other hope did she have against Hela? The woman had been flinging around magic like it was nothing, and Kamala could only assume that she had other tricks up her sleeve. Maybe she really could kill with a touch. It wasn't the kind of thing that seemed wise to test.

The Asgardian darted forward, and Kamala stretched, pulling herself out of reach with a single step. Laughing cruelly, Hela followed, shooting bolts of magic all the while. It reminded Kamala of playing tag, although the game wasn't usually this deadly. She dodged and evaded, thinking fast. She couldn't strike Hela if the woman's skin could kill. For all she knew, she'd smack the Asgardian upside the head and wake up in the afterlife. But she couldn't dodge forever. She'd always been the best at tag, but every once in a while, her opponents got lucky. If that happened here, it would be game over.

She had to change the game. She couldn't hope to stand against Hela, but she knew of somebody who could, and he'd helped her already.

She moved in his direction, trying not to make it too obvious. Hela darted forward like a snake, her fingers coming within millimeters of Kamala's cape. Her mouth dry with fear, Kamala threw herself forward, rolling over Loki's inert form and pulling him with her. Together, they tumbled to the edge of the temple steps and fell down the first. It wasn't that far, but Loki groaned nonetheless.

"I know," she said desperately. "I'm sorry."

Her hands shook as she fumbled for the Eye of Vouk. She'd tucked it into her costume, but it had shifted during the fight, and now she struggled to draw it out. It had snagged on something, and she didn't want to face her death with her costume ripped wide open. How embarrassing would that be? Her cheeks flamed just thinking about it.

"Little rodent," said Hela, her voice dripping with amusement and satisfaction. "You cannot hide from me. I am coming for you, and I am hungry."

Ugh. What did *that* mean? Did Hela really eat people, or was that just a figure of speech? Kamala wasn't sure, but thinking about it reminded her that she hadn't done great in literature class this year. Being a super hero took a lot out of you, and her grades had suffered a little. Hopefully she'd survive long enough to improve them.

Her mind was wandering as panic set in, and she steadied her breath to refocus. She pulled the Eye free and held it up to look at Loki, slouching behind the step and hoping to go unnoticed just a little longer. The pendants were definitely magical, so the Eye should be able to tell her if there was some way to take them off. Some magical clasp she could use. Anything.

The necklace blazed bright in the Eye's vision, and it took her a moment to figure out what she was looking at. All the while, Hela's heels clicked ever closer. She stalked them with slow deliberation, taking delight in the fear she created.

"You should run," she said.

Lightning split the sky with a crack, and the wind picked up, sending a cloud of dust into Kamala's face. She tried not to cough, muffling it with her sleeve. But Loki couldn't help it. His throat rattled as his lungs spasmed, trying to expel the debris.

"There you are," said Hela, satisfied.

Kamala pushed the fear from her mind, looking at the necklace. There! The magic wound around Loki's neck in a continuous circle, but she spotted a weakness where the two pieces had been magically welded together. There was probably a better word for that, and Doctor Strange would know it, but it would do for her purposes. She had to strike there. The spot was miniscule, and if she missed, the magical backlash might kill at least one of them. But if the Sorcerer Supreme's theory was right and Dormammu had to conserve his energy to open the portal, they just might survive.

Besides, she couldn't come up with any other ideas, and no matter what, Loki deserved a chance at freedom. She couldn't stand by and do nothing about that.

She focused, shrinking her wrist and hand until they faded from view. Although she couldn't see them, she could feel just fine, and she reached for the weak spot right next to the pendant. One yank, and it should pull free. She could do this. She had to.

A spiderlike shadow spread over her as Hela leaned over the side to look down the steps toward them. The green light of the portal outlined her head. But Kamala ignored her, focusing on her goal. Her hand shook, and even at this size, it was dangerous. She couldn't afford to fail.

For a moment, she wished that she had backup. She wished Spider-Man was here, making wisecracks in one breath and encouraging her in another. Or Mr Cage, with his quiet strength and parental protectiveness. Or T'Challa, who would punch Hela sky high and then politely offer his hand to help her up. Or Doctor Strange, who knew more than all of the teachers she'd ever had, but still took the time to teach her how to use the Eye of Vouk, all because he thought she was worthy.

But if they could believe in her, if they could accept her as a necessary member of the Shadow Avengers, maybe she ought to believe it, too. After all, hadn't she stood against the planet killer? Hadn't she befriended the Kree when they wouldn't listen to anybody else?

Even Captain Marvel believed in her. She would do them all proud.

"It is time to say goodnight, my pet," said Hela.

"I don't think so," said Kamala.

She pulled the chain free with a convulsive jerk, bracing herself for the lance of magical power that would probably pop her head clean off. But it didn't come.

Loki's eyes opened. They blazed green, but it wasn't the sickening magic that dripped from Dormammu's slaves. These were the eyes of the Asgardian God of Mischief, and they were furious.

He grabbed her by the shoulder and used her to pull himself up. Kamala could feel him shake with the effort, but his expression betrayed none of his weakness. A cloud of fury hung around him, so thick she could almost feel it. No one who looked at him would guess how he trembled. Hela recoiled in surprise as he stood to face her, but she recovered quickly.

"You cannot hope to stand against me, father," she chided. "With Dormammu's power behind me, I am unstoppable. Inevitable. Bow before me or stand aside, lest I crush you beneath my heel."

Loki gritted his teeth.

"I am done with kneeling before my lessers," he snarled.

"So be it."

She lifted her hands, summoning up a great cloud of glowing green magic. It swirled around her, caressing her figure, growing in size and power until Kamala could feel its hum. But Loki was not to be undone. He stared his daughter down, pale but resolute, and held his hands out before him. Energy coalesced between them, crackling with power. It grew and grew, and Kamala could hear things within it – snarling dogs and the flapping of thousands of wings, the call of unidentifiable creatures that somehow sounded hungry. She ought to have been frightened, but somehow, she knew that these things wouldn't hurt her. They were under Loki's control, and for the moment, she was under his protection.

He was the God of Mischief and the lord of illusion, and Loki Laufeyson had had enough.

With a snarl, he unleashed hell on his daughter.

FORTY-FOUR

T'Challa's enhanced senses picked up the sounds of battle as he climbed up the steep steps of Sobek's temple. Thunder rattled in his bones, and bolts of lightning stabbed at the ground with abnormal strength. The electricity in the air made the hair on his arms stand on end despite the comforting cocoon of his panther suit. He didn't need to see the bright flickers of magic atop the ziggurat to know what was happening.

"It has started," he said to the sorcerer who hovered alongside him, his cloak curling around him to protect him from the growing winds.

Doctor Strange nodded, but neither of them paused to discuss their options. The time for planning was over. It would have to be enough.

About halfway up, his earpiece dinged. Shuri had rigged his Kimoyo card to communicate directly through the Panther mask. All he needed to do was touch his temple. When he did so, his sister's voice came through, transmitted directly into his eardrum by the sensitive electronics of the suit. The words were meant for him alone; someone could stand right next to him and not hear a thing.

"Brother," said Shuri, "I have the intruders in custody, and all pockets of resistance are neutralized. I've questioned some of them, but they know nothing useful. They are hired guns with questionable hygiene."

He almost laughed. Only Shuri would make such an observation after a fight.

"Good. And the prisoner?"

"Heimdall is here, but we are keeping him hidden. So far, he seems to have escaped notice, and we have come to a certain understanding that if he tries to kill us, I will feed him to the crocodiles. But he is eager to return home if such a thing becomes possible."

"We will do our best. Keep patrolling in the event of a second wave. If you like, you can send the prisoners back to the city and sentence them to a bath," he replied.

"Thank the heavens. I might never get the stink out of my nose otherwise." She paused. "Come back to me safe, brother."

"I promise," he replied.

He cut off the connection and answered Strange's questioning look with a short explanation, leaving out the bit about the body odor. The sorcerer didn't ask.

They reached the top of the steps, where he quickly evaluated the situation, his claws out and ready to fight. Complete chaos greeted them. It had been some time since he'd visited the temple, and the last time he'd been here, the altar had been whole. Now it sat in shattered pieces on the ground. Although he did not revere Sobek, and the crocodile clan had been extinct for generations, he could not help but feel a pang of regret. When this was all over, he would see about reconstructing it, or at least preserving the pieces that were intact, as a gesture of respect.

But for now, he had work to do. Doctor Strange didn't so much as pause. He levitated toward the portal with an expression of determination. T'Challa hoped they weren't too late to close it. A circular opening about the size of Captain America's shield sat in its center, and through it, T'Challa could glimpse another place where a flickering red sky outlined the broken buildings. Acrid smoke leaked from the hole. None of these things boded well, but he would have to trust that Strange could handle it. In the meantime, he would make sure that none of the enslaved Asgardians could interfere.

There were more of them now. Amora the Enchantress floated in midair, her hands moving in a complex spell as Spider-Man swung toward her on a long length of webbing. Ms Marvel picked up the remains of a crocodile statue and flung it at Hela. The Goddess of Death batted it aside, but it distracted her just long enough for Loki to strike at her with his sword. The weapon blazed with magic as she met it with her own. Somehow, the Shadow Avengers must have freed him from Dormammu's influence. The sight cheered T'Challa. Strange had been right! Dormammu's hold grew weaker as he poured more of his strength into opening the portal. Summoning three more Asgardians only spread him thinner. This defection would change the tide of battle.

At the far end of the temple, lightning roared down, striking the rock. The bright flash temporarily blinded T'Challa, although his mask made some effort to protect his vision. But these bolts were brighter than anything he'd ever seen, and they carried the destructive power of a missile. As he strode closer through the smoke, he could begin to see why.

Thor, the God of Thunder, crouched over the prone form of Luke Cage. The two were locked in a struggle of wills and muscle, and Luke held on, but only barely. Thor had leverage on him, and based on the Unbreakable Man's singed clothing, he'd been hit by lightning a few times already. The strikes would have killed a normal person, but Luke kept on fighting. Despite his best efforts, Thor's hands hovered millimeters over his neck.

T'Challa wasted no time. He launched into action, concentrating all of the kinetic energy in his suit into the fists. It had finally recharged after its earlier depletion, and he could feel the power humming through his gloves. He landed in a crouch behind the two struggling men, planted his feet, and delivered a devastating haymaker to Thor's chiseled chin. The suit discharged, amplifying the blow with a wall of force that ripped Thor from the ground and threw him into the air.

Luke's eyes brightened. "Thanks," he panted.

Thunder rumbled, cutting off T'Challa's response. He turned just in time to see Thor flying at him like a predatory bird swooping down for its prey. Green-tinted lightning swathed his body, matching the pendant that swung at his neck, and his eyes were blank. T'Challa darted to the left, and Luke scrambled to the right. The Asgardian flew right between them. But Thor wouldn't give up that easy. He circled around for another pass, drawing his hammer.

"I'll draw him off. You take him out," said Luke.

No more words were needed. The two heroes met each other's eyes in a moment of unspoken accord. They would trust each other with their lives today, just as they had before and would again.

Thor swung back down, sparks of electricity dripping from his body. They coalesced around the hammer, coating it in a rime of electrical power. He swung down toward them, but Luke stepped forward, planting his feet and puffing out his chest.

"Bring it, Asgardian!" he shouted, his voice ringing with challenge. "Show me what you've got!"

Thor brought it. He soared down without slowing, pulling the hammer back for what was certain to be a devastating strike. T'Challa tensed, all but forgotten in the face of Luke's brazen challenge. At these speeds, he would only get one chance to strike at Thor. If he could only get that necklace off, the Asgardian would join their fight against Dormammu just as his brother had. T'Challa knew this, and he only wished he had learned the secret of removing the pendant. All their efforts to remove Heimdall's had resulted in nothing but pain.

But it was possible. He knew that now, and he would make it happen.

Thor pulled the hammer up over one shoulder and swung it in a sweeping arc that caught Luke Cage square in the chest. Lightning speared the sky, four separate bolts pulling energy from the clouds and pulling it down into the hammer to enhance the already brutal blow. It hit like a thunderclap, driving Luke into the ground up to his ankles. He roared in defiance, trying to pull them free, but it was all happening so quickly. Thor pulled back for another strike.

"Fight it!" yelled Luke. "You're no slave. Fight Dormammu!"

But T'Challa knew that the words would fall on deaf ears.

Thor would be Dormammu's slave so long as the pendant hung on his neck.

So he darted forward, his steps silent like a panther on the hunt. This time, he was going for stealth and speed rather than force. His claws grazed the edge of the chain that hung around Thor's neck. They hooked at the delicate links. One jerk, and he would pull it free.

But the moment that he tried, green fire enveloped them both. Every single muscle in his body locked in place as heat ran through his veins. He could feel an enormous presence, unseen but somehow close. If he could have turned his head, perhaps he could have seen it, but he couldn't move a muscle. He could feel himself falling to the ground, jerking in agony, with no hope of freeing himself from the magical net that had captured him.

"You are too late."

The voice filled his mind, deep and dripping with the power of a thousand worlds. It was the voice of a conqueror. A voice full of hunger. It would have sent shivers down his spine if he'd had the muscle control.

"I am Dormammu, and I am your master now."

FORTY-FIVE

Stephen Strange approached the opening portal with determination. He had closed the others without much difficulty, but he could already see that this one would be different. Its connection to the ley line allowed it to pull energy from the ground, and if he simply severed it, that energy would have to go somewhere. It could cause a catastrophe of worldwide proportions, changing the polarity of the earth, or altering its climate to the point where it could not sustain life. The potential for destruction was sobering, and he would have to proceed carefully.

With each new piece of information, Dormammu's plot made more sense to him. Strange had wondered why his enemy had stopped with a few portals and brought over just a handful of Asgardians when he could have run the world over with them. But he could only spend so much of his previous energy in monitoring his thralls. So, he had chosen the more subtle route, employing Norman Osborn's mortal employees to do the bulk of the dirty work, and summoning the smallest number of Asgardians necessary to complete the task. He'd distracted the Shadow Avengers, keeping their focus on freeing the slaves when they should have been investigating the portals themselves, and his unusually subtle approach had ensured that only a handful of heroes stood here to defy him when the future of the entire Multiverse hung in the balance.

But through the portal, Strange could glimpse the world beyond, and it bore the level of complete destruction that he usually associated with Dormammu. The sky had been blackened, its darkness broken only by the sullen glow of clouds of fire. Broken buildings jutted from the dead ground. Nothing living moved there, nothing except for one enormous figure that stood in wait, silhouetted against the angry sky. Flames burned in the depths of his eyes, and when he spoke, fire would flicker in his mouth.

Dormammu stood in wait for his doorway to open. He held a hand up in greeting. It would have been friendly if not for the magic that dripped from it, eating holes into the ground at his feet. It was an intimidating sight, but Strange understood its meaning more than most. The Dread Sorcerer's magic drained from him at an alarming rate as he poured his will into the growing portal. The strain would have killed most sorcerers already, but Dormammu stood firm and determined, secure in his conviction that he would win. But he would soon reach his limits, and Doctor Strange would be ready for him.

The Sorcerer Supreme met those fiery eyes, eager to pit his mettle against Dormammu's. For a moment, they stared deeply into one another, and Strange felt the pull of the evil sorcerer's will. If he allowed it, they would be shunted off into a mental landscape where they could settle this one-on-one, but as much as he wanted that, he knew it to be a horrible idea.

Dormammu might be drained by the effort of supporting the portal, but he wouldn't hesitate to cheat, locking Strange away until the portal opened. He would have to set aside his personal enmity for the moment. He might not win the war, but that was OK. This was a battle – a world – he wasn't prepared to lose.

It was time to make a stand.

He tore his gaze away and returned to his contemplation of the portal. Individual combat raged around him, but he could not allow himself to be distracted. Not now, with such a delicate magical construct to unravel. This was why he'd created the Shadow Avengers in the first place, to handle all of the non-magical obstacles that he knew Dormammu would throw against them. They would keep the Asgardians off his back while he closed the portal. But first, he would have to encase the area in a protective spell that would ground all the expelled energy, sending it back down into the ley lines from whence it came. Then he could lay down a purification spell that would neutralize the destructive energies of Praeterus. Feeding the power of a dying planet into their live one was not a good idea in any sense of the word. This spell would also counteract the physical effects of the dormamine that had been poured into the ground.

He looked things over one last time to ensure that he hadn't forgotten anything, and then he raised his hands. Magical power coalesced along his fingertips, drawing from the well of energy that surrounds all living things. At that moment, Stephen Strange felt fully alive. He'd been searching for this rush his entire life, driving fast cars and taking on the difficult surgeries that no one else would even consider, all for that fleeting moment when his limbs tingled with adrenaline and every cell in his body sang in unison. As the Sorcerer Supreme, he experienced it all the time. He would never get tired of it, but the knowledge that came with it dampened his glee. For the first time, he truly understood what it meant to stand at the doorway between life and death, with the power to choose.

That very same power had corrupted Dormammu. It was his duty to oppose it.

"This ends now," he said, spreading his hands.

Reality itself responded to the call of the Master of the Mystic Arts. The air tightened around the edge of the temple, randomly flying molecules linking into a cohesive net, drawn in by his will. With a gesture of his hands, the shield closed, locking the combatants and the portal into a half bubble that sealed it from the outside world. Lightning struck, dissipating across its surface. He smiled thinly. Dormammu would have to do better than that.

Valkyrie approached him with her sword in hand and her jaw set with determination. He paused, eyeing her cautiously. Dormammu's pendant still hung at her neck, but her eyes were clear and blue. For the moment, the Master had stayed his hand, but that would cease the moment Strange made a move toward the portal.

She coughed, her face flushed.

"I'm fading fast," she croaked. "That last blast took something out of me."

"I'm sorry."

"But I can still protect you while you work. It would be my honor."

After a moment's consideration, he nodded. Trusting her

was a risk, but working such delicate magic without protection posed risks, too. If one of the slaves broke free and attacked him at exactly the wrong moment, he would fail. Better to face a weakened Asgardian who would fight against Dormammu's influence than one that was fully in the evil sorcerer's thrall.

She stood guard next to him as he poured power into the shield, keeping the combatants from jostling him as he worked. Enchantress and Spider-Man flew towards them, struggling in midair, and she deflected them with a bat of her sword. She caught a bolt of lightning from Thor's hammer with the blade, pouring the electricity into the ground. With every strike, her shoulders grew straighter, but her breath grew thinner.

The Sorcerer Supreme's magic infused the shield, making it glow with a gentle light. He tested the shield, probing it mentally for weaknesses. It had to be perfect before he began. One flaw could quite literally destroy everything.

"You seek to contain me?"

Dormammu's mocking laugh filled his brain. No, he could hear it, coming from the depths of the portal. Dormammu's monstrous figure filled the opening. His head and half his chest were visible. It wouldn't be long before he could step through. Magic flowed from him to patter down onto the ground at an alarming rate. Was it Strange's imagination, or were the flames of his eyes a little dimmer than usual? Could that be a sign that this was the moment to make a stand? It was now or never.

"This world is not yours, Dormammu. And it never will be," said Doctor Strange.

"We will see about that. Asgardians! Kill Doctor Strange!"

As if on strings, the eyes of the enslaved Asgardians turned to him, their irises filled with green fire. Thor. Hela. Enchantress. And Valkyrie. She raised her sword, her expression blank and slack. Her hand trembled, and her breath rattled in her chest, but it didn't matter. He could not hold them all off alone.

"Shadow Avengers! To me!" he yelled.

FORTY-SIX

Kamala watched the enslaved Asgardians turn on Doctor Strange with horror. She and Loki redoubled their efforts to distract Hela. They'd worked surprisingly well together so far. Although she still wasn't willing to risk touching the Goddess of Death, she'd flung just about everything she could reach, distracting the evil Asgardian just enough to create openings for Loki to exploit. She'd embiggened and swiped him out of the way just in the nick of time more than once, buying him time to catch his breath. But now, Hela brushed them off like they were flies. Loki stabbed her in the back. The sword jutted from her flesh, just beneath the shoulder blade, and he sagged from its pommel, remaining upright only through sheer force of will. His body had taken so much abuse. Kamala had helped as much as she could, but still, the exertion had drained him almost to breaking point.

The Asgardians closed in on Doctor Strange, breaking his concentration. The earth shook, ravaged by the energies that surged through it. Kamala and Spider-Man launched themselves at Thor, only to be knocked back by a bolt of lightning. She slammed against one of the only remaining statues left standing atop the ziggurat. She'd thrown most of the other ones already.

She found herself staring at Valkyrie's back. The Asgardian held her sword loosely in one hand, moving it through complicated patterns as she tried to break through to Doctor Strange. Black Panther intercepted her, blocking and twisting to avoid the frantic assault. He limped as he moved, and his suit had torn over one thigh, exposing the long slice cut into his skin. Blood trickled from the wound, but he kept on fighting.

Kamala's eyes locked onto the necklace. She'd taken off Loki's; why couldn't she do it again? Before she could fully think through the idea, she'd lunged forward, darting under another blade as it stabbed forward. She reached forward with one tiny hand, searching for the weak spot right next to the pendant. As her fingers grazed it, she had a moment of sheer panic. What if each necklace was different? Has she just made a fatal mistake? But it was too late.

She grabbed onto the links and pulled, gritting her teeth in anticipation of the magical backlash.

It didn't come. The chain broke loose.

Valkyrie's sword reversed in mid-swing, her muscles quivering with effort. She paused for a moment, shaking her head as if to clear it. Then her lips firmed, and she threw herself into the battle once again, aiding the Shadow Avengers instead of attacking them. But it was too late. Thor's hammer impacted against Doctor Strange's body.

The portal opened.

Kamala stared through the hole in the sky, marveling at the destruction of another world. She wondered if it had been a nice place before Dormammu got to it. If their world would look like that eventually.

"Drive him back!" said Doctor Strange. "The portal will collapse if we can hold him off long enough."

But it seemed hopeless. Dormammu strode toward the nearly open portal, grinning madly.

"Little pig, little pig, let me come in," he said, his voice dripping with malicious glee.

She kept on fighting, but despair dragged at her. They were losing, and she knew it. Their only hope was to release the Asgardians and stand together, but she couldn't get close enough to Thor to tear his pendant off without getting crushed by Mjolnir or fried by lightning. After the fourth aborted try, she turned her attention to the Enchantress, hoping that someone else would manage to turn the tide of this battle before Dormammu crossed the threshold and the world was lost.

If she'd been the betting type, she would have put her money on Doctor Strange. Or Spider-Man. Any of the Shadow Avengers, really. After all, that was what they'd been picked for. They had a habit of pulling out wins against seemingly insurmountable odds.

But she never would have put money on Venom.

The black-suited symbiote sprinted around the fighting heroes and launched himself at the portal. He traveled between worlds with a flash of magic that rattled her bones. On the other side, the symbiote hit Dormammu hard, driving them both back from the opening.

She gaped at the portal, barely able to believe what was happening.

Had Venom just saved the day?

If so, how could they leave him there when the portal closed?

"Asgardians!" she shouted. "Now's your chance to go home before the portal closes. Help Venom and send him back to us!"

"They won't listen, not with the pendants still on them," said T'Challa, panting.

"Let me take care of that," she responded, grinning fiercely.

FORTY-SEVEN

Eddie Brock knew he was being an idiot. He'd run like Parker had suggested, sprinting past the small clusters of Oscorp employees. With the help of the symbiote, he'd snuck past the keen eyed Wakandans and out into the empty jungle beyond. But with every step, he became more and more agitated. He was the lethal protector. What was he doing running from a fight?

It made logical sense, but he just couldn't do it. The symbiote withdrew, leaving him to catch his breath as sweat stuck his shirt to his back. At first, he just marveled at the storm that collected over the temple. Clouds rolled in so fast that it reminded him of an eclipse. All around him, the jungle went quiet as the animals reacted to the unnatural weather. Thunder rumbled across the sky, and giant bolts of green-tinted lightning arced from horizon to horizon. The portal must be opening. Parker and the rest of his hero buddies had obviously crashed and burned. He still hated Parker and always would, but it was too bad about the rest of them. Even if they looked down on him, they still did good work. He wasn't too proud to admit that.

He paused there for a few minutes, watching the lightning stab at the top of the temple. From this angle, he couldn't see them, but he could imagine them still fighting despite the fact that they were getting their butts handed to them on a platter. He could say a lot about those Avengers – much of it insulting – but they didn't give up.

He had to go back. He couldn't have explained the decision for a million dollars. Maybe he just couldn't stand the thought of running. Maybe he was too proud to flee while the others stood to protect the innocent. Or maybe he just really needed to hit something.

Parker would do, but he wasn't picky.

At first, his Other was quiet, although he could sense the question it wanted to ask. But it hesitated for a long moment before it spoke.

We aren't running? it asked.

"No," he replied. "Fighting's what we're good at. The lethal protector doesn't run from a fight. Even if the outcome doesn't look good."

Yes.

"It's a risk, though. I still can't take this thing off. Parker said we could do it eventually, but how do we know when it's safe?"

His fingers hovered over the pendant, unwilling to make contact.

It will be safe when we tear the Master's head from his shoulders. Our freedom is worth it, even if we fail.

"Yeah. Good point." He broke into a loping run, but he didn't have the same innate dexterity that the symbiote had. He crashed through the jungle like the Kool Aid Man through a brick wall. Hopefully the Wakandans had withdrawn, because they'd hear him coming a mile away. "Why didn't you say that before?"

We both needed to think.

"Yeah, well, thinking's not my strong suit. I'd rather sock somebody in the mouth."

Me too, Eddie. The symbiote surged from him in a wave of delight and bloodthirst. His muscles swelled, his head flung back. He couldn't help it; he emitted a shriek of challenge, clenching his fists. *Now we hunt the one who leashed us. We will hunt him, and we will devour him.*

We are Venom, and we will not be caged.

He tore back up the path, past startled Wakandan sentries who threw spears at him just a second too late. But there was no time to engage them, no time to shove those spears down their throats sideways, no matter how badly he wanted to. He shot off a burst of webbing and took to the air, well out of the reach of their weapons. Then he loped up the side of the temple, taking the steps two or three at a time. All the while, he thought about how good it would feel to rip Dormammu's head off his shoulders.

When he reached the top edge, he forced himself to slow. His muscles twitched with the need to inflict pain, to punish the villains for what they'd done. But as much as he wanted to vent his ire on the others, he knew the Asgardians were in the same boat he was. They would turn on their master if given the chance. Together, they had a chance at winning. He just had to give them that chance. So he snuck forward, looking for an opportunity.

He hid behind a crocodile statue, surveying the space. As he did, Doctor Strange raised his hands, summoning up a glistening force field that locked them all away from the rest of the world. Smart. Whatever happened in the cage would stay in the cage. It wouldn't poison the rest of the world around it.

Eddie liked that. It meant he didn't need to hold back.

All around him, the Shadow Avengers battled against enslaved Asgardians. Parker went toe-to-toe with the Enchantress, pitting his speed against her teleportation, his webs against her Dormammu-boosted magic. The two appeared well-matched, with neither of them gaining much of an advantage. Ms Marvel and Loki teamed up their efforts against Hela. As Eddie watched, the Shadow Avenger snatched Loki out of the way of a sweep of Hela's sword, assisting the still-weak God of Mischief in any way she could.

Smart kid.

Black Panther and Luke Cage fought Thor, but the God of Thunder didn't seem fazed. He brought his hammer around for another strike, failing to notice the lithe form of the Panther that darted in close. Black Panther hooked a claw beneath the slave necklace. Eddie's heart leaped into his throat. It didn't work. He could do nothing but watch as the green magical fire covered Thor and the Black Panther, dropping them both to the ground.

Then Thor stood back up. The magic dripped off him, even though it still clung to the Wakandan, making his muscles seize. Luke roared, grabbing Thor around his waist and lifting him from the ground with a heave of his enormous muscles. He threw the Asgardian god into the air, only to have him float back down, borne safely to earth on a cloud of lightning.

"Sweet Christmas," said Luke, shaking his head. "Come on, man. I know you're in there. Fight him off."

"I grow tired of your mewling," said Thor.

He pointed his hammer at Luke, and Eddie winced, squinting in anticipation of another lightning strike. But the hammer emitted a giant green ball of lightning mixed with Dormammu's sickening magic instead. It was about the size of a small elephant, and it hit Luke hard. Then it enveloped him. Eddie couldn't see what happened to him on the inside, but when the ball popped, it left him on the ground next to the Black Panther, barely able to lift his head.

Thor slung his hammer over his shoulder and scanned the battlefield. His glowing eyes fell on Doctor Strange, who had so far managed to escape notice. Thor's mouth curled into a cruel smile that didn't sit well on his face. He started towards Strange.

That was bad. But things got worse fast. As if responding to some unheard order, all of the enslaved Asgardians turned to face the Sorcerer Supreme. He shouted for reinforcements.

"Shadow Avengers! To me!" called Doctor Strange.

The heroes did their best, but the enslaved Asgardians were like automatons, focused on a single task. They shrugged off their attackers, pushing them out of the way and ignoring the strikes that fell on their backs. Loki stabbed Hela; Eddie saw the blade sink in. But she continued as if nothing had happened, her eyes blank. She would bleed out without even realizing it. Dormammu had taken over her will completely.

A lot of things ticked Eddie off, but this one made him really mad. He wanted to tear Dormammu limb from limb, but if he tried, he'd end up just like them. A puppet locked in his own body.

Then it occurred to him – Dormammu didn't know he was here. The Dread Sorcerer had summoned all hands on deck, and he'd missed Eddie. Parker had been right after all. Dormammu must be spinning too many plates to realize he'd stopped controlling him. If Eddie could sneak up to that portal, he'd have one chance. Even if he only got to sock Dormammu in the chin one time before the sorcerer overpowered him, it would be worth it.

This time, he didn't need to give his Other a mental pep talk. They were one now – one thought and one purpose. Despite Venom's bulk, he could move quietly when he wanted to, and all Dormammu's attention was on Doctor Strange. The Asgardian slaves tried desperately to rip the Sorcerer Supreme's head off. The Shadow Avengers and Loki worked to protect him. But the Asgardians were strong, and Dormammu had made them stronger. They absorbed damage as if it was nothing. Despite the heroes' best efforts, the Asgardians closed in on the sorcerer, who spun his spells as quickly as possible. But it wouldn't be enough.

The portal was almost open. Eddie could see Dormammu waiting on the other side, his fiery mouth stretched into a satisfied grin. Lightning struck the ground at an increasing tempo, accompanied by deafening thunder. The ziggurat shook, buffeted by the energies of the portal. Strange waved his hands around faster, his face tight with determination. Eddie couldn't see what he was doing, but it must have been strenuous. Blood began to trickle from one nostril. But it still wasn't enough.

Hela swung her sword. Eddie winced as the weapon carved a brutal arc towards the sorcerer's unprotected neck.

But Strange saw it coming. He sidestepped, but Enchantress popped into the space next to him, shooting a bolt of energy at his feet, driving him back. He dodged again, the space growing tight. His hands kept casting, and his cloak pulled him to and fro, keeping him from harm, but there was nowhere else to go.

Eddie's hands tingled with the need to wade into the battle, even if it meant allying himself with these do-gooders. But throwing himself into the fray now would only reveal himself to Dormammu, and he wasn't about to give up his chance to pummel that monstrous magician. He continued to creep toward the portal. Just a little farther…

Thor swung his hammer. It connected.

The blow drove the breath from Strange's body. He staggered. His hands dropped, releasing the resistance he'd been putting up against the opening portal.

The portal opened with a clang like a giant gong, low and menacing. For a moment, everyone went still. Eddie tensed, preparing to make his move. The Asgardians dripped blood, staggering as they bowed low before their master. The fight had taken a lot out of them, but they still showed no signs of relenting.

"Drive him back!" Stephen Strange gasped. "The portal will collapse if we can hold him off long enough."

It was a great plan, but the Asgardians stood in the way. Thor turned and planted his feet, preparing to protect the portal. Hela and Enchantress flanked him on either side, biding their time. Behind them, Dormammu took a single step toward the open passage between the two realities, savoring his triumph.

"Little pig, little pig, let me come in," he boomed.

His voice made the back of Venom's neck prickle. It sounded

like a gleeful nightmare, like the end of all things. Perhaps it was.

But not if he had anything to do with it. Symbiote and human charged forward without hesitation. Their partnership had been one of strife and blood, a constant struggle to find accord between two vastly different senses of morality. But deep down inside, they were the same. They were both lethal protectors, and they would fight to the death to save what was theirs. Dormammu would not win, and if it meant that they had to sacrifice themselves, well…

It would ruin Parker.

A grin of satisfaction spread across Venom's face as he darted behind the Asgardians. At the last minute, Enchantress spotted him, shouting a warning, but it wasn't quick enough. Venom leaped, putting all his power behind the jump. A world of destruction and emptiness grew before him, but he had the symbiote with him. Nothing would turn him back from his purpose, not even the prospect of being stuck in a strange dimension such as this one.

The pendant flared into action, searing Eddie's mind. He struggled to retain control of himself, trying to hold on against the overwhelming tide of Dormammu's will. It battered at his senses, but his Other was there, too. Together, they weathered the storm. Their hand lifted against their will, but they held back against the urge to shoot a web and divert their course.

Eddie kept picturing Parker's face. He'd have to admit, over and over again, that Eddie Brock had saved the world, while he'd failed. It got better and better the more Eddie thought about it.

Dormammu flung himself at the portal, trying to get there

before Venom, but the symbiote had the advantage. The would-be invader reached the threshold, sticking the toe of his boot across the great divide. Then Venom hit him. The symbiotic bulk drove the sorcerer back. For a moment, the two of them struggled. Dormammu tried desperately to throw the symbiote to the side and hurtle himself through the portal, but Venom held onto his senses with every ounce of will he could muster. As he did, he ensnared his prey with tentacle after tentacle, wrapping up his limbs. It was only a temporary triumph, and he would pay for it later. Maybe he imagined the stunned expressions of the Shadow Avengers on the other side of the portal. Maybe not.

But he didn't have time to watch. Dormammu slammed a giant fist into his face, over and over again, beating it to a pulp. Still, he held on. The portal hadn't closed. Strange had said it would, so why hadn't it done so? He couldn't keep this up much longer.

The sorcerer tore free. Venom slouched on the ground, trying to build up the energy to keep fighting, but everything hurt. He grabbed at Dormammu's ankle, and the sorcerer kicked him free with a vicious movement.

Dormammu stepped toward the portal again.

A figure in full plate armor came hurtling through the portal. Valkyrie swung her sword at her captor as she came, shouting a battle cry. Dormammu batted her aside with a contemptuous expression, but fast on her heels came Thor. The God of Thunder wore an expression of fury and a cloak of lightning. The chain had been removed from his neck, and his eyes were clear and cold. He hefted his hammer, swinging it in wild arcs that drove Dormammu back from the portal.

This was his chance. Maybe Eddie could have his cake and eat it, too. While Dormammu was distracted by the Asgardians, he could escape back through the portal before it closed. The possibility of going home gave him strength when nothing else would have. Now he'd get to appreciate Parker's humiliation in person. Maybe that was petty, but he deserved a little pettiness after saving the world.

He scrambled to his feet, staggering toward the portal. As he did, Enchantress came hurtling in with fire in her eyes. She, too, was pendant-free.

"How dare you enslave me?" she demanded. "Do you know who I am?"

She began to pelt the already beleaguered sorcerer with magic, and Eddie staggered on. Let them have their revenge. They deserved it.

He made his painstaking way to the edge of the portal, his sides heaving. He'd broken something. A few somethings, by the feel of it. They'd heal, but in the meantime, every breath was agony.

Heimdall came hurtling through the portal, shouting a war cry. He joined the battle, his glowing eyes blazing with fury. Dormammu snarled, beset on all sides. But he didn't seize control of Eddie's mind via the pendant that still hung around his neck.

Dormammu's power was depleted! This was Eddie's chance at freedom! He grabbed the chain before he could think twice, bracing himself for the agony that would fill him the moment he touched it. But nothing happened. He tore the chain free with a convulsive jerk. He was free!

He stepped toward the portal, his heart light for the first

time in a long time. The portal began to hum with warning. Eddie didn't know much about magic, but he didn't need a manual to tell him that this thing was about to shut down. He took a step, his toe crossing the line just as Dormammu's had.

Loki and Hela hit him like a freight train, driving him backwards. The two Asgardians crushed him beneath their combined weight. For such thin people, they sure were heavy.

Eddie sent out a few tentacles, wrapping them around the edge of the portal and pulling him in that direction. Finally, he was free. He pushed his painful way back to standing yet again.

The portal winked out of existence, trapping him there. He fell to his knees before the spot where it had stood, shrieking in pain and grief. He would never get home. Instead, he was stuck in this stinking cesspool of a world, with its red skies and shattered buildings, and it was all Parker's fault.

Fury renewed his energy, and he turned to join the fight.

FORTY-EIGHT

The portal closed with a boom that made Stephen Strange's ears ring. The pressure on his head vanished without warning, and he found himself straining to maintain his magic against a resistance that no longer existed. He pulled his power back inside him, marshalling his strength in case this was some trick. But all signs suggested that this was real. They had succeeded in turning the tide at the last possible minute. Relief made his limbs weak. He'd always been a confident person, but at times he'd doubted, and he'd never been so happy to be proven wrong.

Somehow, they'd lucked into the best possible outcome. He would have to study to see exactly how they'd gotten here, but one thing was certain – he'd picked his team well. Although he hadn't been able to anticipate every possibility, they'd adjusted to each new challenge with aplomb. Not only had they rebuffed Dormammu's invasion attempt, but they'd also managed to send back every single one of the Asgardians in the process. At first, Strange had quailed at sending them back to face Dormammu alone, but the Dread Sorcerer was drained from opening the portal. If there was ever a hope of driving him back, this was the time, and the Asgardians had an axe to grind after their long servitude. It would lend them strength.

T'Challa made his way through the rubble that had been an altar to Sobek just a few hours earlier. He paused to pick up the shattered remains of one of the crocodile friezes, setting it aside carefully to ensure its survival. Then he joined Doctor Strange, looking up at the spot where the portal had stood.

"Is it truly over?" asked the Black Panther, his voice strong despite the gashes and gouges carved into his suit and skin.

Strange thought so, but with an adversary as persistent as Dormammu, it was best to be certain. He pulled out the Lantern of Morphesti and activated it. All clear. He double-checked with the Eye of Agamotto. Still nothing.

"I think so," he said, straining to keep the wonder from his voice. He'd learned long ago that one of the keys to being the Sorcerer Supreme was to act like he'd expected this outcome from the start. People didn't like their sorcerers shocked. It didn't inspire confidence.

T'Challa pulled his mask off and gave him a knowing glance, but restrained himself from commenting. The Wakandan king wiped sweat from his brow, surveying the damage.

"I will notify Shuri. We will need to clean up the temple as well. I don't like the idea of leaving that substance in the ground to corrupt our land," he said.

"I will gladly make myself available to assist," replied Strange. "I have purification spells that should help remove some of the magical residue left behind, and I'd welcome your sister's insight into the structure of dormamine." He paused. "And yours, of course."

T'Challa grinned. "Never fear, my friend. I accepted long ago that the lab is my sister's domain."

Strange nodded, and the two men clapped each other on the shoulder before T'Challa hurried off. En route, he stopped to exchange a hand clasp and a few quiet words with Luke. After he'd gone, Strange beckoned to the brawny man, offering his hand.

"I appreciate your quick thinking," he said. "We wouldn't have been successful without it."

"Can I have that in writing?" asked Luke, his voice light.

"I'll have Wong draw up a certificate."

The two men beamed at each other, their past conflict dissolving in the light of their success.

"I suppose I'll go see if the Wakandans could use a hand. Come get me before you go? If you leave without me, I'll have to hitchhike back," said Luke.

"T'Challa has access to a portal that opens at the Sanctum Sanctorum," replied Strange. "But I will check in with you before I leave. I'd like to examine those prisoners anyway. Some of them may carry magical wounds from Dormammu's influence, and those should not go untended."

"Sounds like a plan."

As Luke walked away, Strange turned his attention to the remaining two members of the Shadow Avengers. Spider-Man and Ms Marvel sat together, their heads bowed in collective grief. Regret assailed Doctor Strange. He'd avoided thinking about Venom's sacrifice for as long as he could, but he could do so no longer. He made his way across the temple floor and dropped down next to them.

"I'm sorry," he said.

"I didn't even like the guy," said Spider-Man. "This shouldn't bother me."

But it was clear from the thickness of his voice that it did. Ms Marvel tightened her arms around him, squeezing his shoulder. Strange knew that he should offer some comfort, but he'd never been particularly good at such things. His mind tended to skip over the emotions to the problem that sat behind them.

"Venom may yet be able to return to his rightful reality. I will do some research on this. Do not give up hope," he said.

Spidey nodded. "It's the goofiest thing. I can't stand him, but I'm going to miss him."

"He was a complicated soul," said Strange.

"He sacrificed himself to keep Dormammu out," Ms Marvel pointed out. "That doesn't erase his past, but when the time came, he stood up for what was right."

Spider-Man nodded. "Maybe I was wrong about him. I hate to admit it, but it doesn't change the truth. I've got some thinking to do."

"As do I," said Strange. His pensive tone got their attention, and after a moment of enduring their questioning stares, he explained: "This plot threw me off kilter from its inception, because it is so unlike Dormammu. He tends to be more of a wrecking ball than a subtle sort. It concerns me."

"He *was* working with Norman Osborn," said Spidey. "He specializes in subtle nastiness. I should have brought him in when I had the chance, but I bought his act. Again. Sheesh, how gullible can I be?"

"You believe in people," said Ms Marvel. "That's not a bad thing."

"Yeah, well, I didn't believe in Eddie Brock," said Spidey.

"Maybe if I'd ..." He trailed off, shaking his head. "Never mind. We ought to help clean up. But if you do learn something that could help Eddie, you'll tell me, right? If there's any chance of saving him, I want to help."

"You'll be the first to know," said Strange. "I'd like to continue our Shadow Avengers meetings in the short term, anyway. I am sure that everyone will want to hear about our progress on the cleanup, and perhaps we can find out more information about Osborn's involvement as well."

"I'll see what I can dig up," responded Spidey, brightening at the prospect. "Maybe you'd like to give me a hand, Ms Marvel? We make a pretty good team."

"I'm in," she said, beaming.

FORTY-NINE

Peter Parker's stomach growled as he made his way down the crowded sidewalks toward his subway stop. He paused to check the time, ignoring the annoyed grumbles of pedestrians forced to take three whole steps to get around him. He had just long enough to grab a bite to eat before the Shadow Avengers' meeting. As nice as the Sanctum Sanctorum was, they only had enough munchies when Wong showed up, but after every meeting, it felt like tea came out his pores.

He'd heard a lot of good things about Sal's Pizza, and the place smelled divine. So he swung inside to grab a slice from the hot case. Customers jammed the waiting area, crammed into every available nook and cranny, but he wormed his way up to the counter and ordered a slice of pepperoni that smelled like heaven.

The old guy with the mustache took his money and handed over the change. Peter smiled his thanks and turned to go. As he did, a bright flash of green caught his eye.

It stopped him in his tracks, even though he knew that was

silly. After the events of last week, he'd developed a startle reflex when it came to that color. He'd knocked a two-liter of Mountain Dew off his kitchen counter one morning when he caught sight of it out of the corner of his eye. It would be a while before he could look at that color and not think of Dormammu.

This time, a whole beverage case had caught his eye. More Dew, probably. At least he hadn't kicked it in this time. He smirked a little at his jittery nerves and began to push his way toward the door with the overloaded, aluminum-foiled plate clutched firmly in both hands.

As he made his way past, the sign plastered to the side of the case drew his attention. It read: "Try Osdrink, the drink that glows with energy!"

Peter stopped in his tracks, his blood running cold. So far, he'd struck out on his Oscorp research. Norman had gone to ground after their little tete-a-tete, and Peter had done some digging into the records, but he hadn't come up with much. The Oscorp factories had been churning out dormamine, but he hadn't been able to figure out where it was going. Now he knew, and the possibilities made his blood run cold.

He flung open the door to the drink case, smacking a beefy construction worker with it in the process. The guy made an obscene gesture, and Peter muttered an apology as he grabbed a drink. Hopefully touching the bottle wouldn't contaminate him. He'd have Doctor Strange give him a careful once-over at the meeting. But if the rest of the team hadn't seen this, they needed to. Most of them didn't seem like the energy drink type. They could run through buildings without the need for stimulants, and he was the only one crazy enough to pull all-nighters on a regular basis. Streaming TV had done bad things to his sleep schedule. And then of course there was the hero gig. That, too.

He threw a few bills on the counter to pay for the drink and hurried out of the shop. The subway ride seemed to take forever. He drummed his hands impatiently on his knees, waiting for his stop. Across the aisle, a woman in expensive yoga gear glared at him in annoyance. Before he could apologize, she dug in her bag and pulled out a bottle of Osdrink and took a swig. Peter watched her the rest of the ride, expecting her to sprout an extra set of arms or open a portal to another dimension at the next stop, but she did neither of those things. She did, however, switch seats when one came open, shooting a nervous look in his direction. Maybe he hadn't been staring as surreptitiously as he'd thought.

He got off the subway and sprinted the rest of the way to the Sanctum, pausing only to shrug his costume on before bursting in through the doors. The rest of the Shadow Avengers were already gathered around the meeting table, chatting quietly. They turned as he made his entrance, slamming the plastic bottle of glowing liquid on the table.

"I think I figured out what Osborn is up to," he said. "And it isn't good. Do we have any idea what drinking dormamine could do to people?"

Luke frowned, leaning down to take a closer look at the bottle.

"Do we know for certain that it's the same stuff?" he asked.

"It's listed in the ingredients as a dietary supplement," replied Spidey.

"Of course it is," said Doctor Strange. In response to the

curious looks, he sighed. "It wouldn't be regulated by the FDA. Much easier to push it through to the public that way."

"Well, they're doing a good job of that based on what I've seen. They had a giant case full of this stuff at the pizza place, guys. I saw at least five people drinking it on my way here. They all seemed perfectly normal, but..." Spidey trailed off, unwilling to say what they all were thinking. "I don't know what it will do to them. If people drink this stuff, will they turn into slaves, too?"

"Perhaps worse," said T'Challa. "The Asgardian slaves wore the pendants. When the dormamine is consumed internally, it could be even more powerful."

"Dormammu could subjugate the planet without even setting foot on it." Doctor Strange scowled. "And if it's as widespread as you say, we won't be able to interfere with the distribution."

"That was Norman's backup plan the whole time." Peter sat down bonelessly in his chair. "If only I'd known..."

"So, what do we do?" asked Ms Marvel, looking around the table. "There must be something."

"We need more information," said Doctor Strange thoughtfully. "Spider-Man, see what you can find out about Oscorp's production. We'll look for some way to disrupt it."

"Got it." He nodded, putting a hand on Ms Marvel's shoulder. "We make a good team. Care to give me a hand?"

"I'll give you two," she replied.

"I will work with Shuri to unravel the structure of this substance, if I may take a sample?" asked T'Challa.

"Wong will provide a container. We can split the bottle," said Strange, stroking his beard thoughtfully.

"I'll put the word out. Warn folks not to drink the stuff," suggested Luke. "Round up as many heroes as possible, in case we need backup."

"Good, good," said Strange.

"Doctor Strange?" asked Ms. Marvel nervously. "Are you OK?"

The Shadow Avengers stopped, staring at the Master of the Mystic Arts. He stared blankly down at the table, his gaze unfocused. He twitched, his fingers jerking. Peter's stomach sank. Could Strange himself be under Dormammu's sway? Had Osborn spiked his water cooler or something? He was willing to believe anything at this point; Dormammu just wouldn't give up. But then the doctor's eyes cleared, and he looked around at them, his expression grave.

"I have looked into the future," he said, "and our options are limited. But there are a few roads to success left to us, if we have the strength to take them. Go. Do what you can, and contact me if you are in need of my assistance."

The Shadow Avengers rose from the table with sober expressions. Hands were clasped and hugs exchanged. Then they hurried toward the door, driven by a single purpose. They would stand against Dormammu once more, and they would not fail.

But one Avenger remained. Spider-Man stood at his chair, staring down at the bottle that still sat on the table. The liquid inside cast a sickly green glow on the burnished wood. The web-slinger shook his head.

"We're too late, aren't we?" he said. "This is going to get bad."

"We are not too late. But yes. It will get bad," admitted Doctor Strange.

"What are you going to do? I noticed you sidestepped that question."

"I require magical assistance. An expert on soul manipulation and telepathy. He may be able to provide the key to shielding the populace from the effects of that drink."

"Who? I'll help you look," said Spidey. "Just give me a name."

"Thank you, my friend, but I believe this quest will be mine alone. I do not believe that my quarry is on this plane of existence. There is no time to waste. If we are to free all of humanity from Dormammu's malign influence, I must find Doctor Voodoo."

ACKNOWLEDGMENTS

This book was a dream come true, and it couldn't have happened without a few key people.

I owe some serious thanks to the entire Aconyte team (and Gwen, Marc, and Lottie in particular) for their faith in me.

Gwendolyn Nix, my talented editor, is such a joy to work with. I hate talking on the phone in general, but she's one of the rare exceptions. Thank you, Gwen, for not judging me when I ramble, cheerleading when I need it, and supporting me when things inevitably go sideways.

Stuart Moore, author of *Target: Kree*, is both kind and talented. Sharing books in a series can go extremely well or be a huge headache, but he made it effortless. Stuart, I hope you enjoy where I took the story, and I especially hope I didn't write you into too many corners.

As always, I couldn't do this without my family. Andy, Connor, Lily, and Ryan are patient with my all-consuming need to watch everything Marvel puts out and visit every comic store we pass. Your support and brainstorming help are invaluable, and I love you.

Lastly, I owe a shout out to the rest of my friends and family, who keep me (relatively) sane: Emily Cooperider, Ali Cross, Jennifer Fick, Keith and Lisa Grace, Lee and Maryellen Harris, Sarah Ison, Marian Rugg, the Driveway Drinkers, and a few people I'm sure I will think of about ten minutes after I submit this. I'm sorry. These things are harder to write than you'd think!

ABOUT THE AUTHOR

CARRIE HARRIS is a geek of all trades and proud of it. She's an experienced author of tie-in fiction, former tabletop game executive and published game designer who lives in Utah.

carrieharrisbooks.com
twitter.com/carrharr

WORLD EXPANDING FICTION

Do you have them all?

MARVEL CRISIS PROTOCOL
- ☐ *Target: Kree* by Stuart Moore
- ☑ *Shadow Avengers* by Carrie Harris

MARVEL HEROINES
- ☐ *Domino: Strays* by Tristan Palmgren
- ☐ *Rogue: Untouched* by Alisa Kwitney
- ☐ *Elsa Bloodstone: Bequest* by Cath Lauria
- ☐ *Outlaw: Relentless* by Tristan Palmgren
- ☐ *Black Cat: Discord* by Cath Lauria
- ☐ *Squirrel Girl: Universe* by Tristan Palmgren
  (coming soon)

LEGENDS OF ASGARD
- ☐ *The Head of Mimir* by Richard Lee Byers
- ☐ *The Sword of Surtur* by C L Werner
- ☐ *The Serpent and the Dead* by Anna Stephens
- ☐ *The Rebels of Vanaheim* by Richard Lee Byers
- ☐ *Three Swords* by C L Werner

MULTIVERSE MISSIONS
- ☐ *You Are (Not) Deadpool* by Tim Dedopulos
  (coming soon)
- ☐ *She-Hulk Goes to Murderworld* by Tim Dedopulos
  (coming soon)

MARVEL UNTOLD
- ☐ *The Harrowing of Doom* by David Annandale
- ☐ *Dark Avengers: The Patriot List* by David Guymer
- ☐ *Witches Unleashed* by Carrie Harris
- ☐ *Reign of the Devourer* by David Annandale

XAVIER'S INSTITUTE // SCHOOL OF X
- ☐ *Liberty & Justice for All* by Carrie Harris
- ☐ *First Team* by Robbie MacNiven
- ☐ *Triptych* by Jaleigh Johnson
- ☐ *School of X* edited by Gwendolyn Nix
- ☐ *The Siege of X-41* by Tristan Palmgren *(coming soon)*

EXPLORE OUR WORLD
EXPANDING FICTION

ACONYTE

ACONYTEBOOKS.COM
@ACONYTEBOOKS
ACONYTEBOOKS.COM/NEWSLETTER